D0339371

ABOUT THE AUTHOR

YXTA MAYA MURRAY is the author of *Locas* and *What It Takes to Get to Vegas*. She was a recipient of the 1999 Whiting Writers' Award for fiction. She teaches at Loyola Law School in Los Angeles.

THE CONQUEST

BOOKS BY **YXTA MAYA MURRAY**

Locas

What It Takes to Get to Vegas

rayo *An Imprint of* HarperCollins*Publishers*

THE CONQUEST

a novel

YXTA MAYA MURRAY

A hardcover edition of this book was published in 2002 by Rayo, an imprint of HarperCollins Publishers.

FIRST RAYO PAPERBACK EDITION PUBLISHED 2003.

Book design by Shubhani Sarkar

The Library of Congress has catalogued the hardcover edition as follows:

Murray, Yxta Maya.
    The conquest / Yxta Maya Murray.— 1st. ed.
        p.   cm.

ISBN 0-06-009359-5
    1. Manuscripts—Conservation and restoration—Fiction. 2. Women museum curators—Fiction. 3. Los Angeles (Calif.)—Fiction. 4. Aztec women—Fiction. 5. Authorship—Fiction. 6. Spain—Fiction. I. Title.

PS3563.U832 C66 2002
813'.54—dc21

                                                                    2002069757

ISBN 0-06-009360-9 (pbk.)

03 04 05 06 07 WBC/RRD 10 9 8 7 6 5 4 3 2 1

TO *Virginia Barber*

"[Cortés] carried home a large collection of plants and minerals, as specimens of the natural resources of the country; several wild animals and birds of gaudy plumage; various fabrics of delicate workmanship, especially the gorgeous feather-work; and a number of jugglers, dancers, and buffoons, who greatly astonished the Europeans by the marvellous facility of their performances, and were thought a suitable present for His Holiness, the Pope."

WILLIAM H. PRESCOTT,
History of the Conquest of Mexico

THE CONQUEST

PART One

The museum is dark tonight. The shadows are cut by a few lamps, which cast a veil of light on the bronzes displayed in this gallery. Naked, shimmering girls and bearded satyrs turn supple in the glow, almost as if they might come alive any moment and turn a discerning eye upon their observer. I move from the room and out of the wing, stepping onto the courtyard with its flower and water gardens floating in blue light. Beyond the precipice of the hill upon which the museum stands lies the black ocean indistinguishable from the sky. It is a white-air, January evening, perfect weather for Jean Paul Getty's ghost to wander, dazzled, through the limestone halls his money built. I stretch my sweater tighter around my shoulders and enter the library.

Even at midnight a few scholars' lamps burn from various corners, and the silence is threaded by the sound of a pencil on a page. Ancient, magnificent books sleep on the shelves, such as these medieval medical texts dispensing deadly advice on leechings and applications of mercury. I pass the fading tenth-century copy of Epicurus, with its recipes for sea urchins with honey and roast flamingo with mint. Here are the fifteenth-century chivalric novels in their lovely cameo bindings. And the eighth-century Aztec calendar with its themes of blood and grain.

I reach my desk. I turn on my lamp and pick up the old book that lies here. I run my fingers on the spine, the rotting leather. The tooled headbands and marbled papers, the rippled vellum leaves filled with beautiful script. Centuries ago a tawny fugitive dipped her pen into an inkwell and wrote these words long after the soldiers and bondsmen gave her up for dead. Later, the eons bit their teeth into this book. In a few years it will die unless this hinge is reglued and the tattered parts of the leaves and covers are patched.

That is my job. My name is Sara Rosario González, and I am thirty-two years old.

I'm a rare book restorer.

EVERY DAY I COME HERE to do the slow and painstaking work on this volume. It often takes me into the early hours of the morning. As I examine the flaws on a leaf I will become distracted by the words written on it. The story. I have no trouble imagining its author. The tawny woman bent over these leaves, slowly painting the letters in their telling style. After two pages she raised her head to watch a bird outside of her window. The green hills of Spain stretched farther than she could see. A soldier with a red plume in his helmet whipped his steed across the knolls, but such sights did not frighten her any longer, as she had learned to take refuge in disguises. She smiled, and returned to the book that now rests under my hands.

It is a late sixteenth-century folio, untitled, and bound in oxblood morocco; the text of vernacular Spanish is written on vellum in formal Rotunda script. The narrative tells of a female Aztec juggler brought to Europe by Hernán Cortés, and she has many adventures including fighting with the Ottomans, abandoning herself to the pleasures of Titian's Venice, and plotting the assassination of the Holy Roman Emperor Charles V. We believe it was composed in Cáceres, Spain, circa 1570, and because of stylographic similarities to other texts most scholars agree that it was authored by one Padre Miguel Santiago de Pasamonte, a hedonistic and probably insane Hieronymite monk who wrote a series of scandalous novels a full twenty years before Cervantes penned *Don Quixote*. My boss here at the Getty, Teresa Shaughnessey, is in these theorists' camp.

It appears that I am the sole dissenter to their hypothesis. I believe, as I've said, that a woman wrote this folio, and an Aztec woman at that. Perhaps it is fiction, perhaps not. Historical accounts of Aztec slaves' passage from Tenochtitlán to the Vatican will be found in annals from that era. And although this book contains accounts of magic, it was written in a credulous age, when the passionate still saw spirits and monsters mingling with human neighbors.

I've also dared to give it a title: *The Conquest*.

If I prove my hypothesis I will be as clever as any necromancer, for all the dark women of history have lost their tongues. If I show my colleagues that an Aztec woman wrote this book, it will be as if I'd tapped on the shoulder of the great volcano Ixtacihuatl and bade her speak.

And that's exactly what I'll do.

THE NIGHT IS DEEPENING. Saturday night, so that this place is a clock-stopped island beyond which lies an electric and protean Los Angeles filled with revelers. I am the last of the scholars left here, and it is my favorite time in the museum, when I can fancy the duchesses and devils stepping down from their canvases and waltzing together through the black halls.

I can work now with no distraction but my own imagination. My tools are simple. White gloves, a bone folder, knitting needles, glue, and thin, milky sheets of linen and Japanese paper, which I will graft to the book's body in much the same way the surgeon repairs the body of a patient whose heart has been punctured by illness.

No, I will say that the process reminds me instead of a sweetheart reconstructing a destroyed love letter. The first time I held one of these relics—it was a thirteenth-century manuscript of an Aztec poet, for I tend to seek projects that relate to my race—I remember the impression that I possessed a message from a revenant suitor pining for the love of a beautiful woman. I glanced up, then, at these shelves of sleeping books and thought how each hid the ember of a hot heart that beat after passions now long forgotten.

This fact holds unbearable ramifications. Doesn't it?

Or is it a blessing?

Here is my answer to that question:

My mother, Beatrice, who was a great one for telling me bedtime tales, once regaled me with a fable about an alchemist named Tzotzil who lived during the epoch of the Earth's infancy. Sitting by my side and stroking my hair as the bedroom window darkened, she said that though the planet then was still so new that it yielded, at the slightest touch, all the gifts and fruits that might sate its inhabitants' appetites, Tzotzil anticipated the current world's predilection for dispiritedness and longing.

Tzotzil was lonely, my mother told me, whispering into my ear as my eyes grew heavy with sleep.

In his despair, he visited the cave of the fortune-teller Atitlán, and explained that despite all his wealth he was still poor in matters of the heart. Atitlán agreeably cast a spell, and his crystal ball revealed a sylph with hair as black as ink and eyes that were the tenderest shade of blue. Yet, despite the girl's seeming perfection—she had the breasts of a mermaid, a dragon's talent for debate, and an ability to eat a roast griffin in one sitting—Atitlán augured that she had one critical flaw, as she would not be born for five thousand years.

Now, this is certainly very bad news for a lover, but Tzotzil, who had almost swooned with passion when he saw the image in the crystal, resolved to communicate his ardor to his intended. He tawed a goat hide, cast a homing spell on it, and then wrote a sonnet to the future girl.

He died soon after, Mother murmured, as I sank deeper and deeper into my pillow. And what was worse, as the eons passed, and the Earth cracked and soldered itself into new shapes, Tzotzil's sonnet was handled by so many collectors that by the time Anactoria was in her thirtieth year, they had whittled the vellum into no more than a trash scrap.

Anactoria, black-haired, blue-eyed, cantankerous, famous for her heroic acts of gastronomy, walked along the sea cliffs one day, and looked on the ground. There, she saw a rough piece of paper with words printed on it. She picked it up and read: *O you rosy-armed Anactoria, only Tzotzil may claim your heart.*

Anactoria thought it odd that this fragment would contain her name, although due to her carefree disposition she was more amused than disturbed. As a consequence of her exotic culinary inclinations, however, a curious thought entered her head. On impulse, she rolled up the scrap and ate it. And this was a mistake.

For as soon as the words hit her bloodstream, its homing charm spread out to all her cells and she found herself possessed by a delirious longing for a lonely alchemist named Tzotzil. She sat down on the sea cliffs and stared out into the ocean, drunk with passion.

Anactoria gazed out at the sea, dreaming a dream that was

woven when the world was newly born. The girl with the temper of a dragon, the cunning to eat a griffin, the beauty of a mermaid, had now been poisoned by a poem.

Mother raised her eyebrows and drew her face near, kissing both of my eyelids and cheek and nose and chin, while I struggled to fend off my dreams long enough to hear the story's ending.

I still remember it:

Anactoria died years later, an old woman, and in love.

THIS FAIRY TALE, told in a mixture of my mother's voice and my own, comforts me sometimes on weekend evenings when I sit in my office, musing over some ancient codex, only to look up and see the night dancing behind my window.

I imagine then that I am holding a missive from some long-passed true love, some antediluvian cartographer who drew these priapic sea serpents or this lusty nereid with me in mind.

But then the fantasy fades. I have no Tzotzil or Anactoria in my past or future because I *am* both Tzotzil and Anactoria, in that I suffer from a sickness of memory for the real and the imagined. I don't think I was designed to be born in this age of forgetting. Although there *is* the problem of too much recollection, as nostalgics struggle to exist in the present tense long enough to dive into that electric night with its discos and tangerine martinis.

And what's worse than this lack of fit is the fact that I, too, have a lover I can't forget, and no marvelous excuse like Anactoria's. My beloved lives right now, and here, in Southern California. In fact, we went to high school together.

His name is Captain Karl Sullivan, and he'll soon be engaged to another woman.

THE 6:00 A.M. SUN showers down on the highway, which stretches before me the next morning like a long dark promise. I haven't slept all night, as I worked at the Getty until dawn, making some progress on a particularly damaged section of *The Conquest*. Now I look out of my window to see new commuter settlements of condominiums and brand-new baby mansions flanking the 5, though bright orange poppies glow from the intermittent spaces of neglected fields still safe from progress.

I'm in my car, driving south to Oceanside, toward the Marine base of Camp Pendleton. This is where Karl lives.

I pick up my cell phone and dial his number.

"Hello?" He has been asleep.

"Are you alone?" I ask.

"Sara?"

"I just wanted you to know that I'm coming over."

I hear the sounds of sheets rustling, and I can picture him morning-rumpled, with his great dark hair mercilessly shorn and his rangy, furry frame half-nude in flannel pajamas.

"Wait a minute, wait just a second, I don't have my head screwed on yet," he says. I hear something knock over, and his grumbling. "You're coming—what? I thought we said we should keep clear of each other."

"*You* said."

"I'm seeing Claire later today, though. I don't think that your coming over is the best idea."

"Well, I do. I'll be there around eight. I just want to say hi. I haven't seen you in four months."

"You're driving two hours to just say hi?"

"That's right."

"That's kind of a long . . . are you all right?"

"I'm fine."

"I mean, you know—"

"I know you're getting engaged." Now I say his name in a voice he recognizes, a voice I've used with him before.

He doesn't say anything for a few seconds. "I sure haven't heard that voice in a while. You sound good."

"And I'll be feeling that way when I get over there."

"I really don't know if it's the best idea."

"You don't have anything to worry about."

"Just my old heart, right?" he asks.

"Is that so bad?"

"Well, I kind of need it beating if I want to keep walking around."

I snuggle the phone under my chin, do a quick dogleg around an old brown Ford and then a shiny Toyota. I'm doing about ninety-five. "I'll get it beating."

"Oh." He laughs. "*You* haven't changed." I can hear him rustle out of bed, and start moving around his bedroom. "So, what have you been up to?"

"We're making small talk?"

"I want to know, I haven't seen you. *God*, it's good to hear you. It knocks me flat, to tell you the truth. And no, seriously, are you doing all right? Do you need anything?"

"Yes."

"Anything I can *give* you."

I roll down the window and let the wind come in, and it whips my hair around my face. "Look, Karl, do you want to see me?"

Another long pause.

"Do you want to see me?"

"Yes," he says, finally. "Yeah, I do."

And then he hangs up.

I press on the gas, flick on the radio and hum along to the music.

I am brimming with feeling, just from that short conversation. There are those who are lucky enough to meet someone special when they're just beginning to notice the world—that unshelled age of fifteen, in my experience—and the first mold that they make of themselves takes part of its shape from that person. Decades later, they can still reach through the years and touch that pure egg. When they say your name it's like a secret code.

This is who Karl is to me, and why I can't forget him.

1982, MILLIKAN HIGH SCHOOL, in Long Beach, California.

I notice it's more attractive in retrospect.

Tenth grade. Post-*Roots*, pre-*Brideshead Revisited*, the days of the Hillside Strangler and the Hostages, this is the period when we'd all just fled the terra firma of Big Bird and Baby Alive and begun an alarmingly accelerated process of cell division: The girls developing overnight these shocking bulbs that poked out from Duran-Duran concert T-shirts and round little behinds that they packed inside jeans that were so tight that some of them would later be diagnosed with nerve damage; the boys walking around with their books held at strange low angles, their Levi's drooping around their flat cracker butts as they negotiated the lunchtime racial and music-appreciation geography, there being several phyla of rocker and racial minority. For here were the Goths with kabuki black-and-white-painted faces, the Punks with fake Cockney accents and pink Mohawks held up by Hair Net and egg whites, then the public school preppy oxymorons adjacent to the Asian, black, and brown kids, all in nonmiscegenating cliques, as segregated as prison inmates.

By the end of my sophomore year, I had long opted to spend most of my time sitting under the school's large, peripheral jacaranda tree and reading (anything, from *Middlemarch* to Stephen King's *Christine* to *Shogun* to *Anna Karenina*). A heroic shyness persuaded me that I did not mind being apart from these politics, as I could discover dramas and friendships in the society of books that seemed just as exciting, and maybe more benign, than the alliances and duels I observed from that perch. I imagined I emanated an intellectual glamour beneath my tree, though I see now that I emitted an invisible toxin, like the poison put off by a frightened frog—except that I *was* interested in integrating with one new whippet-thin student from Bakersfield, California, a kid with dark llama eyes and a huge smile out of which shone a thicket of unstraightened teeth. Within the first few days of his matriculation, I knew he was called Sullivan, and that he was already making a name for himself in math class. Still, the prospect of actually speaking to this heartbreaker seemed as impossible as holding forth with the Loch Ness Monster until the heady day of the beach party organized by the school administration to reward its honors students.

The fling was held at Bolsa Chica Beach, where the sand's soft as velvet and the ectomorphs prance in the surf like seraphim all day long. I fled my fellow students through the strand until I found an undisturbed patch of surf on which I could swim and sunbathe out of eyeshot. After an hour or so, the tall dark boy wandered into my vicinity. He stood on the dry sand and made patterns in it with his huge feet.

"Hello, there," Karl said.

"Hello," I said back, as if in a dream.

"You're that girl always reading under the tree, aren't you? I tried to catch your eye a while back, but you might as well have like a DO NOT DISTURB sign swinging from your nose. Mind if I paddle around here a while?"

No, I said, I didn't mind.

We swam there together all afternoon, although we didn't talk much. But I did watch how the waves left a shining skin on his arms and handsome chest. I noticed his hair standing in wet clumps and the way he shook himself like a puppy; I admired the striations of muscle cross-hatching his back. When a swell tumbled him into the water he would stand up fast, laughing through the seawater. What he could be doing on my patch of sand, I could only half-imagine, and a crazy joy began flinging itself through me, especially when he attempted to show off by swimming against the darkening current.

"That's what they teach you in lifeguard training," he explained, panting dramatically.

"Are you a lifeguard?"

He shook his head. "I read about it."

It was almost dusk by now. From the far edge of the beach, a few of his friends stumbled over the dunes. When they spotted us they waved and yelled at him to get in the car.

"Wait," I said. "I have something to tell you."

He looked at me and grinned. "What?"

I shrugged. He waved his friends off, and they left.

I dove back under the water and stayed there, thinking of what I could say that would impress him. When I had to come up for air again, he peered at me through the gloaming, with his arms crossed against the cold.

The next thing I knew, I started telling him a story.

Out of some freak and delicious inspiration, I led him into the glittering water, up to our waists, and entertained him with a famous romance about an Aztec princess and her doomed groom while the waves broke over our shoulders. *She wanted to remove her dress for his pleasure,* I told him, shocked not only at my brazenness but the new and incredible fluidity of my tongue. *She loosened the ribbon of her gown so it fell to her feet.* I didn't even resemble the queer fish called Sara González at that moment, but felt dangerous and happy and entirely fluent at seduction. I floated around him, whispering in the shadows, while he stared at my mouth. It was in that moment that I discovered my only talent, which is to tell Karl Sullivan stories, and I felt strong enough to mesmerize him all night.

But even then, I didn't finish what I'd started.

"Now isn't that something," he said. "You kind of got a knack for tall talking, don't you?"

I shrugged. "Maybe."

"So how does it end?"

"I'll tell you the rest later," I said.

"You promise?"

I promised.

It was dusk; the stars peered from between the clouds. We did seal dives in the water and stared out at the disappearing indigo. I saw a blue spiderweb of veins over the smooth shell of his pectoral as he hovered in the black water, looking at me and not saying anything.

"What?"

"I'm poor," he blurted, grinning again so his tilted teeth showed. He gestured at the sky. "I like astronomy. Rockets and all that? Doesn't matter if you're rich or what up there—like Gordo Cooper. You heard of him?"

"No."

"He was an astronaut. That was pure brains at work. He got to see *everything*."

"Everything like what?"

"Like what? Star nurseries. He got to see the constellations. The whole Milky Way. And up that high, it's supposed to be really something. You peer out of the little window in the shuttle, and Earth doesn't look any bigger than a nickel."

I stood in the cooling water as Karl began to tell me what made him so crazy about the stars—about how, in Bakersfield years before, he'd first started looking to the skies because it seemed like the one place where a body could stretch out as much as it liked and not worry about getting yelled at, or poked, or smacked on the ear.

Tempers were likely to run high enough in the Sullivan house, which was stocked with four boys and a widower dad who tried to make ends meet on a welder's pay. Mr. Sullivan taught his sons what a hard hand had to do with being a man, although Karl left the leather jackets and fistfights to his three older and gigantic brothers, who ate like locusts and practiced their karate chops on his head. There had been a year or two when things were so tight he'd wound up sharing a bed with the biggest of them, and his resulting cold uncovered toes and bruised cranium often led him to take refuge outside, especially in the summertime, when he could lie in the soft grass and gaze up at the unclaimed space booming as far as he could see, while paying special attention to that empty, white, glowing world lighting the sage fields around him. What he wanted most, though, was a virgin land that no one had ever seen before, let alone scuffed up with their shoes (as had happened in 1967), so he could really know what it was like to "be there first." This possibility had been presented to him in the sixth grade, when he learned Einstein's idea that the universe was in a state of constant expansion—and what better place for a boy sick of tight spaces and secondhands than the endlessly new desert between the stars?

"See," he continued now, "if you're smart enough? They have a space program out in Texas, and they'll slingshot you up there. Mission specialists is what they call them. One day that'll be me, I hope."

I tried to imagine Karl dressed in a space suit and dancing past asteroids, hopscotching white dwarfs, and leaping into the dark, mysterious sea where time could be crushed smaller than a cashew and a man could stretch out as much as he wanted.

But then those images faded, all at once, as the only thing I could concentrate on now was how he had suddenly taken my hand.

He reached under the waves to take hold of my wrist and traced the veins with a tender thumb. He laced our fingers together and then looked straight into my eyes.

"You look really pretty like this, under the moon," he said, and smiled.

I'VE HEARD PEOPLE SAY they didn't appreciate their best days until they were long over, but I knew what was happening to me when I spent time with Karl.

On Saturday nights he'd iron his collar so it was stiff as a sail, and take me out to Bob's Big Boy, where we'd laugh our cans off over petroleum-thick cups of coffee and the best banana splits. The boy didn't have enough cash to buy me much in the way of roses from a florist, so he'd go gallivanting all over town with a pair of scissors to gather me strange and beautiful bouquets snagged from parks and wild-grown vacant lots, and he'd cook me up tuna sandwich picnics that we'd eat on the beach, where the black and glistening ocean view was better than any movie. I was never shy with Karl, not on the occasion of our first, heady, tooth-knocking kiss, or even later, when we lost our virginity during a skipped fifth period (he'd rested his cheek against my shoulder and held on to me for dear life). About once a month, too, we'd go to the Griffith Observatory, where he'd yell about the ersatz Universe booming over our heads, and I even attended one of Karl's KISS concerts where I screamed at the glams barfing blood while he squeezed me in delight—but it didn't matter what we did, as I knew there was no one but him and it was all gold down to the marrow.

I had a hard time of it when he flew off to attend the U.S. Naval Academy in Annapolis, Maryland, to prepare for his future as an astronaut. I coped by crossing off the days on the calendar and flying out there for the proms, where the midshipmen danced like Frankensteins and the dates all dressed like Easter eggs, and I made him duck into the Ladies so as to strip off his uniform with my hot little hands. He gave his salary to the phone company, as well, when he joined the Marines and moved to Quantico, Virginia, in 1989 to train on UH-1H "Huey" helicopters, but we'd always see fireworks when we got back together, and I had my own education keeping me busy. After high school, I hiked up to Stanford University, where I'd spend the next six years studying literature and book arts. I missed him so much it gave me chest pains, but Karl and I still managed to settle into the patterns of our long-distance relationship.

I settled well enough into school, too. Stanford was a place where I started to feel some of my blank spots fill in, though I did sometimes find I couldn't quite describe in our calls and letters what was happening to me at college, what happened to me even the first moment I wandered into the university library and discovered those volumes of Tolstoy, Wharton, Gogol, Paz, Eliot, and Shakespeare just waiting to be plucked and swallowed. The novels I read helped me see the world itself like a piece of fiction (written by a series of hands that were a different color from my own), and the brand-new ideas of my professors could fill me with excitement so intense it bordered on fear. But, more than that, when I sat in the library, and especially in the rare-book room with its crumbling totems—I just felt like I belonged there. Libraries and museums, any place with collections, reminded me of my mother, Beatrice, who, while she lived, was passionate about history and its beautiful fetishes. It is a happy and crazy kind of feeling to know you've stumbled upon a place where you could live forever, and that's what I knew then: Even in my freshman year I planned on a future in book restoration. I'd sit in those corridors, inhaling the musty scents and wondering about the secrets that must be hidden in those volumes—not just the rumors and love tales contained in their pages, but what wars they'd weathered, whose hands had rubbed them with such affection that they now crumbled into dust, even what crimes had been committed to own them.

And then the semester would end, and I would finally see Karl again.

I tried to recount these transformations for him, just as he tried to show me the ways in which his more concrete dreams of space were widening something inside of *him*, but if these subjects were not quite understood, there was still no lack of discoveries to make in one another. I've registered every change in his handsome cast, such as the bulky muscles and the elegant lines his face assumed when his teeth learned to behave. And I loved to return to that permanent knot of blue veins on his chest, which reminds me of the nebulas he talked of, with one arm behind his head, the other's fingertips tracing the constellations he wanted to visit when accepted to the Lyndon B. Johnson Space Center in Houston.

As for me, I grew two inches, breasts of some consequence, as well as what he called "bohemian" ideas and a ravenous erotic appetite.

"I've pictured you in your birthday suit while jumping out of planes," he said in Quantico after a four-month separation. "I once woke up in the middle of a dream making *kissing* noises only to find myself surrounded by some what I would call impolite marines. I've chewed enough ugly food to choke a rhino, and I've been made to stand at attention in the cold dawn without any protection but my skivvies and a prayer. I have paid my dues to Uncle Sam, madam, and right now I'm going to get some payback myself by getting made love to by the sexiest woman in the whole U.S. of A."

But we always would wait before we jumped into things, so that I could whisper one of my sweet somethings in his ear. Since that first night at the ocean I'd continued to romance Karl with my stories and no seduction could commence until I picked up the trail of the last tale I'd started. Having ripped off my lovemaking method from the classics, I never told him the end of a saga before beginning a new one: As my plots tugged, loosened, unknotted (and then ramified and tangled again), I would put my mouth on his neck, or his jaw, brushing a lip against his eyelid, unbuttoning his shirt until we were twined together on the bed and had no more breath for stories. I beguiled him with sci-fi epics in the sultry weather of southern motel rooms, and I bewitched him with pornographic chronicles in thin-walled university dorms; I smuggled westerns into the narrow but obliging beds of marine barracks and whispered murder mysteries while disrobing his Sara-starved body in the backseats of rented cars.

In 1992 Karl was transferred to North Carolina, and asked me to move in with him before we got married. How could I resist, or want to? I gladly took the plunge by abandoning my plans for a Ph.D., and at the age of twenty-three found myself in the small, nearly Latino-free town adjacent to Camp LeJeune.

We rented an apartment, which I decorated with Frida Kahlo prints and a modest Swedish dinette; I would have liked to devote two walls of shelves to my library, but we discovered there was only sufficient room for the smallest pine bookcase, and so I packed most of my volumes away in a closet. This was temporary, of course (we both said), and I noted also that these days I didn't have that much time for reading, as I was so busy planning the wedding—and *saving* (an activity that can take its own chunk out of the day, I learned), since we didn't have sufficient money for my ring. Despite these new responsibilities, the first months flew; we made love like monkeys and on weekend mornings I'd ride him piggyback while he raced along the shore, hollering happily about our future sons and my exquisite behind. "I can't wait to get this little body pregnant," he'd laugh, hiking me up higher, "I can't wait to see you all big and pretty with our baby inside you." "When I move you up to Houston, I'd better keep you away from Ground Control because those guys won't be able to handle the distraction." When he talked like this, it made me happy, but sometimes I could also sense a set of unspoken plans vanish into thin air; once or twice I tried to bring up those memories of my mother I'd had in the university library, as well as my ambitions to bind ancient books, but the thoughts sounded strange in this new environment where I had somehow inherited a set of foreign expectations, and a fully fleshed-out role of U.S.M.C. fiancée.

When I thought about applying for museum jobs or continuing with my Ph.D., I had a hard time reconciling those ambitions with the examples of other busy base wives, which showed that the commitment necessary to be a success at this life should take up every second of the day—and would compete too much with the bewitching and jealous mistress that is forensic bibliopegy. The most intimidating experiences I had were at the fêtes attended by officers' wives, snacking amiably on barbecue while describing, with great and obscene humor, the herculean strength needed to bolster temperamental flyboys as well as endure sometimes solitary months and near-single motherhood. It was during this period that I developed my everlasting respect for military brides, those healthy-thighed gals hoisting tots over busy hips and somehow managing not to go batshit while their husbands set off for sea or air or, as in my case, outer space.

With a growing sense of befuddlement I set about planning

the ceremony, ordering assorted fabric swatches and samples of candied almonds and arranging meetings with the priest at the local church. Whenever I imagined Karl pressing his mouth to my neck as I told him one of my stories, my bafflement disappeared in a snap. But soon after, while looking for a catalogue of galactically bad wedding dresses or suggested chicken-rich menus, I might pass by the book-packed closet and grow light-headed with the sensation that I'd misplaced something important. Rich memories of the university library would waft back to me then, as well as that feeling of a friendly maternal haunting I'd had in the rare-book room—something that could still divert me to such an extent I began to make an assortment of fumbles in my wedding planning. After a scandalous number of menu gaffes and missed appointments with the priest, Karl and I started to have our first disagreements, during which he once said, "If you need more time, you say so. Be straight with me, okay?"

"What are you talking about?" I asked.

"I love you, and you know that. But don't forget I'm not a ball to be kicked around."

I denied any misgivings, and the truth is I didn't fathom my own alarm until a few spare months before the wedding. It was almost all prepared, the Jordan almonds, the bridal train with its seed pearls, the salmon or beef and the honeymoon in Oahu, everything except for my naked finger waiting for its twinkling diamond. Unfortunately, I forgot the ring when on a Friday afternoon I wandered past a Fayetteville used-book shop and saw in the window something so astonishing, a volume so celebrated that even in the stunted infancy of my high-end bibliophilia I knew it to be an incomparable find: A foxed, faded, bumped, and D.J.–free first of Borges's *El Jardín de Senderos que se Bifurcan*, which did not look like anything so special until I turned to the brandy-tinted title page and saw that the great man had inscribed the octavo to his publisher, Victoria Ocampo: "*A Victoria, con la gratitud, la admiración y el antiguo afecto de Jorge Luis Borges, 1942.*" This I knew was a neglected relic of Argentine genius and its famous midwife! It was an original evidence of a Latino golden age—though it needed a new clamshell, it would have to be cleaned and resewn, and once I restored the marbled endpapers they would glow like jewels. How had it gotten here? Who had set Jorge out in the sun? In the wrong hands, if purchased by the wrong buyer, it could be dead in a few years.

As if in a dream, I walked into that shop and, rather than save our money for my wedding ring, I spent it all on that book. "You did what? You bought *what*?" Karl asked me later that night, his eyeballs boggling when I slipped my prize from its paper sack. In the end, this revelation catalyzed additional and more painful disclosures about my befuddlement and his mounting hurt feelings, which found keen expression in his treatment of the octavo. Though he tried to hold the precious Borges with the greatest delicacy in consideration of its cost, other motives intervened: As the fingers of his right hand clutched at the volume with nervous delicacy, his right shoulder appeared influenced by a contrary attitude, and the tiny battle in his body caused him to half-drop, half-fling it onto the floor—a gesture that further damaged the volume's spine and seemed to be a harbinger of the dashing of all my bookish dreams.

"I'm sorry," he blurted after a few seconds, and crouched down to retrieve the volume. "But I sure don't understand this. All our money on an old book. *Your ring* gone on this . . . *book*. A book you can get in the library! I can't tell you the things I had to do to save all that money. Or what a happy jackass I was just scrimping and socking it away." He wove his jaw from side to side. "So, I don't know what you could have been thinking, except maybe it's that you don't want to get married."

I tried to explain it to him, saying that I wasn't ready for the military life, and that I wanted to leave the base and take him with me, but he shook his head.

"I don't want you anyplace but here, with me. What are you going to do, you're going to go to California? I can't go to California. I can't quit the Marines! We can work something out for the two of us out here, can't we? Because even if I wanted to—you can't ask me to leave the force. It's how I'm going to get up there. It's the only way I'm getting *up there*." He frowned at me, his forehead reddening. "Don't you know that about me by now?"

And while we stared at each other in the kitchen, I saw what he saw again, just as I did on our first night at the ocean. I saw Karl breaking free of his childhood straits by whizzing through the galaxy, as light as popcorn, as free as a quark, stretching out through space's dark matter and stars that expanded and contracted like his own heart. But I knew then, too, that I was heading back to school so that I could get my hands again on those fragile bindings I first saw in the rare-book room and find the secrets tucked under their hides. Though I could barely explain my motives to Karl, the memories I'd had while sitting among the folios, and the curiosity those books sparked in me, were leading me to make some strange and painful decisions. And those enchantments weren't nearly done with me yet.

IN THE NEXT FEW MONTHS, we stalled our plans for the ceremony; soon after I reinstated my plans for a Ph.D. and traveled back to Northern California, only to then return south when I was hired by the Getty. In the decade since, Karl's moved around too. There were the years in North Carolina and Pensacola, and he even had a stint overseas before he settled in Camp Pendleton nearly a year ago. I would not say we've "weathered" all these transitions that well—for the past eight years Karl and I have been in the protracted phase of our recurring relationship, meaning we break up, then make up, then break up all over again, the latter being occasioned more and more, not just by his transfers, but also, I'll admit, because of my work. Though Karl is the more itinerant and far-flung, I have often been the more scarce.

My interest in incunabula (our tongue-coaxing, musical, sexually evocative word for old books in the most general sense) only intensified the years following our engagement, and I've found that in this profession there is no shortage of enigmas to lure me from my lover. What have I been looking for in the Getty's gorgeous, and yet incomplete, archives? *Proof of my own past*, to be blunt. In 1997, for example, I wrote only one letter to Karl during a period of nearly six months, as I became buried in a failed quest to reconstruct the catalogue of the famous, burned Aztec library, known as *Amoxcalli*, which I saw mentioned in our unbound 1632 copy of Bernal Díaz del Castillo's *History of the Conquest of New Spain*. And that was only the beginning. I disappeared for months after finding the remnants of Nahuatl marginalia in a disintegrating 1543 volume of Copernicus, and also after discovering what appeared to be ancient Mixtec graffiti annotating a beautifully gilded, though badly sewn Andalusian Qur'an. I spent three incommunicative seasons trying to track down the bloody, and I suspect, royal provenance of Benito Juárez's family Bible after stumbling upon a Parisian bookmark tucked between its pages (France-friendly Maximilian occupied Mexico in 1864), and even longer attempting to trace the true name of the Venezuelan (or Chilean) who anteceded Defoe's Man Friday in the 1719 *Robinson Crusoe* I restored—efforts that have led to many (I have been assured) "interesting theories," "close calls," and "provocative conjectures," but, in the end, no concrete results other than the impairment of my relationship—until now. My current project, the search for the narrator of *The Conquest*, I am sure, is different.

But whatever its merits, this last dereliction has been the worst: I began the effort around the same time that Karl moved to Pendleton, and have since committed innumerable romantic delinquencies such as missing dinners, phone calls, and the ubiquitous bring-a-date parties.

And so yes—Karl and I have had our ups and downs. I have exhibited very bad judgment vis-à-vis the home-office time ratio on account of my passion for the clandestine life of literature. But as I told him, and continue to do so, I know that barracks, marriage, and books can eventually mix. I've read about Emily Dickinson's living with no company but her poems and the famous bibliopegist Roger Payne doddering around in his solitude and drink—all those examples of busy brains who couldn't mix the world with work—and I do not want to wind up like that. And even with my romance misdemeanors and my anxiety about committing to the Marines, I have never questioned that my future would someday include a big wedding with a bad band, or a batch of sweet fetuses with periodontal problems.

What I am saying is, I did not believe it was possible that he could want to be with anyone else.

But only a few months ago, during one of the evenings that I missed, Karl attended a Marine barbecue at a retired General's San Diego manor—some emetic orgy of hot dogs, ground cow, stigmatized shoulders hoisting Coors cans to mouths flabbering out some extremely feminist mariner's anthem—and in the midst of all this lathered humanity, my darling Karl saw, in the way a pilgrim or opium addict might see an angel, a rose-cheeked, honey-colored girl, she of the button nose and Irish-flamed hair and savage appetite to change her name.

Claire O'Connell.

I have seen this rival with my own two eyes, three months before I made the present trip down south—the party at which

Karl beheld this vision was hosted by her General grandfather, and out of what I believe could only be some subliminal self-sabotage, he'd told me the name of the avenue upon which the historic meeting occurred: "El Cielito." When I heard the distracted tone in his voice, I'd set aside my research for the first time in two seasons to drive to that pretty Oceanside sky street. I steered up the leafy road lined with majestic old arts-and-crafts alcazars, many of which were complete with the grand, old, Adirondack-perfect porches I could just imagine throwing myself down upon. I will not get into the details of how long I parked on that shady lane attempting to absorb the scene of the crime, but it was just long enough for me to witness Karl walk out of one of the manors, with an orchid-cheeked redhead in tow, whom he then began to frisk with his big, busy hands. That was a more covert kind of operation, as he didn't spot me then, but I did make my presence known a few days after that when I demanded that he talk to me, and he obliged by telling me much more than I wanted to know. First came the harrowing details—she was a nonretired General's daughter (the Marine genes ran in the family) ready-made for base culture, she was wild about him, and she did not exhibit any tendencies toward library-induced absenteeism or other kinds of conjugal truancy. The worst information, though, was nonverbal. Karl stopped talking, and stood in the doorway, staring, as all the color drained from his face so that the only clue he remained alive lay in his huge and burning eyes.

"I think that I love her," he said.

"Liar," I told him. And I still believe that's true.

Matters have not improved, though. Karl admitted to me a while ago that he was thinking about marrying this woman, and so I obviously have no other choice but to use all my skills to bring him back to my bed. Or, more precisely, my one skill. Once Karl and I began having our troubles, I began to see the stories I've always told him in a different light. They're not just love poems, but are also spells and spirit knots that can come to the aid of a negligent and desperate lover. They resemble the enchantments of other, more famous weavers I've read about—the Arabian slave beguiling her king out of murder, a translator tempting a general through the jungles of New Spain, or ocean witches singing of the spreading plains of Troy.

Beware, my boy! The greatest temptation a mariner will ever be tested by is in the arms of the beautiful sylph who rises before his prow, her hair a mass of glittering plants and her mouth a soft weapon as she sings to him of the past. I am not so stunning as all that, though I'm rich-skinned like my father, Reynaldo, who is the color of a panel of oak, that rough and lovely dark. I have very straight black hair that falls to my waist and nearly black eyes behind vintage cat-rims. I resemble a Mexican Shirley Jackson, I think, librarian-like, hirsutulous, and secretly prurient.

But I can be more dangerous than I appear.

Only Karl knows this, though. And this is why, when I arrive at Oceanside, none of the nearby marines raises any alarm. I slip under their guns like any other innocent girl. It's a quiet, glowing day, without one hint of recklessness in the golden air. The morning has bloomed here, so the sun freshens this garrison with a sweet clear light that I imagine filters through Karl's window and onto his bed where he lies right now, fully dressed, staring at the ceiling, and waiting for me to ruin all of his plans.

THE SECOND-FLOOR APARTMENT where Karl lives is a generous-sized one bedroom with just enough space for at least three bookcases. As I push through the open door I see it is decorated with the old prints and bridal dinette that I bought in the months when I planned our wedding. Karl emerges from the kitchen when he hears me enter. His hair has grown out from his usual cactus buzz so small curls struggle to form around his ears, and the corners of his mouth flutter before he smiles, then reaches down to give me a gentle and nervous hug.

"Hi there," he says, pressing his hands on my spine, then holding them there for a second before extracting himself.

"It's good to see you."

He looks down at what I'm wearing, and his smile widens. "Hey, didn't I—no, I *bought* you that dress."

"Yes, you did."

"When was that?"

"Back in North Carolina."

"I remember that. I remember that day. You kept on—" He makes a gesture with his hand.

"—twirling the skirt around."

"Right. You were trying to get me to waltz or do some of that crazy ballroom dancing." He laughs, then looks down. "Well, it still looks nice on you."

He hesitates, and then walks as far away from the bedroom as possible, into the den, though I notice that the tips of his ears are glowing bright red.

As I sit on an easy chair, he chooses the sofa on the other side of the room. He puts his huge hands on his knees and stares at them with a panicked expression, as if they might reach for me against his will.

"Your hair's grown," I say.

He rubs his hand over his pate. "I should be more careful, or else my head'll stop looking like a jar. I'll get a B.C. cut tomorrow."

A "B.C. cut" is short for a "birth-control haircut"—an apt nickname for the Marine coiffures that make the men look so awful, they are guaranteed to avoid the procreative complications risked by more attractive members of their gender.

"Keep it long," I say, "you look handsome."

Now silence, as we look at each other across the distance of the room. Karl presses his knuckle against his mouth and shakes his head.

"I'm sorry," he says.

"There's no need to be sorry."

"Yeah, well. I am."

"We don't have to get into that right now. I wanted to see you."

"Maybe not as much as you thought. Because I can't say that anything's changed since the last time we talked." A blush begins to spread around his eyes, then he smashes a cheek with the flat of his hand and presses his lips together.

I stand up from the easy chair, though I don't approach him yet. I'm wearing a sweater over the dress he bought me in North Carolina, and also a knit cap, which I slide off. Despite his resolve, I see Karl flick his eyes up, and I dangle my hair like a lure as I move around the room. There are a few signs of the girlfriend—a crystal giraffe gawking from a side table, an absence of dust, a thin scent from, it seems, the bowels of Victoria's Secret. Worst of all is the photo of Claire O'Connell, which I look right through before leaning up on a windowsill which resembles the one in a Pensacola apartment I'd rested my hands on when Karl and I were engaged in a happier dialogue about two years ago. The blush that spreads from his eyes to his whole head tells me that he gets the reference; without speaking both of us now remember that afternoon when I licked his ribs with my thigh. I gaze at him from this narrow seat, letting him know that I know, and after the air thickens between us I let my eyes wander back around the room, to the pile of aerospace testing books stacked on the coffee table.

"Are you trying out for the program again?" I ask.

He nods. "Every chance I can until I make it. I'm hoping my flying Hueys gives me an edge, though I guess Houston likes jets better."

The space center in Houston admits only a few contenders a year, and so many hotshots apply you have a better chance of making it to the moon by sprouting a pair of wings than getting up in one of those cans. As a way to avoid any squeamish discussions, he goes straight into this subject, and when he touches on the topic of the new findings on Mars the old glimmer shows up in his eyes. I have told him this before, and it's true, that there's something in me that says he *will* make it. When I think of him shooting through space, a dark light shoots through me too, so I want to unhook each button of his shirt and press my mouth to the blue star on his chest, then watch that stiff lip of his start fluttering.

"Claire's uncle went up once," he says.

I look out the window and click my nails against the sill.

"Just on an orbit to fix the Hubble when it was imaging the Eagle Nebula," he continues, "but he got to go. I asked him how it was up there, and you know what he said?"

I lift a shoulder, drop it.

"He told me it was like—this was so wild, I couldn't forget it. He said it was like meeting the woman you're going to marry. He said he looked out from the shuttle's window and saw Earth, a little bit bigger than his nose. And right then he loved it and missed it more than anything. The whole planet! He said he was floating up there, homesick as a kid at camp, and he just couldn't *wait* to dig his heels into some old-fashioned terra firma." Karl scuffs his hands against his knees. "I've been thinking about that ever since."

"I think I can understand how he felt." I ease up off the windowsill and stare him down for ten, then twenty seconds, a minute, until he stares at my mouth, forgetting.

Then he remembers the problem.

"What are we doing here?"

"Nothing. Catching up."

" 'Catching up.' " He gets wistful here. "Is that what this is?"

I move closer to him.

He shakes his head. "There's other people to think about now. And also, you and I have already tried all of this over and over. *You* didn't want it."

"I didn't want to get married."

"To me. You didn't want to marry me."

"You know that's not true. I didn't want it just *yet*."

Karl touches his fingertips together in a careful way and stares at the delicate structure of his hands. "Well. I'm getting married."

I sit next to him on the sofa. I unbutton my sweater. Then I say, "You love me."

He doesn't deny it, and I take his hand.

"Sara."

I take off my glasses. I slip off my sweater, and I can feel my hair on my neck and arms. "Where did we leave off the last time?"

"What do you mean?"

"You don't remember?"

He closes his eyes. "You not talking about our"—he hesitates here—"game?"

"Yes."

"Ho no, I really just don't think we should get into that."

I graze his forearm with two fingers. "You didn't mind so much before, did you?" I can see the pulse in his throat.

"That was before."

"Before I had you naked in my bed and I was telling you a story. Though I didn't finish it, did I?"

He doesn't say anything.

"Aren't you curious how it ends?" I run the side of my hand up his spine, then brush my jaw against his shoulder.

He lets out a breath, and then starts to laugh again. "Oh, come on. You're getting me all rattled."

"I know you're curious," I go on. "I know you've thought about it. I could just whisper the last part to you now, like a secret. And then I'll leave."

He looks down. We're so close I can feel his breath on my cheek and jaw. He remains quiet for a while, studying his knees. But finally he says, "I want to hear it."

And that's all the encouragement I need. I take his hand and pull him from the den to his spartan bedroom, with its oak bureau and plain but accommodating bed.

I put my lips to his ear.

There is no greater pleasure than whispering my tales to Karl, and he listens to me with his eyes closed, so that I imagine the words drifting into him like an intoxicating smoke. I continue the story I left off with last time—a fable of a goddess tricked by the devil into drinking from the stream of amnesia so that she forgets her own powers.

When I am finished he opens his eyes.

"Did you like it?"

He reaches up and touches my face, and I take his hand to kiss the palm and very lightly bite his finger.

"I liked it," he says. "But you're a danger to my nerves."

"Well, here's another. There was a girl who lived five hundred years ago, who was brought as a slave to Europe. She was very beautiful, with dark, dark eyes, and a knife she strapped to her thigh."

I slip my hands over his face. I touch his shoulders through his shirt, then cup his chest with my hands. I pull him down, using some strength. My thigh is on his waist. My hair glides across his throat.

"In the fifteenth century, Hernán Cortés brought over a troupe of performers from the New World as presents for the Pope. And he didn't know it but one of those performers, the girl, who was disguised as a boy, intended to sacrifice an emperor in retaliation for Europe's crimes against Mexico."

Karl looks at me across the bed, thinking. Then he puts his fingers on my lips and I climb on top of him.

"Tell me what happened."

"Can you imagine what a time to be alive, Europe in the middle of the 1500s? There was the war with the Ottoman Empire, the Catholics' fight with Martin Luther, the sack of Rome, the sack of Peru, and in the middle of it all is Charles V, the dumb and greedy king she wants to murder. Although there *is* a complication."

"What?"

"She falls in love. With someone she's not supposed to."

He grins. "Who?"

I lean down and inhale his breath. I touch my mouth to his mouth and to his eyelids. I love this lip, this scent. I was there when he got this scar on his wrist while cooking dinner. I know every color in his eyes.

"Someone who touches her like this." His shirt opens, revealing ribs like white scrolls. His muscles jump under my hands. Here is the delicate network of veins tracing his upper arm. His hipbone like a hard knot I could untie.

He moves under me. Again he asks: "Who?"

But I don't answer that question.

I make love to him instead. The entire time I keep my hand pressed to the blue star on his chest, which flushes and trembles. I scale his body and fasten myself to every furrow, every place where I can grasp a good hold, until he is curled inside the net of my hair, startled and blinking.

"Good God," he says.

I rest my cheek on his stomach and watch the changing

weather outside of the window, and try to put the way I feel into words but come up with a color instead. There's a painting I love—*Starry Night* by Edvard Munch, which hangs in the west pavilion of the Getty. It shows the sky the way the sky would dream of itself if it fell asleep, draped in a deep, moon-pure blue. If the sky were this kind of blue you would swim in it.

That color is how I feel.

"I'll tell you the rest of the story later," I finally say.

I slip my sweater back on, my glasses, my cap, while he is still in disarray with his arm flung over his eyes.

"Don't feel bad," I tell him.

"Our problem was never the loving and the hugging and the squeezing. We never had any trouble in that department. It's other things that kept us from being together."

"They don't matter," I say, "and you know it."

Now I kiss him and leave.

2.

Standing in the Getty's courtyard the morning
after seeing Karl, I warm my hands against a
paper cup of coffee and look out at the ocean miles
away. No one is here but the birds and the guards, it's
so early. The cold weather glazes the magnificent
buildings and sage grass. Steam from the coffee cup
makes shapes in the air. Charcoal figures wearing
stiff-brimmed hats move behind the windows.

Stunned from too little sleep and blinking at the
dawn, I am still waking up. My imagination is the
most supple at times like this, during the early hours
when I can still feel connected to my dreams. Memories and trifles float and bump through my mind like
dark leaves in water.

I sip my coffee, thinking of Karl, and the way he
looked on the bed the day before. The thought makes
me feel a little raw. I let myself drift into other fantasies, recollections.

It is not hard to do in a place like this.

Standing here, I could believe myself the queen of a
deserted Greek kingdom in the far, far, future. Modern
battlements of travertine rise out of the sea mist, and
the polished stone floor spreads like a perfect Sahara

beneath my feet; here are the yarwoods, birds of paradise, the oaks and lavender; here is the heroic ocean, like another piece in this vast collection.

Getty, our benefactor, would have hated it. His biographers note that he preferred the look of old Italian villas or English mansions, as they helped maintain his hallucination that he was a British lord and no ordinary son of Minneapolis. All of his resources were devoted to this fiction—as they certainly were not invested in his family (he was married five times) or his friends (a notorious miser, he installed pay phones for guests at his Surrey estate). The only thing that mattered to him was cold and glittering rarities. He wanted to be remembered as a Medici. He wanted to live forever.

What a terrific failure. We remember not just his philanthropy but also his personal delinquencies and strange death (he passed, fully dressed in a Savile Row suit, ignoring his cancer pangs as he attempted to do paperwork at his desk). Sometimes I imagine Getty's shade floating through the museum's piazza and frightening the patrons by howling at the Schindler references, the feminist interpretations and Spanish translations. Instead of a simulacrum of the British Museum's hushed, gloved propriety, this poor shade sees hordes of minorities thronging through the halls of contemporary architecture.

Minorities like me. I've worked here for over six years and can think of few things better than spending my days in this cloister. At the moment the watery light spills over the galleries' faces of pale stone, a fossil-studded Tivoli travertine from the same quarry used to build St. Peter's Basilica. The rock glows shell-pale, with spots of light glinting off embedded crystals and the bone prints left by sea creatures that used to swim with Neptune. I am leaning up against the west pavilion's rotunda, and in a nearby stone I notice the skeleton of a leaf, each delicate vein perfectly preserved. A similar fossil will probably be found in Peter's Basilica, as identical rock was installed by Michelangelo's men during that great period of its construction, though the gold that floods its halls and lit the altar where Urban VIII prayed hailed from a different source—the melted American gods and glittering streambeds that once ran scarlet from murders committed in that same saint's name.

I love the museum because it is a garden of such secret histories. For the past few years, I've made a home in this place, surrounded by these relics of lost empires and the breath of the great dead. It's in the Getty that I've learned I have a knack for resurrecting and protecting a history that not everyone else can see, and it is one of the greatest passions in my life. I spend all my days, all my weekends, all my evenings at it, unless I'm with Karl. He has trouble understanding why I work as hard as I do, but I'm still looking for proof of my own past in these pages that I mend—maybe a foreign name obscured under a false title, the dusky blood in the provenance, an unexpected tint in the skin of a genius—any afterimage of the dark continents burned by the *lumen gratiae* of these brilliant civilizations protected by the Getty, and, more generally, anything that might rattle the cage of this perfect collection I feel so many things about. I suppose you could say I'm an eccentric looking for something that doesn't exist, like that famous cracked knight who saw a princess Dulcinea in the big-hipped girl busy slopping pigs. But though some of my esteemed colleagues do levy such slanders my way, they don't ruffle my whiskers even a little bit. When I do find these arcana—that is, now, when I do *establish* them—I know I'll have started to realize the aspiration that used to grip me when I'd dream my afternoons away in the university library, and when I'd think of my mother, as she's the one who first planted in me this hunger for our own burned and buried past.

Though she didn't imagine that I would ever wind up here.

She trained me from an early age to distrust this kind of zoo. And working as a conservator at the Getty does have a whiff of collaboration to it—I catalogue the gods plucked from dead temples; I store soldiers' stories in gilded rooms, even as those same soldiers burned other, strange libraries. A Mexican, she taught me, and a woman, can only have a uneasy rapport with these menageries. My mother died two decades ago, but I know that if she were still here she would tell me to quit this job that I love. She would want me to be an *enemy* of museums, donning a black cowl and stealing into archives to filch mummies, medals, idols, amphorae, in order to send them back to their homes.

But those are not my methods. I admire Mr. Getty's jewels with a Mexican eye. Sometimes I feel like a happy spy who lives in the emperor's castle.

If my mother were alive today, I'd tell her that I'm working toward her ends from the opposite angle.

ALL OF US CAN identify accidents and inspirations experienced in early years that have guided us through our lives. My accident, my inspiration for all my work, has been my mother, Beatrice, though this may sound strange, as she was a magnificent criminal. And I mean that literally! She was a dazzling felon, cardamom-dark and black-eyed like her family in Jalisco, Mexico, and predisposed to poetry and illegality on account of a worldview that regarded everything around her as hijacked. After she and her mother immigrated here in 1944, my grandmother fell ill, and the impoverished young Beatrice thereafter suffered an adventure that I do not know too many details of, except that it involved being the consort of a wealthy Anglo man who expected liberal compensation for his patronage. As a consequence of this bargain, she developed a high-strung pessimism: She became a person who no longer could "believe everything she read"; she did not "judge books by their covers." And her incredulity did not soften after she met my father, Reynaldo, or experienced mother-hood. She never forgot to look at the world with a subaltern's eyes, and her skepticism flourished, perhaps too much, as, bit by bit, she eventually rejected a quantity of the premises that underwrite much social intercourse, which is the classic strategy of neurotics, novelists, and thieves.

To witness this development was also, as it turns out, a perfect education for a future custodian of incunabula.

When I was nine years old Mother took me to a show of pre-Hispanic artifacts at a Long Beach museum, a retrospective so provocatively exotic that it stunned the tongues of our town's art circle. I still remember the docents whispering among the ithy-phallic sculptures, cagily pointing to the nonpornographic motifs, and pressing their faces up to the glass traps holding naked war-riors wielding knives, nubile servant girls bearing grain.

Beatrice stopped in front of one display of a scrap of very large, old, thick paper upon which faded drawings of singing men could be seen. When I looked down at the sign I saw that the paper was a rare remnant of an *amoxtli*, or a sixteenth-century Mesoameri-can book, made of the amate tree's crushed bark and inscribed in red and black ink by Nahuatl sages.

My mother remained in front of the bolted glass box that held the relic. She stayed there and stared at it for a very long time.

"All of this is stolen," she told me finally. "Did you know that?"

I only looked at her. She took a breath; her lips wavered.

"I am so homesick," she said.

She stared at the fragment for another moment then reached up and jiggled the bolt that locked the box. By virtue of a lucky negligence, the curator had forgotten to fasten it. It sprang open without any effort and the front glass panel slid open. She reached inside and fingered the page. No bells rang; the guard had turned the other way; docents chattered in another room. She lifted it from its plinth and rolled it into a scroll that she tucked into her bag. One patron, over by the Mayan stelae, gaped.

And then we left.

At home, we unrolled the soft and flaking page onto my parents' bed and looked at it. It was printed with spare drawings of an old man sitting before an assembled group of youths. Scrolls emanated from the elder's mouth—symbols that I would learn later are the pictographic signs for the speech of a *tlamatini*, or master of flower and song.

I finally got up the nerve to ask "Why'd you take it?" after about half an hour. Several people had already called us (we hadn't answered the phone), and some of them had been pounding on our door.

My mother smiled at me and let out her braids, shook her hair.

At this point the doorbell rang, and the knocking started up again.

I was terrified. I asked her again, why she had taken it.

"Why'd I take it? Because it didn't belong to them, that's why. It made me mad, *hija*. These museums are just like a big lie, you know? And those people, their eyes have no idea what they're looking at when they see the pretty pictures. To them it's invisible! They are looking at *me*, and they don't know it. They are looking at *you*. They might as well put us in one of those glass boxes. You get me?"

Now the knocking was louder. I heard the words, Museum Security.

"Oh, *sssssh*, don't get nervous," she continued. "I can see it is hard to understand. And later, your father will say, *Oh, your mother. What a crazy-brain! What a nut case! Forget all that business she told you.* And it will be even more confusing. But between you and me, Sara, if you want to be a smart girl, my advice is for you to remember everything."

"Mom, you *stole* something from the museum."

"Yes, okay. I guess so. You could call it that. Your dad, he will call it that. This guy outside the door with the thumping will call it that. But *to steal, to lie*—these things are all upside down and sideways for me. Other people say those words, and I hear *blah blah blah.* And in this case—sure, those words have zero meaning. This book, what used to be this book, it was ripped off a long time ago before I ever saw it. But I already told you about that, didn't I? About the libraries?"

I shook my head, shrugged.

"I have told you so many stories, but not that one?" She traced the drawing with her fingers. The beads around her neck and wrists clicked. "Oh, you should know it, you'll run through life with the brains of an iguana if you don't. So, okay: *Years* back, a very hardheaded kid, a soldier named Bernal, followed General Cortés into the heart of Mexico, looking for gold. They wandered through the hot jungle, always moving to the right, so that this Spanish boy thought he was circling down to the center of the Earth or even Hell itself, but of course it would not be an *infierno* until he got there. When they finally arrived at the great city, filled with the temples and the gardens and the beautiful strangers who looked something like you and me, this soldier, he could not believe his eyes. Were these people animals? he wondered. Were they devils? So wild they looked with their black skin—they were pagans, surely. And more important, such creatures could not have any use for gold.

"And this idea, this gold, that is what kept him moving, though he was skinny as a chicken, and he was so tired. These dark girls, he thought, they will pour hot water into a gold bath and clean me with their soft hands when I am through with them. He planned to drink from cups of gold and bring a hundred perfect emeralds back to his wife. He gripped at his sword, dragging himself through the town, until he came upon a temple. At last, he said to himself, I will make my fortune here! This must be the place where they hide the treasure! And he was right. When he entered it, he saw that it was filled with *nothing but these books*. Worthless! the idiot shouted. I am tricked! he yelled. Or maybe, *just maybe* he looked at one of these books. Maybe he saw how it perfect it was, and he put it into his pocket because he knew that *here* was the real gold. Maybe this paper here comes from the book he stole. But even if he was so smart that he could see he had found the true treasure, it did not matter. For now he could already smell smoke. He saw the flames eating the books. As he had stood there, trying to read these pages, the other soldiers had already set this magnificent library on fire."

My mother stopped talking. The phone now rang. There were voices behind the front door and another loud series of knocks.

She winced, but fixed her eyes on me, and touched me with her cold hand.

"Do you see what I'm trying to tell you?"

She looked lovely and strange, and I knew then that she wasn't like other people in some very important ways. I could smell her perfume—tuberose. I pressed my palm to the dark paper and the image of the man with the scroll on his tongue. And I didn't have the heart to tell her that I didn't see, I didn't understand her, at all.

MY MOTHER WAS ARRESTED that evening for grand theft (the *amoxtli* remnant, even then, was worth almost one hundred and fifty thousand dollars), although my father, Reynaldo, was able to get the charges dropped by encouraging the view that she was experiencing a tragic but temporary klepto distress. "Why you want to break my heart like this, *corazón*?" I heard him asking her that night, through my bedroom wall. "*Mi* little flower, *mi preciosa loca con la cabeza quebrada*, all I want is for *you* to be happy. I give my *life* for this happiness, you know that. But my baby, my birdbrain, you can't go stealing that shit from the museum!" Mother didn't answer his arguments or inquiries, and instead cried all night. I know that he couldn't decipher her motives any more than I; she never explained them to him, either. She died sixteen months later of a undiagnosed and congenital heart condition known as atrial septal defect, which is nothing more complicated than a hole in the heart, and after she was gone, subjects like this became off-limits because it hurt like hell to talk about them out loud.

But I was afraid to forget her, and collected everything that I could and stored her inside of me—every eyelash, the tones her voice could take, the clicking of the beads around her wrists and throat. When I got older, those memories did help me. I finally figured out that on that afternoon she had, within the limitations of her opportunities and era, tried to redress a nearly five-hundred-year-old theft—though this was a revelation that eventually tutored me to see the world, like her, "upside down and sideways." By the time I reached college, I had already begun to look inside books, museums, sculpture gardens, and not to observe what lay on the surface of the images assembled there, but to detect some secret that might lie beneath them—some evidence of that crime she'd tried to redress, some other history that escaped the bonfires—and that's been forgotten for centuries. It is a method of seeing that I have retained. This odd habit of always peering under the skin of things has also kept my mother alive for me, and so bright in my mind that lately I've begun to think it is not always so good. I hope that when I disrupt something in this *beautiful* museum I will feel better about her death and her obsessions, which is why I work so hard. It is the reason I left Camp LeJeune and came to this temple built in Jean Paul

Getty's memory. It is the reason I have not always been as available to Karl as I should.

It is also why I have now devoted myself to this old, contested book I call *The Conquest*.

THIS BOOK IS A CHARM. When I hold it I imagine all the dead men who once read it, the monks and the soldiers gasping at its racy sections. I can see financiers thumbing it like a shilling shocker and young girls sneaking peeks at the accounts of battle behind governesses' backs.

This book is a mystery.

Although the folio's plain morocco binding and Rotunda script dates it to sixteenth-century Spain, there is no record of its origin or early history. For over two hundred years it might have lain under glass in a palace or moldered in a barn—although it was most certainly stolen, perhaps several times. Nevertheless, we have no way of knowing, and so possess no obligations concerning its rightful owners, as it survives these eras without a trace until the year 1813, when it emerges in Madrid during the Peninsular Wars.

After Napoleon gave Spain to his fumbling brother as a gift, King Joseph did little more with his rule than aggravate the natives and the tough, tough British. He did, however, have the foresight to hire a highly efficient majordomo who catalogued each of the Crown's treasures. From these records we learn that included in the temporary sovereign's cache were a stable of jet Andalusians, Charles V's own gold tableware, a giant carved emerald from the Americas, and this modestly bound folio.

Maybe the King read it on the throne to take his mind off his losses, as the mountain guerrillas descended in the dark. Commander Jourdan assembled his staggering troops while Arthur

Wellesley's men stormed the countryside now black with musket smoke and cannon scars. Joseph ignored the sound of fire by losing himself in a scandalous passage of the book while irregulars approached his doors with daggers in hand.

Joseph fled with his treasures to Paris, and after that to Bordentown, New Jersey, where he would live for the following twenty years. The folio was sold there, and lingered in rich-paneled libraries for the next century and a half, remaining largely unhandled because of translation difficulties—although I like to imagine some curious, bilingual debutante reading it, and becoming corrupted by its blasphemous and erotic content.

An anonymous seller put it up for sale last year, at a famous auction house in New York. Despite the folio's bad repair, the word had already spread that it was a recovered work of the insane novelist Padre de Pasamonte and so the lot spurred lively bidding. Still, there is no purse like the Getty's and we purchased it for an astonishing sum.

And so now, in a way, it's mine.

I AM EXAMINING the folio at my desk, as blue light ripples in from the windows. The lab where I work sits on the bottom floor of the library, and is a large, white, open space housing several paper conservationists. The color in the room comes from the objects scattered casually on tables and windowsills: a seventeenth-century gilded Bible someone pulled down from storage; a Murano glass horse; oxblood pottery vases filled with blue bearded irises extending pollen tongues; rosewood lettering pens. There is also the oak book press, and a Benedictine book of hours from the fifteenth century. This last item sits on the table across from mine, at which my boss Teresa Shaughnessey sits and appears to labor over the book's fading illuminations. She bends her yellow-kerchiefed head over the pages;

from under the paisley cotton tight gold scrolls of hair reflect the morning light—this is the first growth since her chemotherapy ended eight months before. Her fine pale face, with its wedges of cheekbone and the gray eyes with their small fringe of bronze lashes, hovers over a picture of Bathsheba posing near a fountain in a transparent dress as David admires her from a window in a tower. Age and oxygen distress the portrait; when Teresa touches the fountain with her finger the page tints her flesh with crumbled blue, though this does not make her snatch her hand away.

"I can go get you a pair of gloves if you want me to," I say.

"No thanks." She smiles up at me. "Don't look so nervous, I'm not *hurting* it, sweetheart."

"The paint's coming off."

She looks at her finger and smiles. "So it is!" Closing the book, she props her elbows on it and cups her chin in her hands. "You'll never guess where I went last night. I had the most naughty and *delicious* evening!"

"I don't know. Let's see—a strip club?"

"No, I gorged on those months ago. And all that flapping about does get on the nerves, I have to say. I went to this fantastic club in Hollywood where these pretty little girls played some sort of feminist acid rock until four in the morning. Amazing! They wore tiny dresses made of . . . some kind of electric tape, I believe, strategically placed, and they had the most wonderfully filthy mouths. All very fuck this and fuck that, phallus this, prick that, while they flung their pink hair about like Medusas. It was not as vulgar as it must sound. It was almost beautiful, like one of those fabulous car crashes by Carlos Almaraz."

I shake my head at her.

"Aren't you quite too young to be a prude, Sara? I wish you could have come, but then you would have had to stay up until two o'clock in the morning, and I know that *you* like to be asleep by eight."

"That's not true."

"It is unless you're having another one of your flings with that paramour of yours. Karl, the dashing sailor."

"The dashing marine—whom I did see yesterday, I'll have you know."

"Well, bravo. At least there's that. But you should come out with me some evening—there are the most absurd things to see in this town after dark. Not that I would have known it a year ago. Sweetie, I was just like you, so angelic and responsible and, excuse me, boring. And after the hospital . . . you know, I realized— What have I been doing all these years? Spending it here, alone? Watching the damned television? Now, of course, I go to clubs, I go out dancing, and then there are my lovely parties,"—here, her voice lowered into a whisper—"In fact, I think I will invite a few friends to the museum next month for another soirée. What do you think? Canapés? Champagne, foie gras? A giant tiramisu?"

"No foie gras," I say.

Teresa continues ticking off her menu for the next of her secret parties (secret, at least from the Getty's trustees) that are a kind of museum geek's equivalent of the goings-on in the basement of Studio 54 during the early 70s. They are scandalous extravaganzas, which only a select few are invited to, as they are constructed around the premise of gallivanting around the museum as if it were your own home, where you can prop your feet up on the eighteenth-century silk divan once owned by Napoleon and sip gimlets from gold goblets that littered the tables of Rudolf II.

I've told her a million times that her fêtes are unethical, and probably even felonious, even if they're events at which the most mousy curators, antiquities experts, historians, restorers, and archaeologists go positively bananas with fun. But she ignores me. Before each party, Teresa pays off the guards, and after the museum has closed she turns off the alarms in one or two galleries, then removes the silk ropes from the antique settles and fauteuils and hauls out the Louis XIV silver from Decorative Arts. By midnight, the place is jumping. Scholars french-kiss and sip Cosmopolitans on neoclassical chaise longues, or attempt to dance to the low jazz bubbling from a boom box, taking time-outs to peer up at the Rembrandts, Turners, Titians, getting as close to the work as they like. No whoop whoop sounds when they get within sixteen inches of the French canvas or Aztec calendar; no warning bells shriek when they drink from an Etruscan chalice or slip on the pure gold armband made by sixth-century Mayans. A month ago a squib of duck liver did flop onto the peach satin of a rococo sofa, and last winter a drunk Egyptologist left a light lipstick imprint on a Vermeer when she tried to kiss it—disasters that I spent frantic weeks remedying. I play a kind of cop at these parties, armed with Q-Tips and foaming soap, terrified of red wine, and go especially crackers when anybody gets close to the pre-Columbian artifacts, but even I have to admit that our inventory doesn't show one theft and no one has blown the whistle on Teresa. As she points out, she's only satisfying an inno-cent fetish: The experts who have committed themselves to preserv-ing precious artifacts also have a mania for touching and using them—many say they've felt closer to the eras of their obsession when they can handle their relics like ordinary things.

If you'd asked any of them a year ago, though, not one would have guessed that Teresa Shaughnessey, Ph.D., winner of a Guggenheim, a MacArthur "genius" grant, onetime lecturer at Harvard in book arts, author of three monographs on Padeloup bindings and two on fore-edge paintings, should be the one to give them the opportunity.

For twenty long years she was the undisputed queen of incunabula restoration, having devoted her life energies to the problems of faded watered-silk endpapers, disintegrating German Girdle books, the three best ways to restore the delicate miniatures of Domenico Ghirlandaio. She was respected, yes, but not well-liked. She was not known by anyone well enough to be liked. Dr. Shaughnessey, as we called her, wore her hair in a tight little bun and bulky snowflake-patterned sweaters that could not drown her huge breasts; she shuffled down the hallways with her head tilted in a strange birdlike angle toward the ground and made eye contact with no one. Occasionally, she would peer up from her work and give a colleague a shy smile, but then snap her eyes right back down to work. And there were rumors that Dr. Shaughnessey held eccentric conversations either with herself or with her books—rumors that I started, actually, since we shared an office and I'd occasionally catch her in the midst of some comic observations, or even laughing at one of her own jokes, but as soon as she saw me she turned as quiet as a cat.

Then she became sick. This, again, was rumor, as she simply vanished for six months, and the disappearance was shrouded in an eerie silence. When she returned, though, we knew from the different shape of her sweater and her sleek head that the stories were true. And it was not just the cosmetics that had changed. During her first week back, when I referred to her by the title I always used, she placed her hand on my shoulder, then asked me to call her by her first name. I obliged; she took me to lunch, and our intimacy dates from that afternoon. She was confiding, though exhausted from her treatment. She told me that despite her fatigue she had started meeting people, going dancing, and in general trying to "gobble up the gorgeous world." She also said she was going to quit.

"I have discovered that I've made the terrible error of substituting *objects* for people in my life," she said, chewing on her sandwich. "Quite depressing, really. Dashes of paint on a canvas take the place of lovers. Leather and paper replace a child. History?! My hallowed passion! It is nothing more than a phantom, which though entertaining cannot be *kissed*. It simply does not exist—try to touch it in a hospital, Sara, while you are imprisoned in all that gleaming progress. It disappears like ether! There is no *real* life in a *Morte d'Arthur*, is there? No matter how gorgeous the binding? Happiness does not reside in Gutenberg's ink. Not even in your precious Mexican calendars, I think, dear. Everything should be used up, swallowed up! *Not* saved. Not hoarded like the bones of saints. And I *do* see this place as a kind of fantastic tomb. What I am saying to you is, this is a long-delayed offer of friendship. I was *such* an idiot for keeping to myself for so long. It is also, however, a good-bye. I am quitting the museum to become . . . I don't know. A travel agent, perhaps. A dog groomer. Something a bit more substantial, I hope."

But she wouldn't get her wish. The Getty would not let her go—not its most gifted restorer, not the woman who had resurrected Joachim of Fiore's *Vaticinia Pontificum* from a few scraps of dirty vellum into a glowing scripture! Not the magician who had conjured Francesco Alvarotti's glittering *Consilia et allegationes* out of a heap of filthy leather! They offered her money, then more money, then so much she had to stay. On her own terms, though—which are, I have to say, essentially dangerous to the historical project. She is a kind of saboteur. Most of her efforts to restore books have ceased, since she doesn't see the effort as worthwhile any longer, and believes even the greatest, most beautiful works should be allowed to molder gracefully into the ground or, better yet, be worn down to smooth nubs after being handled, touched, experienced directly, and not in the white-gloved way we currently interact with the great relics. And so she will filch a precious folio from storage and bring it to a local middle school, where she'll let the students leaf through the vivid pages (after washing their hands, at least). And so she'll let the moldering folios' pages bloom with perilous green gardens (I am trying to fix these in my spare time). And so the parties, where all the laws of preservation-observation are suspended—which she continues talking about now.

"You *are* coming?" she asks. "It's going to be an amazing time. I'm holding it in the south pavilion, with all the rococo. And I think I'll drag out some of the gowns from storage, like the ones we bought last year, supposedly worn by Veronica Franco?"

"I don't think I can make it. I have a lot of work to do."

"Not on *that*?" She points at *The Conquest*. "You could finish it during work hours, shouldn't take you more than six months. *If* you want to do it, that is."

"I want to do it."

"I certainly don't see what all your fuss is about. Like I've said before, I think this whole business is ludicrous."

"What we do is not ludicrous, Teresa."

"Well, I think you're particularly consumed with this one, in any event. And have you catalogued it yet? Under *de Pasamonte*?"

"I'm still working on my theory."

"Yes, my sweet, I have noticed that you seem to be in the thrall of another one of your bat-brained hypotheses. File it under *Peter Pan* for all I care, but for Christ's sake don't get fixated."

"Unlike some people I care if the cataloguing's accurate."

Teresa closes her book of hours and looks at me. "If you *insist*—I will go over this with you. *Again*. Unfortunately for you, I am nearly an expert on our old padre. In 1560, '66, '68, de Pasamonte writes *Las Tres Furias*, *La Noche Triste*, and *El Santo de España*—books with the same simple morocco, what looks to be the same handwriting. Am I wrong? No. And they have the same themes, the same narrative style."

"But those books were signed. And I don't think a man wrote this. I don't think a *Spaniard* could have written this book."

"Well, Mr. Joyce made old Molly Bloom up, didn't he?"

"This is different."

"And how is this so very different?"

I can feel my face flush. I look down and flip the book's pages. "I don't know. I just think it is."

"Well, I'm not going to press you on it anymore. I can see you're getting upset."

"I'm not upset."

"Of course you are! You're a sensitive one! And I used to be just like you, worrying and bollixing over every little thing. But that's not what I wanted to talk to you about today. I only want you to come to my party. *Do* come. It will be such a blast!"

I tilt my head up at her, and smile. "Actually, I may not be able to for another reason."

"Which is?"

"Karl. I hope I'll be seeing him that night."

"Oh dear, there's no competing with a naked man, even I know that. So, in that case, I will let you off. But just this once."

Grinning, she reopens her book of hours, and turns away from me. On the page in front of her, Bathsheba continues shimmering half-naked by the fountain; David gawks from his tower.

I return to *The Conquest*.

I OPEN THE FRONT board to the first flyleaf. Immediately, a scent of dust and age reaches me, and after that the faded words.

Reading has always been like dreaming for me, and I have to settle into a story much as the mind slowly rises from sleep into the night's strange forest. If I'm reading a love story, let's say a tragedy, some feature of the beloved's comes into focus first—Anna Karenina's eyes, dark as wine, then the glimmer of a gold thread in her dress. Sensations overlap from page to page like lines of music, for on top of the dress and eyes is Karl's face, or my mother's. Next comes the thread of a mazurka, pale breath in the train station, then the face of Tolstoy, white-bearded and dying in Astapovo. Last, there's the feel of the book under my hand.

The book is a body and your mind will mold to its individual curves much in the way it will to any other lover—at least, until it buckles beyond use.

That's where I come in.

The folio's text block has almost completely loosened from the case; the spine has broken. The morocco peels back from the boards and there is a canker of mold on the last twenty pages, which, besides damaging the vellum, also obscures the script. I spent several months studying the best approach to its restoration, and then cleaned the leather and sized and washed the leaves. Now I am onto the next stage, which is repairing the ulcered sections of the book's skin with the Japanese paper, dyed the same old-blood color as the morocco. The leaves will be mended with this same, undyed paper. For the text, I'll mix an ink of my own recipe—a silky, mink-colored ink, an ink like the one Cervantes once used—and repaint the Rotunda characters with one of Teresa's beautiful rosewood lettering pens.

But not *too* well. Out of respect for all of the dead, some sign of the centuries should stay. And besides, the book is a different thing now than when it was first written. The author's hands were once here (delicate, I'm sure, a small brown woman's hands, and not a pale monk's), but also thieves', and a thieving king's, and eons of New Jersey scions. To remind readers of this history I won't repair this scar on the back board, or even repaint the less faded letters.

I now lift the book off the desk, and flakes of vellum come off on my palms. Every time I pick up this volume, microscopic bits must erode onto my skin or travel from my fingers up to my lips, and in this way my cells absorb them like a poison or an oral vaccine.

the
CONqUEST

A few years ago, while perusing a volume on extreme cases of philobiblism for my own amusement, I read about a psychotic who loved books so much he ate them julienned and pan-roasted with potatoes, bell peppers, and a little garlic. Bibliophagia, I think was the diagnosis. I wondered what effect the works of Dickens would have on such a gourmand, as opposed to, say, those of Balzac or Schopenhauer.

I wonder what effect this book might be having on me.

Something is loosening inside of me; I feel a new transparency, a susceptibility. At night I have difficulty getting to sleep, as I'm plagued by fantasies. I imagine myself outside of Karl's apartment, looking up at his window from the shadows. I'd like to serenade him as the Italians did; I would sing an aria from *Don Giovanni* before scaling his balcony and kissing his mouth so that I am perched, thrilled, in thin air.

Maybe the girl who wrote these pages is running through me like a drug borne on a scrap of paper. A girl Teresa thinks was a wayward monk. A love affair no one but me thinks really existed. I think this mysterious narrator is affecting me somehow. She makes me want to go to extremes. After feasting on her story, I feel brave enough to scale a tower for Karl. I would ignore the limitations of my era and sex and win him in sword battle like a sixteenth-century century *magnifico*. I would embrace him in the long, wet grass until he remembered no other name but my own.

I turn the flyleaf. I read.

3.

I, who am now called Helen, was raised from birth to be an Aztec king's wife, but the only thing I ever wanted to do was be a juggler.

My borrowed name was not made, however, by either the throne or the small red balls I could float in the air like a sorceress. Instead I found myself a slave, a silk-draped concubine, and an assassin.

I became all of these things because of the Spaniards.

THE SHORE OF MEXICO, 1528.

After my kindred stoned Montezuma to death and Cortés torched Tenochtitlán into cinders, the Spanish general ordered his soldiers to load his ships with the last of the gold, some fine examples of our jewels and feather work, and finally a small collection of buffoons and dancers and jugglers—including the greatest juggler who ever lived, the magnificent Maxixa—who, Cortés thought, might impress his own countrymen.

Although I am a woman, and thus not eligible to practice the high art of jugglery, I taught myself the craft, in secret, from a very young age. I can spin ninety-two spheres in the air at one time. I have transformed gold balls into twirling birds.

It is the only talent that I have.

And so that spring, when the acrobats and clowns climbed the gangplanks of the general's gleaming ships, I donned the juggler's uniform of deer hide and face paint, thus obscuring my sex, and followed them, juggling, as if it were the most natural course of all.

My exiled brothers gave me strange looks but not one mentioned my fraud to the Spaniards. They had enough worries on their minds.

They would have applauded me, though, if they knew the real reason I went to Europe. I am the last of a long line of royal Aztecs. My beloved father, Tlakaelel, when he lived, had been prince of a great and wealthy province, and a fierce patriot who knew the power of his ancestors. He said to me once that "the only way to survive this life, daughter, is to hold our grandfathers deep in our hearts. Only the man, or girl, who girds her heart tightly enough that she preserves in it the hearts that lived before her makes a shield so strong that the arrows of villains, or perhaps even time itself, cannot pierce it." My father also taught me the wisdom of vengeance. He cautioned me to keep in mind always the enemy's debt to our honor, and said no shed blood, no act of burning a temple or book or father would remain unremembered, or unanswered.

As I am his living kin, and of honorable blood, that answer would be mine.

In his last few moments, when he knew that my mother and all ten of my brothers had died from fire and starvation, Father took my hand and whispered his final charge.

"Kill these savages' king in revenge for their crimes."

On April 1 (this date comes from the calender I learned in Rome) I stood on the prow of the Spaniards' ship with my red and gold balls stashed in my many pockets, and an obsidian knife strapped against my thigh. I watched as General Cortés kissed his Mexican lover—a beautiful and clever traitor—on the shore.

And then we set sail.

THE MORE THE YEARS pass, the more my old home shines in my mind. The horrors have almost all vanished and I can see again the great library before it was burned; the zoos of birds and tigers; the gardens. For me, now, home resembles the priests' Paradise most of all, which makes me wonder if "memory" is simply another word for "imagination."

But it was so beautiful.

We built the city of Tenochtitlán on water, and so we walked on water the same as Charles V's Christ. We lived in a floating pleasure garden of spice trees and red maguey, and we worshiped at giant stone temples where young men, transformed into gods, were draped with white and pink petals. We anointed these men-gods with oils and emeralds before the holy sacrifice. Later the banquet tables buckled under the roast goat, corn, tomatoes, cactus, and the sacred feast made out of the sacrificed man. One could not look at his horrible face, the flowers in his hair, but one taste of his body ensured rain and corn for the entire year.

These were some of the most glamorous nights of my life. At the banquets the jugglers and buffoons performed for the Emperor's enjoyment until dawn, and we were permitted to watch along. One holy evening—the blackest evening of the year, where no moon nor star cut the dream-tinted darkness of the sky, only the gold torches blazing—on this evening Maxixa spun one hundred silver spheres at a time so that it appeared as if the jeweled air itself were at his command. The very heavens seemed at his bidding, for as the one-hundredth sphere dazzled up through the aerosphere a change could be felt in the wind, which fanned about us like giant bats. All was anima in that second, the rocks, the watching trees, I could feel Epicurus' atoms like sparks on my skin. Quietly we stared at the silver-sprinkled sky and the endless black beyond. Then a moon appeared, larger than a god. The one-hundred-and-first sphere.

The moon, I tell you. The great Maxixa summoned the moon.

It hovered behind him like a pet bird. And as he juggled, I remember, his body vibrated with joy.

It was that night I developed my lifelong passion. To this day, I still possess no larger ambition than to be as excellent a juggler as that man.

But it was not to be so.

INSTEAD, I WAS DESTINED to become one of Montezuma's 1,000 wives.

The Emperor's seraglio was a castle made of precious woods and mammoth amethysts that served as pink windows to the outside world. When guards passed back and forth in front of these windows they could see hazy, round shapes there. Sometimes, the braver girls pressed their mouths and naked breasts against the transparent stone to tease them, even though discovery would mean certain death.

Their many privileges had made them reckless.

The Emperor, enjoying intelligent conversation as much as the pleasures of the flesh, withdrew the prohibition on the education of women where his wives were concerned. He summoned the court's astronomers and poets to tutor his women. A number became accomplished poets themselves, and wrote the most beautiful love songs I believe have ever been sung in the history of the universe. Others mapped the stars with a genius greater than Copernicus'. Still others developed mathematical formulas that tackled the mysteries of sun and moon.

Nevertheless, their talents lay trapped behind ebony and pink jewels, except for the day when the Emperor called upon them in the interests of pleasure.

Montezuma preferred to take his wives in an open-air bed at the center of his famous garden. I saw him touching the shining body of his eight-hundred-and-thirty-second wife one day, when I stood behind a spice tree, spying and shivering with excitement. His skin looked as soft and red-brown as the earth and his long black hair swept over the jaguar-eyed girl. Their moans made the faces of the nearby sentries ripple with frustration.

I, who had never experienced love before, gripped onto the spice tree as if it were a friendly body. Lightning flashed inside my ribs. I hoped that such pleasure awaited me too, and soon.

But one week later, a giant brown creature galloped into the garden. Perched on this monster was a white-

skinned liar named Cortés, or (some thought) Quetzalcoatl, who spoke through his Mexican translator.

Within the year, most of us were dead.

꩜ I THINK MY HEART should have died in
those cinders of Tenochtitlán.

I think my heart should have been starved out of my
body as my father's life was starved out of his body.

But there were nights, on the Spaniards' ship, when
I would look out onto the dark moon of the ocean and
feel something flicker within me.

Perhaps it was my desire for revenge that heated my
heart.

Or, the desire for the feeling I had once when I gripped
the spice tree and saw the jaguar-eyed girl. Not one lover,
male or female, had yet printed my body with theirs. I
consider love and juggling two of life's highest callings.

But whom would I love now?

For a moment, I thought of tucking myself under the
dark waves that covered the world, and of swimming
down to where the seashells and skeletons live.

But for the beauty of the moon upon the water, I
would have done it.

꩜ EVER SINCE I BEGAN reading The Conquest, the
quick strange voice of its narrator, Helen, has stayed with me. I
move through Los Angeles with her book in my mind, descending
from the museum to walk and drive through the city's morass
while translating her story in a private tongue.

The Getty perches on top of its alp, like an awesome white

palace that exists out of time. White trams, commuting to and from the parking lots, transport the visitors and employees away from the snarled cars, the blaring radios, the smells of cooking and the noise and laughter, up to these white galleries of stone, the fixed and beautiful vividness of a Rembrandt or a Turner against the muted, perfect walls.

And then, back down they go again. (Though for me it is never for long.)

In my '97 Camry, on the tree-lined 110 freeway, I tell Helen's story to myself. I try to stay close to an English that might hold the Spanish she penned on the old vellum, which is the malediction poured into a slave's ear but also the adept tongue of a lover. While I drive home today, I zip past the gorgeous indestructible oaks and the bedraggled elms chugging oxygen up to the ozone like a last lost hope until I settle next to another Camry, this one a burgundy '99 with a decal of the Mexican flag glued onto the rear windshield alongside a Goth-font insignia for the rock band Metallica. After a while I notice that inside the car is a family with three children, all of whom are looking at me with bewilderment, and I realize that I have been reciting pages of *The Conquest* out loud in my car and making facial expressions.

I wave at the kids, and they wave back, yelling things I can't hear. One of the smaller girls, a round little dryad with caramel skin and large plastic glasses, bears a resemblance to me when I was her age, about eight. She now stares at me without blinking; a habit I am sure others think peculiar. She wears gold buttons in ears that were probably pierced a few days after she was born.

When their father zips around a blue Miata to get into the fast lane, I can just see their little hands still waving, and then they disappear.

And now my thoughts drift away again, floating over the shiny humps of cars, the trees and green sequined signs. I begin again to puzzle over Helen's scenes, and the riddle of mingling high Spanish with my English designs. I have no trouble leaving this place and returning to the story.

ITALY'S GREEN SHORES *made me so homesick for the deeper green of our dead jungle. The second I saw it looming over the blue, I considered running my knife through Cortés's neck then and there, despite the talisman of St. Peter he wore about his neck.*

I already knew he was no god, regardless of the portents that confused the Emperor. Scurvy had made us all bleed.

Days after landing, we entered a Rome already gilded with my old world's gold, and which was especially bright with flowers and flags now to celebrate the recent return of His Holiness. The Pope, Clement VII, a onetime conspirator with France and thus no great friend of Spain's king, had just emerged from exile in Viterbo after the so-called Sack of Rome and now lived in a giant, gleaming palace.

The Vatican is as white as the dead bones that helped build it.

CORTÉS GAVE US AS *a present to the Pope, along with gold holy relics and the sacred headdress of our Emperor. The relics and headdress were installed in the Vatican's ethnographic museum, and we were installed in a small apartment. On my fifteenth birthday, I was baptized by Clement VII himself after being given a good scrub by an ugly nun. It was because of her* anatomical revelations concerning what she'd seen in my bath that he gave me the name of Helen, despite my insistence on continuing to wear the juggler's uniform. He called Maxixa Alberto.

I will not disclose my original, true name, for it is as precious as blood itself. The Pope's St. Augustine once wrote that the soul resides in the blood, and so its unnecessary spillage is a heresy.

To me, my soul resides in my name. To speak it out loud would be my own bloodletting and so I am content to let it remain a mystery.

Not that the Pope was interested in hearing it.

He didn't seem much interested in us at all, and we stayed caged in our apartment for three of the 'Romans' weeks. Our only visitors were nuns, priests, janitors, and cooks, who assembled at our doorway to stare at us like stunned fish. They were a curious lot dressed up like shadows and with their strange plucked faces. They also appeared to suffer from an excess of nerves. On the fifth day of our incarceration two of my exiled brothers, in order to ward off melancholy, began stroking each other as men will do. Each of us averted our eyes in order to give them their privacy, but the priests and nuns were quite impolite and began screeching as soon as Nezahualpilli inserted his member into Cacama's arse.

While the Catholics flapped about I noticed one nun who did not react as the others did. Dressed in the same shadow fashion as her friends, she nevertheless possessed a beautiful, exotic face. Her pale, high bones and wide brow were so fair I could have etched her in the white sands of my home's shore. Her eyes were the same color as the giant emeralds our artisans once carved into the shapes of flowers. Her mouth was the same stain as red maguey.

She was staring at me.

Being blessed with a handsome bosom, I was surprised that my charade did not scandalize the Italians, but I later learned they thought us so eccentric they would not have been surprised had I been born half-fish or walked on hooves. This nun, however, let her eyes linger on my swells and a secret happiness lit her countenance as her eyes traveled back up to mine. This woman saw the human in me. As her colleagues attempted to pry my brothers apart she threaded through the commotion so that we stood face-to-face, and I noticed in those magnificent eyes the same lovely look I once spied in the jaguar gaze of Montezuma's wife.

In gratitude I recited a love poem written by an ancient king to one of his wives, and I spoke it soft enough so only she could hear:

"You have shoulders of gold, and the scent of water in
    spring.
Bring flowers to my heart, beauty. Do not abandon
    this warrior! I will kiss your fresh mouth.
I desire your skin, your voice, your small, soft hand."

Of course the nun could not understand the words I gave her.

Or could she? Perhaps she felt what was beneath them.

Out of her dark robes came a white hand. She pressed it to mine and smiled at me.

I could feel the life flickering inside me again.

Then the priests wrenched the lovers apart and carried them off, we were sure, as sacrifices. My friend threaded back from where she came and all the Catholics began kissing the weapons they hung around their necks—the same powerful sticks Cortés used to kill us. After that they fled in a whirl of black.

Now we were alone.

For days afterwards, my kindred's unhappiness was so great many spoke of starving themselves to death. Others suggested we strangle the priests and thus commit suicide indirectly by virtue of the Pope's guards' guns.

I did not encourage such talk. Although I had imagined death by drowning once, that flickering inside me sparked still. The truth is, I felt a terrible happiness to be alive. After so much murder, any sign of love or life that I spied filled me with the most sublime joy if I could ignore my phantoms of blood and slag. There was sweetness in the nun's white hand, or the sight of the formal garden outside of the window. Even the Italians' delicious food such as the strange spit-roasted beasts decorated with feathers and ribbons (and brought to us on silver plates melted down from our gods) inspired in me an ambition to live. Also, the rich, bacon-scented turnip greens simmering in copper pots. Or the cunning sugar sculptures of trees and fish, which I imagined were shaped for me by the beautiful nun's own fingers.

No, I could not starve myself to death.

I had to stay alive at least long enough to fulfill my father's charge.

But my cell mates continued planning their ends.

Maxixa, our leader, would sit in a corner wearing his deerskin rags, tossing one or two spheres toward the ceiling. I noticed when the talk grew too hot he began sending thirty or forty of them up like small stars. After a while, the men would stop plotting to enjoy the filigreed air and his other miracles. Once, he made it rain inside so everyone, from the Pope to the lowest slave, was soaked to the skin. Another time he created a rainbow in the sky, and as we stared at it he tucked his spheres in his various pockets, then looked at us.

"When this Pope asks us to perform, I will make his heart stop," he said.

We knew he could do it.

MAXIXA HAD BEEN APPRENTICED *to the famous juggler Quauhpopoca from the age of three, and quickly exceeded his tutor's own talents. The man and the boy lived in a cave on the outskirts of town and honed their wizardry. The city people understood that a great talent was upon them when, at ten, the boy balanced thirty-seven spheres on a cloud and then made it hail. That was almost forty years ago.*

Now, of course, he was known as the man who could command the moon like a falcon on a leash. But how?

After we had been imprisoned for ten weeks, I asked him to tell me his secrets.

He turned and aimed his hawk eyes down at me.

"Daughter," he said. "You believe that I have a secret? Some trick I hide under my sleeve perhaps? Foolish girl, my secret is that I have none! I possess only passion! My gift teases then slips away from me like a woman, and the only thing I can do is attend to her as I

would a wife who tortures me with stinginess. *Practice, practice, practice is my one lure. There is no more jealous lover than juggling. If I stroke the talent just softly enough, if I praise her with the right words and lay the most perfect bed, this bitch, this seductress will approach defenseless and mold herself under my hands. No, she is not my gift, she is a gift to me, and if I do not set the proper conditions and wait for her, she will not appear. Every day I wake wondering if she is gone."*

This was not the instruction I had been hoping for.

Still, I followed his advice. I practiced antipodal juggling as I propped myself in a handstand. I attempted the fantastic feats of legerdemain, including making sixty spheres, three silver plates, and Maxixa himself disappear. I also learned the high art of sword swallowing.

My brothers followed suit, for example Ixtlilxochitl with his marvelous S-shaped nose practicing his buffoonery and the crane-thin Camargo honing his acrobatics, and soon everyone was back to our contortions and plate spinning, with Maxixa presiding over us like a genie.

Then finally, after more than a month, two priests appeared at the door, ducking to avoid the flying crockery.

"The Pope commands a performance."

POPE CLEMENT VII, *bastard son of one Giulio de' Medici, was a weak-chinned man with liquid eyes who was utterly unprepared to contend with the Martin Luthers of his future. A soft-minded aesthete, he had recently commissioned work on the glorious paintings of one Raphael, and summoned us to appear before him in the Stanze d'Eliodoro, an apartment in the papal palace*

of Nicholas III. This room was filled with a gentle light that danced across Raphael's *The Liberation of St. Peter*, a fresco showing a giant gold god bending over the shackled body of an old man who wore a strange, flat, round gold hat.

We, as it happens, were already familiar with this St. Peter due to the talisman Cortés had worn around his neck, but thankfully we would not be receiving any more of his religious instruction today.

The Pope now sat on his throne. A nearby priest gesticulated madly for us to begin.

Maxixa, armed with his one hundred silver spheres, stepped forward.

We held our breath.

THE GREAT MAXIXA, student of the famous Quauh-popoca, ruler of hail and rainbow and moon, genius juggler of the sixteenth century, stood before this chinless weakling and prepared to stop his heart.

He quickly threw fifty spheres in the air and began weaving one of his spells. The spheres danced in the empyrean like flying fish and the Pope, along with each priest, each nun, including (I now saw) my soft-palmed girl, stared upwards with expressions they did not wear even in prayer.

Maxixa's body trembled with joy as he added, ten, next twenty spheres more. And then, as the eighty balls flew too fast for the eye to follow, we could hear it: The underwater sound of a heart beating.

Hup-hup. Hup-hup.

The Pope's heart.

Clement VII wavered in his throne and we could see

his eyelids flickering just then, as if he were tripping into a light sleep. Here ten more spheres were added, thrown up like rain. Hup-hup. At one hundred the Pope would be dead.

But just at that moment, Maxixa made a mistake.

Raphael's mural gleamed before us in the afternoon light filtering through the windows. The light beams reflecting off the mural's brilliant colors attracted Maxixa, who has always had something of a weakness for beauty.

He looked at the mural and recognized the old shackled man there, from the amulet that had adorned Cortés's neck.

At that deadly sight, Maxixa's body stopped trembling. Next, all ninety spheres fell to the ground in a silver shower. Maxixa followed them, slumping into a faint, as his genius leapt out of his body like a ghost. And here the Pope, suddenly wide awake, and all the priests and nuns sat up to clap in wild appreciation.

Clement VII never knew that St. Peter saved his life.

I had hated that saint for longer than a year by this time, as did my brothers, and today we hated him with an even more bitter dread.

He cost us everything we had.

AT HOME IN PASADENA, I sit on my garden porch, still translating to myself, and watch the dusk sift onto the wide black streets, the bosky trees. The sidewalks and granite lamp-posts and the driveway-choking S.U.V.s reflect the particular blue of this hour. In a Greene-and-Greene knockoff bungalow across the way (my house is built in this same style, as Pasadena is one of

L.A.'s few havens for nostalgics), a frantic dalmatian scrambles its giant paws on a window while a family man, a Korean neighbor of mine whose name I do not know, parks his sedan, then stumbles over a hose and a toppled silver Razor scooter on his way up to his front door.

In the midst of my reverie, I watch him enter his house—lit with stained-glass lamps and decorated with California Impressionist oil reproductions—and greet his loving family despite the dalmatian's insistence on offering him a vigorous series of embraces.

They sit at their dining room table to eat dinner, frowning over their food, raising their heads and laughing, a small crying one among them wreaking some commotion, and the father's responding kisses—all this I can see from my porch. The moon is barely visible in the sky. The house windows brighten when the light lowers.

The dusk pools in my lap, as I hold the Spanish and English phrases in my mouth. I have all the time I need to memorize passages from the folio and study them. I have all the space and quiet a scholar might want to pursue the clues coded in those old beautiful pages. Nothing here will disturb me, no voice or tumult or sound of snoring or embraces from large families, no kisses and sly jokes told in the night.

It is lovely this evening, the soft drifting blue dark. No foot appears on my porch step; in my home no child with large plastic glasses agitates the precise arrangement of volumes on their shelves. I have total freedom to work, and loneliness, and doubt about my choices. I enjoy unhampered access to these secrets and feasts of words that I have been on the lookout for since the day my mother asked me to understand her theft of the *amoxtli* fragment in a way that was not tragic.

I have the book. The soft, ancient vellum leaves. The large and dramatic hand-*ductus*. I can still remember the days when I began to decipher the pages. That stumbling feeling of discovery. That wonder of what was real, how much could be autobiography. The intimate sensation of adjusting to the author's rhythm, the tuning of the ear so that you might hear that close, whispering lover's confidence. And the anticipation of what might happen next.

PART *two*

4.

After our failure to assassinate the Pope, His Holiness, in His magnificent ignorance, summoned us again and again to perform for him in the Stanze d'Eliodoro. We complied by leaping through hoops made out of each other's arms (this was the sinuous-nosed Ixtlilxochitl) and balancing ourselves on two fingers (here, the crane-thin Camargo), all within sight of the gold-hatted saint who had presided over our fathers' murders. At each show Maxixa would try to levitate the one hundred balls in the air only to watch ninety fall. There were no more rainbows or housebound hails. No more planets beckoned like dogs. No Catholic heart suspended in its deadly work. His talent had fled him, and would not return for eleven years (although when it did, he almost brought the sky itself crashing to the ground).

The Pope, in his appreciation, showered the now gray-faced, dull-eyed Maxixa with rich gifts of a mink coat and his own coach and driver. The man never understood that every exhibition was only a spectacular failure.

For my part, I stood in the corner juggling my spheres and trying to ignore any feelings of mirth, but I must admit it was difficult at times. I was doing what I loved with all the time in the world and every juggling resource. It was during this period that I perfected the juggling of up to fifty spheres, as well as the more impressive art of juggling knives, which were specially forged for me out of our stolen silver by the Pope's own smith, and which had to be turned precisely four times in the air in order to be caught by their pearl handles. This was a dangerous occupation for someone who still saw the spirits of her clan flit through the Vatican's chapels—I often saw my father Tlakaelel in these first few months in the corner of our apartment, with his face marked by blood and his mouth distended into a scream. Because of these memories, there were days when I saw a dagger in the air before me and contemplated letting it sink into my breast.

What, or rather who, stopped these thoughts was the nun applauding in the back row, behind the guards and priests.

My sweet girl came to each performance.

SHE VISITED ME DURING the second month of our incarceration, appearing in the doorway like a shade except for the two sparkling, and very alive emerald eyes.

She had been assigned to civilize me. She did.

Her name was Caterina.

DEEP INSIDE THE Vatican's splendid gardens grows a small bower of lime trees which hides a secret and verdant lair. The air was scented by the lime blossoms and jeweled, that summer, by a sparkling light rushing through the leaves like water.

Caterina, undone, had hair the same color as that light. And a long white body that was not like Maxixa's moon nor the silvered waves nor the daggers I orbited above my breast but only like itself, rare and incomparable. Caterina, neither Catholic nor European nor woman nor man, but only my sweetheart who met me in that green room.

The first day she laid me on a silk shawl and began, very slowly, to kiss only my neck and whisper incomprehensible words. From there she moved, up and down, in sections. My collarbone, my bottom lip. My hipbone and the tender skin under the knee, with the glossy stuff of her hair on my skin. Looking up at the sky of leaves I felt myself spread out, shivering, and disembodied.

I felt this way before when I saw our city burned, and it had made me frightened.

But now I felt this way because I had fallen in love.

CATERINA LUCIA *Gloria de Carranza was of pure royal blood, her mother harking back to Italian dukes and her father from a Spanish count, but de Carranza's constant presence at the casinos of Toledo threatened the fortune of his young and comely, if somewhat queer, daughter.*

Gossip noted that the girl had too fine an affinity for books, and, as everyone knew, literacy did not bode well for the soundness of the mind nor womb. The child, almost a lady at fifteen, made something of a spectacle of herself on summer days by forgoing the traditional courtship-dance ritual of the morisca, instead preferring to sit by the Tagus with her rosy-cheeked nurse and read fairy tales out loud. According to those closest to the house, the girl inherited her eccentricities from her father, himself an impulsive man who was known to have once played penny-prick for eighteen hours straight—and at a notorious gambling house frequented by various jades and Ganymedes, at that.

As gossip expected, de Carranza's indulgences eventually did bring the family to a bad end.

At one of his penny-prick marathons, de Carranza lost nearly five thousand pesos to the wealthy, vindictive, and infamously flatulent Marquis de Aragón, who was known to share an intimacy with Francisco Jiménez de Cisneros, the Inquisitor General and thus overseer of all heresy trials. The panicked de Carranza fled to his offices to examine his books, only to discover that not even the sale of his castle would cover his debts, and in his desperation he offered the only jewel the unmarried Marquis might value over gold.

His daughter.

Caterina was to be married in six months, in a white silk gown and a veil so long and wide it could clothe four families with a taste for Ronda lace. The Marquis, however, was an impatient rogue, and a few days after the wager he bribed his way into Caterina's bedchamber in order to sample his winnings.

Later, he said he was nearly blinded by the devilish specter he saw there.

Under the bedclothes he spied two forms tussling about in a frenzy, and throwing back the sheets he discovered his fiancée engaged in a most precise and expert pleasuring of her rosy-cheeked nurse, who was twisting about like Lilith. Then, staggering back against the girl's nightstand, he came upon an equally great sin. A volume of epic poetry. He picked it up and saw that it was Ovid's *Metamorphoses*.

Both the fucking and the possession of this banned book were capital offenses under the Inquisition, and within the month the Marquis owned yet another castle. De Carranza, his wife, and the nurse were jailed as concealers and heretics. Caterina, as a lovely and ignorant virgin, was able to avoid the stake by taking her orders.

By the time I met her she had been a nun for thirteen years.

"It's not as bad as you might think," she told me, after I learned enough Italian and Spanish to understand her. "Especially if one may forget the horrors of the past. So forget, my angel, forget everything! There is no country for the memorious, only longing with no home. And besides, there is so much to enjoy here. Certainly this life has its difficulties—the kneeling and the scraping, which of course can do nothing but madden a proud girl like myself. And then there are the mandatory silences, the hideous heat in summer—the wardrobe, my sweet, you can have no idea. Many's the day I wear my robes without a stitch on underneath, and amuse myself by imagining what the Pope might say if I flashed him a breast or a bit of pudenda. I might guess he'd have something of a laugh before he had them cut my head off."

She touched my cheek and smiled.

"But no, life can be quite pleasant if you only learn that there are certain tricks. Stuffing your bed with pillows in the shape of a body before running off with a paramour, stupidities of that order. Getting dispensations to attend His Holiness's marvelous parties. Hiding one's books, certainly. And the books! Every banned volume is here, under this roof! The guards are more than happy to indulge a sister's appetite for poetry in exchange for 'gifts'—not that any of them are worth two sneezes as lovers. That's where the women come in. I have tasted the fruits of the highest nobility. One of my ladies, the Countess Mathilde of Quaragna, a woman widely known throughout Europe for her piety and grace, is actually at heart the most delicious scoundrel who once kissed me for three hours in a silk bed—that cat! You must meet her."

Here Caterina laughed, and taking my hand in hers, began tracing my palm's lines with her lips.

"But I have to say"—and here she called me not "Helen" but my true name, which I had whispered to her in confidence—"I have never, never met a girl quite like you."

Now her mouth moved up my arm, and then to my neck.

I closed my eyes.

I LIVED WITH my brothers at the Vatican for the next two years. During this period the ghosts of my clan, who had at first astounded me, bloody and screaming, in every corner, now seemed to fade into ever lighter and lighter shades until they nearly disappeared. I later realized that ghosts, though incorporeal, need to be fed much as the human body does in order to stay alive. But not with meat: with memory.

Only two revolutions of the Roman calendar had passed but already I was in mortal danger of forgetting, and because of my happiness. It is treason to admit this, but those years as the Pope's slave were some of the most pleasure-filled in my life, as it was the first time I had such perfect access to what I cherish most—love and juggling.

As I have mentioned, Caterina's papal mission was to civilize me, and she did. She showed me what raptures hide in the bed and the book, giving equal attention to each discipline. And I was an agile pupil. Her faithful friend the Countess Mathilde—a majestic, fleshy mountain of a woman, who dressed up for His Holiness in star-shaped beauty patches and gigantic farthingales—was besotted (and wealthy) enough to provide us with stolen Edens on some afternoons. And so you might have found me, if you had been a spy, spread out naked on pink silk in a country castle empty except for a few discreet servants to provide our wasted bodies the honeyed fruits they needed to stay alive—for my sweetheart did exhaust me.

One of our most strenuous occupations was what she called the Eternal Kiss. After we bathed in rose-strewn water, she would command me to close my eyes then lay me down on that silk (or the grass patch in the Vatican garden, or a friendly marchioness's gold-encrusted bed in Milan) and put her tender mouth to me. What proceeded was the most delicate voyage, I swear, into heaven itself. After two hours with her lips on my skin my body's borders dissolved and I became as incorporeal as the ancestors who had glimmered at me from the shadows. I was a ruby on her tongue, is that it? I felt myself as honey and saffron in her mouth? Can I describe the lightning in my breast? Her white fingers finding red pleasure? All I can tell you is that I was dead and resurrected with her expert charms and soft breath—and then, as I still panted, my taskmaster patiently, strenuously instructed me in these same skills.

Oh, her gold hair on the pillow. Her eyes glinting.

But there would be no sleep. Caterina, you see, always liked a scrap of poetry after her conquests.

She was my tutor, after all.

The approved fields of study for a nun and a slave could only be the high teachings of Christ and servants' etiquette, perhaps a little embroidery. My professor tended to veer from this curriculum, having discovered that the raptures of bed and book are more related than one might realize. She taught me that vertebra, for example, comes from the Latin versus, which means line, and so is connected, also, to verse.

And it was true, I saw. Her spine was a line of poetry. I ran my fingers down each large pearl.

She was a word-mad girl. I remember the day she rolled over in bed, grasping a small pamphlet to her chest.

"I have a most wonderful present for you," she said. "Here, in my hands, are the sonnets Petrarch wrote to his great amor, the glorious Laura! One of my old lovers, the wife of a brilliant professor (although I must say that he is also an absolutely hideous monkey), tells me that there is a theory amongst the scholars that the girl never existed, and was only a figment of the poet's fevered imagination. But I do not believe these base rumors. No, I am sure that such exquisite lyrics could only have sprung from the pen of a man who adored a flesh-and-blood creature, a living mermaid, a goddess, just as I worship you, my darling."

She bent over the pages, and fed Petrarch's longings to me word by word, until I understood them:

Thoughts of you are arrows, your face a sun, desire a fire; and with all these weapons Love pierces me, dazzles me, and melts me; and your angelic singing and your words, with your sweet breath against which I cannot defend myself, are the breeze before which my life flees.

She wept over this song, "Don't you love it?"

As I remember this moment now, I feel young again. If I could only show you how beautiful she looked with her fingers touching strange language. But I cannot.

For that afternoon passed years and years ago, when I was still an innocent in the world.

MY OTHER OBSESSION filled the hours when I could not kiss or recite songs with Caterina. By the time Clement VII signed the Peace of Barcelona with Charles V, I could alight up to sixty spheres, a record untouched by anyone else in our troupe except its leader. We also taught ourselves the magnificent craft of equestrian juggling, and could gallop in surrounding fields on the Pope's black Andalusians tossing all manner of knives and balls at each other as no one had ever seen before.

These were not the only hobbies my brothers were employed in, however. Like myself, many of them had discovered the delights that could be found in this god's house—the fact is that for all of our fidelity to our King's memory, and all of our grief, most of us had been no better than Montezuma's dogs back home. Some of my kindred gorged on the truffled pheasant and wine, while others became the fancy men of the harem of nuns and maids gliding about. Caterina told me that there had been a rash of excommunications as of late, which coincided with a shocking number of dusky babes delivered in the convents. As these milk-skinned creatures seemed to us the very spice of exotic sex, apparently our darkness had the same effect on them, and while we viewed our opposites as monsters and devils we were also passionately committed to getting each other in the sack.

As a consequence, my brothers grew fat and lustrous with satisfaction. We had to abandon the human pyramid exhibitions, as well as the contortion tricks. Each of us was so dazzled with happiness, however, these sacrifices were of no great moment.

That is, each of us was happy except for one.

Maxixa.

He withered day by day. He was so thin he resembled a dying tree. His eyes, which once had flames burning inside of them, were now snuffed and gray, and he handled his magic spheres with all the joy of a chained ape. In truth, he was not a juggler any longer, but was simply a tosser of balls. He did not even appear to mourn his genius. Instead, he would sit in the corner, manipulating one of my knives, hallucinating.

"Oh my sons, oh my daughter, I see before me the smoking world. I see the temples of Huitzilopochtli shattered on the ground. I see your mothers and fathers in this very room, here now, stained with ash, their hair ripped from their heads, and in such numbers it amazes me you mouse-minded oafs appear to witness nothing at all. Have you gone blind? Are you senseless now with your fucking and your food? These shades' sorrow is a river that pours into me day and night and demands hot revenge, but this old and wasted body is too weak to satisfy its ungentle task. Oh, oh me, oh my gods, I am a vessel of tears. And as this spirit, blackened by fire and bleeding, implores me at this very moment, I am too weak to give it any comfort."

At first, we tried to persuade Maxixa out of his horrors. The ghosts had disappeared for each of us long ago. But we could not. After a while we continued our exercises even as he sat there, wailing. We knew that his perfect mind had been shattered beyond any repair.

And so when the day came that the Pope received a visitor, the famous painter Titian, and we were called upon to give yet another performance, we knew that there might be trouble.

For the great Maxixa, the magician of magicians, was no more.

THE ESTEEMED VENETIAN PAINTER Titian graced our presence with a brief visit before he and Clement VII traveled to Bologna, where their Charles V would be crowned as the Holy Roman Emperor. Forty-two years old, and with a long curly flax-colored beard, the man was a wizard with a brush and about to embark upon the most successful stage of his career. Caterina, who once saw prints of his and sketched them, had already familiarized me with his work. Once I was able to adjust my eye to these Europeans' precious schemes—for we Aztecs sculpted and painted the human form in a way that more closely reveals its rough soul—I knew he deserved the highest compliment: Titian painted women as expertly and voluptuously as Caterina kissed them.

Yes, my eye, like my mind, did adjust. It became hungry for their art. My favorite piece of his was the glorious Sacred and Profane Love, which could only have been painted with women like us in mind. It shows, unmistakably, two Sapphists, one a fine lady dressed in silk and frills, the other rosily nude except for a brief veil over the sex and a spill of red scarf over one arm. They rest upon a fountain, dreaming of love, and are separated by a curious Cupid.

What kind of man could have painted such women? He was a visionary with the taste of a pornographer and an ego larger than the Pope's! The great artist came into the Pontifical palace all color and bombast and terrified the nuns, who swore that he gazed upon them with such a penetrating eye he could see the pink treasures beneath their robes. These rumors only stimulated my curiosity, and I decided I must meet him. When I heard he stayed at the Borgia apartments, I stole a servant's uniform and crept in there to find him bent over a desk, sketching. He looked up and gave me a fierce squint.

"A barbarian," he said. "How very interesting." He reached out his hand. "Come here, child."

Out of hospitality I permitted him a few cheeky gropes, though the moment he touched me I recognized nothing erotic nor disciplinarian in that hand. Instead, he inspected my body like a scientist—thinking me some strange brute recently delivered from the jungle. He examined closely the colors of my skin, exclaiming all the while, then peered into my eyes to marvel at my black irises, and finally succeeded in offending even my clement temper by probing my mouth to examine the solid whiteness of my teeth. I had seen the Pope's stable boys do as much with the Andalusians.

"What in holy hell do you think you're doing?" I asked.

And at the sound of my voice, speaking in perfect Italian, he fainted dead away. It had not even occurred to him that the beast before him could speak!

Nevertheless, within the hour, after some recitation of Sappho and Petrarch, I had the poor beggar madly in love with me.

"Come to Venice," he pleaded. "I must paint you. I'll give you anything that you want."

By this time his hands were on my breasts. I shrugged.

After a bit more of this comedy, the clock struck one, and I remembered it was time for our pre-performance practice. As quickly as I'd entered, I turned and left again, giving him a swift kiss on his shiny head.

I thought him a remarkably impressionable creature.

AT THREE O'CLOCK SHARP my brothers and I assembled for what would be our last performance.

The Pope in his glittering robes entered the Stanze d'Eliodoro, and the audience members prostrated themselves before him like one broken body before taking their seats. I saw my lover in the back row, her face polished with happiness. The plump Countess Mathilde attended as well, her gigantic skirts taking up three chairs. Titian sat within two seats of His Holiness's throne, the painter's thin cheeks showing spots of color as he stared at me like a starving spaniel—while I could not help gaping at Maxixa, who stood next to me, ashen-faced, muttering at nothing, his spheres dropping out of his pockets.

And here, as always, a priest gesticulated madly for us to begin.

We opened with the knives. Eighteen silver daggers were launched with all the deadly charm of vipers and caught expertly, each time, by their pearl handles. Weight juggling came next, as Ixtlilxochitl flung cannon balls up to the ceiling and caught them on the back of his neck as if they had only been feathers. Now we amazed the gallery with the Icarian art of foot-juggling, with eight of us propelling gaudy gold missiles perilously close to Raphael's ceiling frescoes.

Never had we been in such fine form as today with our timing, our precision, our wordless and instinctual anticipation of each other's actions—except Maxixa, who merely shuffled a sphere or two between his fingers and continued muttering at the walls.

The end of the show neared. Soon it would be time for the famous finale: Maxixa's spectacular Dance of the Dying Heart. But when the moment arrived he only chanted his sorry prayer for his ghosts, and so I tucked my arsenal of one hundred silver spheres into my pockets and stepped to the center of the stage. Breathless, I prepared to attempt what could not be done in the presence of that St. Peter.

But it was the Pope's favorite act, after all.

I sent twenty in the air at once, and in that moment I knew I owned the air. Now, out of nowhere appeared thirty, fifty, and I quickly exceeded my genius by handling sixty, then seventy! All went dim with the bodily, nay, lusty joy of my mastery, and at seventy-five some spark cracked the climate. It was as if each atom were lit by a secret fire. The sky outside the window darkened and the faintest glimmer of a rainbow appeared. Then, as eighty angels whirled above me and the room filled with thunder and shouts, some other sound entered my ear, soft as a footfall yet loud enough to snuff my brothers' cheers.

Hup hup. Hup hup.

The Pope's eyelids fluttered.

Eighty-two now eighty-five now ninety.

Hup. Hup.

Ninety-two. The Pope slumped and my body trembled with joy as the aerosphere clenched like a fist from my magic.

But then, all was lost. Maxixa began singing an awful, strange song.

"Do you see them? My sons and my daughter, do you see them?"

Suddenly, the spirits of loved ones shimmered again before us, filling the room to bursting. Transparent women bearing the horrible wounds from the Spaniards' lances spoke our true names. Men starved down to eyes and bones from the months' long siege of Tenochtitlán beat their ruined breasts. And our ancestors, however ravaged their ghostly bodies, had donned for us their finest costumes of gilt and infant skin to remind us of what had once been.

It could not be endured.

Ninety-two spheres rained to the ground. My brothers and I bent before our dead families, weeping. Maxixa ran at the Pope and tried to kill him with his bare hands, only to then be charged with the worst capital offense Rome could fathom.

In this fury, I pressed my face to the floor and begged forgiveness from the gods. Then I felt a hand on my shoulder.

When I looked up I saw my father.

He was so thin and old, I did not know how he could have the strength to travel to this place. But it was his sadness that I could not take. His eyes told me again his old counsel that only the heart that retains the hearts of its ancestors may survive this life. That no act of bloodshed nor world burning should go unpaid. They reminded me of my life's forgotten charge, which was to kill these savages' king.

And how could I not sacrifice all to accomplish that errand when I saw his beloved face?

The Europeans thought us quite mad, as we were praying and shrieking to the invisible dead. The Pope, surrounded by his guards, fled the room with his gold robes fluttering through the door. Even my girl was horrified by the sight of me shrieking before thin air. I caught her eye as I was dragged from my father by burly guards, and I knew her terror and confusion.

Only Titian, the artist, remained calm.

The next day he bribed the sentries now posted at our door and asked for a conference with me.

"Dear Helen, I am not frightened by your superstitions, and my offer remains open," he said, pressing his delicate hands together. "You think me an old man, but I can give you the world. I live in a grand mansion in Venice and I will fulfill your every wish if you allow me to paint you. Gossip says that I am, if you have not already heard this, a man of some power and influence. I can introduce you to many people, including the Emperor himself. I will bring you to his coronation in Bologna, I will bring you to Paris, we can travel to the moon if you like. Only say yes."

Had I heard him correctly—did he say he would introduce me to Charles V? Could I, as a guest of this famous painter, get close enough to rip that king's heart out and satisfy my dear shade?

I took Titian's hand.

"Yes."

WE WERE TO LEAVE the Vatican three days later—for the Pope had no objection to my departure. Maxixa had already absconded on one of the Andalusians, as no chains or prisons could hold that clever necromancer. My brothers were also planning their escapes.

But I, because of Titian's fancy, could simply walk free out the door.

The Countess Mathilde, at Caterina's request, provided me with some traveling clothes, and I found myself dressed in a curious, if gorgeous, uniform of lace and burgundy silk. In the mirror, I could not find the apprentice juggler but instead discovered a pretty but baffling hybrid beast.

"I can see why she is so taken with you," the kind Countess said to me. Still, I was in no mood for self-admiration.

It came time to say good-bye to my love.

Caterina brought me to the bower where we had first kissed, and wound herself around my body so gently I would have abandoned my plan, but she pressed herself to me once, hard, and would not hear talk of my staying.

"Be happy, my sweet girl," she said, crying. "Forget me, forget everything. Be well."

And then she disappeared through the trees.

It was at this moment I knew how hard the task is that my father once described to me, that of girding one's heart. I felt my heart unraveling, and thought all my sadness would drown and kill me.

Nevertheless, my body lived. I remembered my father's last words and I left that place.

BOLOGNA, SPRING, 1530.

One of my most surprising discoveries was how similar these aliens were to ourselves. I quickly determined that the savages' Emperor was no different from my own, dead king, in that both men suffered from the same curious taenia solium—an insidious hunger, as if they had been infected by a worm of sorts, and the only foods that could satisfy them were submitting bodies and foreign soil. Montezuma fed on Tlascala, Cempoalla, Tezcuco, and Charles craved not just all of Europe, but the silk and spice-rich Ottoman Empire besides.

Well, eventually they both learned that the world is too large to fit into any mouth.

Charles V, having gained a sorry legacy from his father, Philip the Handsome, and his mother, Joanna the Mad, was a fleshy, pelican-jawed schemer who owned Spain, Naples, Sicily, the Low Countries, and Austria—and this was just his beginning. Now that he had broken the rebellious Clement VII's Francophile aspirations via the Sack of Rome, he was about to be crowned Holy Emperor of the Roman Empire.

This was to happen in three days, in the Basilica of San Petronio, and before the cream of Italian society.

As Titian's new muse, I would be invited along, and I in turn would also invite a secret guest:

The obsidian blade tucked between my thighs.

IN THE HOLIDAY BEFORE the assassination, Titian wished to lavish gifts on me in the style to which, he said, goddesses should become accustomed. He brought me to the Portico de Pavaglione and described the shops like treasure chests scattered through the city: Would I like a fox cape from the finest furrier of Italy? Silk woven by the wee-handed nymphs of Lucca? Lace of the fineness and delicacy of ice crystals?

"Pick anything you like, dear Helen," he said. "Pick everything you like."

None of these luxuries held any attraction for me yet, for they are all learned tastes. As I stood there, I could only think of my sweetheart with her beautiful white fingers on Petrarch's verses.

I looked up at Titian and smiled. "I would like books, please."

"Books make dangerous devils out of women," he said.

Still, he bought me everything I could desire and more.

I now owned a slim Petrarch, dressed in gilded leather; a precious illegal Ovid wrapped in red calf; a waggish black market copy of Aretino's Lewd Verses—

for Aretino was one of Titian's personal friends. My patron also presented me with an edition of Dante's *Divine Comedy* hand-printed by Aldus Manutius himself. It was in there I read:

> Among the bitter sorb-trees, it seems undue
> When the sweet fig in season comes to fruit.

It was after I tasted Dante that I understood why words and images are patrolled by emperors, for they are dangerous things. Montezuma prohibited women from carving gods or painting our language onto white bark, and these Europeans burn books without mercy.

They know what they are doing.

Beauty is a perilous distraction. I had come here to pluck the life out of a king's breast but my voluptuous inclinations drew me to a gold girl and paintings of gentle, broken-bodied saints that confounded me. The white killing teeth of St. Peter had now been softened in my memory by Raphael. And Sappho's love songs could lull me into such distracting lust that I might begin all manner of rubbing and writhing about in my bedclothes, searching for satisfaction.

No, I could not ever forget that my only inheritance was Dante's bitter tree, even if I wanted to suck all these bright fruits in my mouth.

THE NEXT MORNING my patron dressed me in a canary Lucca silk gown with striped fur trim that made me resemble a tiger. Privately, I tucked my dagger into a diamond-strung garter.

Nothing but the best for the king's coronation.

The unfinished church of San Petronio sparkled in the early sun. The flower of European nobility was here, lords with starched ruffs, the ladies imprisoned in their dresses, each crushing past the temple's marble, pink as angel skin, or its reliefs of the Temptation. Titian pointed to each frieze, talking of the sculptor Jacopo della Quercia and showing me the rich curves of Eve, that soft betrayer.

"Do you know the story?" he asked.

I nodded, for I had heard of this girl from Caterina.

"Once," I began, "there was a woman perfect in form and intelligence, and when God saw her He knew He had made a matchless ruler of men, children, and beasts. To prepare her for this task, He offered her a gift more priceless than the gold of Montezuma: He plucked an apple from the Tree of Knowledge, and said to her, 'Will you promise not to disclose the secrets I show you? Not even to your husband, and no matter how much he wheedles or pleads?'

" 'I promise,' Eve answered, and then ate.

"Upon her first taste, she knew all the mysteries of the world. She understood the stars, and the great zephyr that smothers the sun every night. She understood the science of rain, and she could speak to the man in the moon.

"But soon Adam, who knew no greater occupation than scratching his arse against the yew tree, grew jealous.

" 'Tell me your secrets,' he wheedled. 'While you perform experiments in botany and agriculture, I am left home with nothing to do.'

"Out of her great love for her husband, Eve sinned by feeding her husband a slice of the apple. Within the hour

Adam had eaten all the tree's fruit, chopped it down, and sat by a giant applewood bonfire, warm, fat, and pungent with wind.

"Understandably, she was punished."

I now folded my hands against my skirt and smiled at Titian.

He shook his head and laughed. "What a strange child you are, my sweet Helen."

When he began babbling about an altogether innocent Adam and the feeble wit of women, I realized how these Europeans fear the truth. These old bats and warthogs feeding on the blood of my fathers must see such angels in their mirrors! Even this painter who should have eyes as clear as a god's lives in a dream. But I did not argue. I only took his hand and led him inside.

CHARLES V, WITH HIS FACE of a bullfrog, sat on a throne at the front of the church and prepared to receive the Pope's crown. As my patron and I had been required to sit toward the back, I found myself separated from my prey by a gang of guards and civet-scented magníficos jostling for position inside of this sequined temple.

A palace like this would break my homesick heart. Everything in here seemed lit with the fire of my lost empire. Gold shimmered from the crucifix, dripped from ladies' necks, shone from inside the dark maws of ermine-wrapped bishops. On the walls were unfinished, gilded murals of Satan devouring Moors. A gorgeous ricercar poured out of a jeweled organ. Black ghosts of frankincense billowed from gold censers and drugged my limbs.

Yet, Charles was waiting for me. When Titian turned his head, I slipped away and threaded through the crowd.

I moved past dukes with diamonds in their ears. Past the countesses with heart-shaped silk patches covering skin ulcers. Through the clouds of musk, brushing against soft fox capes, past scimitars sharp enough to slice a girl like cake.

I neared that frog-faced monarch, the obsidian blade scraping my thighs.

But oh gods, oh God, just before I was close enough to harpoon his heart, I suddenly found myself tangled up with three muttonheaded ambassadors who were rowing over one of the front seats.

"Out of my way, you ninnywit!" growled the fat delegate from Fiarra, as he plucked the beard of his brother from Genoa.

Then the ambassador to Siena began beating them both about the skulls. "You damned doodles! You shallowbrains!"

Soon each of the three had one of the others by the beard, creating such an ugly barricade that I, thinking of no other option, began pinching them all on their buttocks, and this caused a chorus of deafening screaming and what with other blithering the guards instantly threw the lot of us out.

I discovered myself sprawled out on the portico, bruised like a pear, and separated from the King by locked doors and even more guards.

The three ambassadors gawked at me, and began muttering about the color of my skin. I showed them my blade.

They fled like hens.

An hour later, the church doors opened. The rabble came stamping out. Titian rushed up to me and pressed me to his chest.

"Helen, my heart, where did you go?"

I did not answer. I stared at the sky and wished myself dead. I had failed. I had failed my father. Somewhere beyond my reach, Charles V was already on his way to Austria.

There seemed nothing else to do, but I knew still that the asp would put me beyond all hope.

I looked at Titian. "Take me home."

He kissed both my hands and did not understand what I meant. The next day, we sailed for Venice.

5.

There is, in the paintings and chronicles of sixteenth-century Venice, a dearth of information about the lives of ordinary women. The images that have been left to us are of famous courtesans, mad queens, and countesses who are better remembered for their wardrobes than their philosophies or crimes. The record of the Aztecs imported to the region during this period is even more sparse. They are rarely called by their own names, and are regarded as remarkable only for their animal-like qualities and the rumors of their cannibal habits, at least by the nobles and painters whose jottings make up the larger part of these annals.

It is nearly eleven at night now, and on the eve of one of Teresa's scandalous parties, which rollicks in a gallery not two hundred yards away from me, as I am in my favorite place—on the second floor of the library, inside the cool womb of the Special Collections, which contains a Fort Knox vault filled with the rare histories of such Venetians. I am continuing my search for any signs of Helen, which might prove that the book I am restoring was written by an Aztec woman. I've spent days and nights paging through rumbling annals, letters, also more recent scholarly works on the Doge's city; I've peered inside of Titian's paintings like a spy, and just for one glimpse of her. I can't stop thinking of her. I lie in bed at night imagining her body under the lime trees, and her hands grazing the soft form of Eve before she enters the church. I can picture her as she stands on the edge of the Republic and stares at the water, and the look on her face as she suddenly remembers with great clarity what her home looked like, although she hasn't laid eyes on it in years.

The past is a private place for the historian, the conservator. When reading about the longings of a long-dead girl I remember another woman who felt similarly boxed and lost. I want to discover Helen here, inside of these books, so that I know that my mother's confidence in the stolen, invisible, and untraced was not false.

I am going to mark the juggler's name in the pages of history, despite the certainties of my colleagues that she never existed. As I've noted, because of similarities in hand-*ductus* and narrative style, they attribute *The Conquest* to Padre Miguel de Pasamonte. Not much is known about this monk except that he was a small and quiet man whose physical modesty belied hedonistic, even heretical tendencies. He kept a lover in Spain—a bluestocking and notorious voluptuary named Sofía Suárez. Various reports describe her as very beautiful and unshy about matters of literature and the flesh, and she is the author of a large and candid body of letters proving her expertise in poetry and carnal pleasure (though sadly, only a few to the monk himself survive). Most think of her as de Pasamonte's muse.

And if so, what a woman she must have been! His tales of prohibited passions, war, and dark magic aroused such fervor amid a society chafing under the sterile rigors of the Inquisition that riots would break out on the days that bootleg copies of his book *Las Tres Furias* were distributed, and epidemics of witchcraft and sodomy were linked to the novel as well. The Crown was so incensed by these crimes that it assigned one thousand guards to discover the anonymous author. They eventually determined de Pasamonte's identity through tips from fellow monks, and descended upon his cloister in the winter of 1561—though when they broke down his doors he had already escaped on horseback. The guards only found manuscripts of three more books in his room which were confiscated by order of His Holiness, and an old hunchback maid weeping and praying to the Holy Mother. There were later reports of de Pasamonte sightings in Rome and Turkey and two more of his books were published in the next decade—these being titled *La Noche Triste* and *El Santo de España*. But after the 1570s no more is heard of him, presumably because of his death.

I have already been contacted by several de Pasamonte scholars who are nearly frantic at the prospect of handling one of his original works. I told each of them that I think they're mistaken. De Pasamonte's books indicate a hothouse imagination supplied with such fantastic gods and monsters and harlots and giants that you can see the stamp of madness on him, as in Swift or Lewis Carroll. But there is a lucidity, as well as an intimacy of tone in *The Conquest* that isn't present in the others, also a familiarity with women's lives and the Aztecs' stolen culture, which I think can only have come from a genuine Helen. For months I've been combing the libraries for any sign of her, starting out with the records on the Vatican, but nothing turned up in those annals. Next I turned to her years in Venice, and it's there I learned how little ordinary women figure in this history. For a long time, I was only able to sketch a picture of the world in which Titian and his equals lived.

What I've found, up to today, is this:

It is the late 1530s in the Republic, which is even now sinking into the rank canals. The moneyed, illiterate women of the region are nowhere to be seen or heard in public spaces, but masked noblemen stumble over the cobblestone roads, and Jews and prostitutes, marked by yellow badges, wander through the walkways. In the open-air marketplace slaves are paraded before the yelling rabble, along with fragile Murano glass, livestock, and antiques. Turning away from this sight and making your way down a side street, you are apt to become lost in this city-maze, where the blue alleys wind like smoke, except that here is a courtesan, her hair dressed like horns and her feet hobbled in thirty-inch chopines; she is balanced by two servants. They carry her up to the door of a fine palazzo, and a butler allows her into the crowded dining room, where Titian hosts a party for his friend, the poet Pietro Aretino.

Today I think I found Helen inside of this room.

In the first third of the sixteenth century, there lived a member of the Venetian clergy named Fra Donatello Tosello who had an obsessive habit of recording every meal and every prostitute that he ever consumed—and the Getty owns a first print run of his journals. As a squat, hairless, and carbuncular epicurean, his ugliness was only matched by his legendary appetite, which was so ravenous, and at the same time so discerning, that he became a sought-after guest at many dinner parties where the primary entertainment was watching an endless stream of delicacies disappear into his jaw.

I am not only talking about food.

Fra Tosello was a hero to most men. He had once bedded three sisters while tasting capon, and was rumored to have conquered the virgin daughter of an Ottoman and an entire demijohn of wine in one fifteen-minute holiday. His reputation, moreover, was burnished by the pages of his famous diary which, in his vanity, he printed for his friends. Unfortunately for the Father, Venice was stocked not only with whores and butchers who furnished his cravings but also with Inquisition spies, and he didn't have the same talent for escape as his brother de Pasamonte. In 1540, after his diary found its way into an informant's hands, he would be convicted of heresy and punished by imprisonment and fasting. On the third day of his incarceration, Fra Tosello looked around his tiny, dark, flea-filled cell, and then at the heel of bread that was to serve as his dinner. Apparently these deprivations were too much for his fat little heart, for he committed suicide that night, using his belt as a noose.

Still, on August 23, 1538, during Titian's party for Aretino, there is no sign of Tosello's bad end. It is not an unusual evening and largely goes unmentioned by his biographers. He breaks no gastronomic nor priapic records, although he does seem in good form. Translated, he writes:

> Our friend Titian provided a most commendable table of Sausages & Splendid cutlets in Coffins & a fine, Fat Liver, grilled Florentine style. I spiced this repast with one saucy trollop, one Marcolina whom Our Lord has found fit to bless with a Magnificent pair of Breasts, which the Dear Girl nearly killed me with, tho' Death by suffocation on such Heavenly Pillows would not be too dear a price for the exquisite Agonies I endured Tonight . . .

Although Tosello is known for his tireless gluttony, his endurance on the page is just as impressive. His diary extends to thirteen volumes in all, and his entry for this particular night continues for nearly twenty pages, with detailed descriptions of suckling pigs and wenches. It's easy to get lost in this dissertation, but a careful reader will find a very interesting passage toward the end:

> [Titian] is dying for love of a new Vixen, a child Black as Night & ill-tempered as the Devil but with a figure deserving of much

lusty pinching. She spent most of the night Brooding & Sighing but when I asked for one small Kiss the Heathen brandished a strange Poniard and promised to slit my fat throat, etc.

I put my fingers to these sentences. I know that this is Helen staring out the rippled window of Titian's home and onto the blue-dark canals of Venice. She dresses in the same high fashions as the courtesans and noblewomen who take the whores' cues—a low-cut crimson bodice strung with silver thread and pearls, a red skirt carefully slashed to reveal the layers of watered silk undergarments. Fra Tosello careens toward her and she gently tucks a dagger beneath the folds of his chin . . .

And I am here, touching the ghost of her in an old book (I have taken off my gloves), which is so fragile it must be kept in this cool tomb, like saints' bones or the small body of Tutankhamen—while nearby, scholars jig away in galleries, drinking, reveling, violating all the charters of conservation on account of my boss, Teresa Shaughnessey, who should be standing by my side, looking at these pages! Moving away from the reading table, I button up my sweater and slip on the jacket I'd slung behind my chair. Now I swipe my key card and let myself out of Special Collections, so that I can persuade or drag her away from this party.

THE SOUTH PAVILION of the Getty contains two first-floor galleries filled with seventeenth- and eighteenth-century decorative and fine arts. Massive portraits of noblemen and -women hang here, the subjects apple-cheeked, still stern, advertising their great glossy beards and dogs and glittering signet rings, or snowy breasts and flossy locks. During the day a pale and lovely light shimmers through the windows, filling the salons with a gold-velvety medium in which motes as bright as mica float. It polishes not just the Tilliard settees and *boissatine* commodes,

Giradon's bronze *Pluto Abducting Proserpine*, but also the Orientalist tapestries showing emperors toying with their exotic slaves, providing the only note of the bloody enterprise in Mexico, Africa, and the wider swath of the Ottoman Empire, that fed these adjacent noblemen who once plucked the fruits of the courtesans posing as raped goddesses.

Each day the tourists come to observe these artifacts under the bored glare of guards. Teresa thinks it awful, this sanitized experience, and even I can understand her point: You can tell from their folding faces what a hard business this looking is—what is it exactly that they should *see*, during the ten seconds they have the art to themselves? The expert lines of Proserpine's ransacked body? The virtuoso rendering of Oriental eyes? They whisper to each other, pointing out details—never getting close enough that the alarms sound, or a sentry admonishes them—or they listen to the docent tapes plugged into their Walkmans.

Once it was all different. Undemocratic, yes, as these pieces were hung in palaces. But these works presided over the daily intimacies of a handful of people, watching them, glowering over them, like consciences or monsters. They could be touched and breathed on. A different ritual of looking was observed. A noble girl, say, born in sixteenth-century Venice and with her eye flavored by that age, once snuck into her father's study and stole a dram of wine to celebrate the secret wildness she felt zinging and zooming inside of her. Up on a wall here—for nudes were not appropriate for common rooms, where ladies might dwell—she saw Giorgione's *Sleeping Venus*, all luminous ivory haunches and breasts like pears and the tender belly. No one was there to tutor any of her reactions. No one would tell her the Venus did *not* look like a particular whore she once saw staggering outside her window. And since those laws were suspended in that shadowed room, where she gazed and sipped from the purloined wine, the

painting rushed up to meet her and entered her mind, as dangerous and sweet as a new idea.

This is, in some ways, the equivalent of the experience that
Teresa gives to her friends when she throws her secret parties
here, and so why I have never reported her even if they make me
wildly nervous.

I move out of the library, across the courtyard, now flooded with
blue shadows stained here and there with pearl from landscape
lighting, and enter the south pavilion from which a thin thread of
jazz can be heard. Inside the galleries, scholars, curators, artists, and
restorers drink white wine from ciboria made of Roman glass and
paw each other on eighteenth-century fainting couches, *lits à la
Turque*. Brie and crackers (not, on my request, pâté) are served on
Baroque silver, gin and tonics are poured into fourth-century
amphorae rhytons. In a corner, a woman wearing only a slip slides
into a fantastic canary-yellow gown, trimmed with a rich striped fur,
which was reputedly designed for the Venetian courtesan Veronica
Franco. Ebullient men and women have adorned themselves with
Restoration tiaras and pre-Columbian amulets (I relieve the revelers of these last items), so they glitter and tinkle with jewels. The
scene is repulsive and gladdening at the same time. One historian
parries with a filigreed sword from early 1500s Spain, that may have
been used in duels or to slay natives. People sit on divans, paging
through ancient breviaries, psalters; others glide their fingers over
the bronzes, laughing.

Strange bits of conversation float around me:

"Did you ever try to cook from Apicius?"

"What did you make, dormouse?"

"Barracuda with raisins, creamed kid with lovage. Honey
cakes."

"Barracuda? How'd it turn out?"

"Terrible. Disgusting. Worse than disgusting."

"Sounds authentic, then. You didn't use forks, right?"

"Did I what?"

"At your dinner. Did you use forks?"

"No."

"Because they weren't used at all until the eleventh century, and weren't fashionable until the seventeenth."

"I *know*."

The small crowd sways and dances to the music. Everyone seems giddy and slightly drunk. Teresa, wearing a silver silk dress and a bright red chiffon scarf tied around her hair, stands to the side under one of the portraits of noblemen while the woman wearing the slip continues fitting herself inside Franco's dress. Two friends help her drag the giant yellow puff over her head, and ease her into the tiny waist, no small trick without a corset. But the woman, too bony for the A-line dress she arrived in, is able to fit inside the gown without much trouble. It transforms her from a dun-colored academic into a smashing leopard-looking girl, glistening in restored silk and fur.

"What an orgy," I say, sidling up to Teresa.

She nods. "Exactly."

"Try to make sure they don't stain anything. Or steal anything."

"They're scholars, connoisseurs, *artists*, not thieves. They're not idiots."

"Just, please, watch them?"

"I *will*, I promise. But look how absolutely happy everyone is. No one will hurt a thing. *Much*." She turns to look at me, then widens her smile. "And I am so pleased that you could come! I thought you'd be too busy snoodling that big sailor of yours."

"Actually, I came here to show you something."

"You're not working, you drudge!"

"A little bit. And I think I found . . . a page in a diary."

"What's this about?" She stares at me. "Oh Lord, not that book again."

"Just for a second."

"You *maniac*."

I pull on her elbow, until she finally agrees.

"In one second, I swear. Let's just admire this pretty girl first. What a princess you look, sweetheart!"

The woman in the yellow gown seems to bloom inside the antique stuff, as if she has just splashed a magic tonic on her somber face. A blush spreads up to her forehead and her hair swirls over her bare shoulders. The silk has suffered a little from the centuries, despite its repair, but gold still smolders inside the delicate threads, reflecting gleams on her white skin and tiny breasts that float inside the giant silk cups. These stay standing only by virtue of the cunning fur straps—replicas, I think, and striped like the hide of some giant African cat.

"I did my thesis on Franco," she says. "I always wanted to touch something she'd owned—a book she'd read, pair of reading glasses. This goes beyond my wildest . . . God, I'm *gorgeous*!" She stares down at herself. "I imagined her something like me, though. I'd read about the way she looked; she was small, I thought. Small-waisted and -breasted. Huh."

"*Is* it Venetian?" a woman in one of the Restoration tiaras asks. "Looks Bolognese to me."

"Is there a difference in styles?"

"Subtle, but yes. And I'm not quite sure the gown's from the proper period to be Franco's."

The woman smooths her hands down on the skirt. "Oh, I hope it is. I hope she wore this."

I look again at the color of the silk and the tiger fur looped over the small shoulders. The great skirt hangs in soft folds, shedding light. I draw a connection to my own subject in an instant—I have no trouble conjuring quick brown limbs and "a handsome bosom" inside that lustrous substance, flickering behind her as she stalks across the Portico di Pavaglione, shopping for books and fox capes, plotting murder. Isn't it just like the dress Helen wrote about? Could it be? Now *I* want to crawl inside the memento because of this fantasy. I'd like to get close to even one living fiber of her; touch one filament of that heritage. But as I think of myself stepping into that gown, struggling inside the wasp girdle as the ancient threads split, the gold silk strains, shreds—in a strange effort to inhabit, even prove, her existence—I stop and have to laugh at myself. I am getting obsessed, aren't I? I'm seeing Helen wherever I look.

I take Teresa's elbow again. "Let's go."

BACK AT THE READING room in Special Collections, Teresa bends over Tosello's diary and squints at the lines. I stand next to her and we both hover over the book, which looks like it's spent years underwater. Studying the distressed pages, I imagine the blue canals of Venice, the smoky poisoned air, hundreds of lavish meals served by rosy-breasted coquettes.

"What do you think of this?" I point to the page. "Here, in this paragraph."

She reads, then stands up and shakes her head.

"Now, I told you I don't care whom you catalogue it under, those things don't really interest me that much anymore."

"It interests me."

"Then I don't think you'll much like what I have to say—which is, this seems to be something of a lark of yours, unfortunately. I don't see this proving anything."

"But this shows Titian had a nonwhite mistress. And the poniard?"

"It could be anyone. African, Turkish. Venetians fancied dusky 'orientals.' Then there's the writing style of our author. The descriptions of magic, the emphasis on the supernatural, this is *all* signature de Pasamonte. And Caterina's resemblance to Sofía Suárez is too close, it simply must be a reference. She was blond, half Italian. *And* she was in a convent for many years. Have you read her letters?"

I pick up Tosello's diary. "Years ago."

"We do own the originals, you know. We bought them years back, when people were just beginning to get interested in that pair. It's one of the reasons we were drawn to this new book of de Pasamonte's, as a way to flesh out the collection. And they're quite amazing. The letters that survive are mostly to members of her salon, and that lover of hers, the girl. There *is* a lot in there. I'm sure you remember, she writes about convent life? Her Italian mother? There's some famous portrait of her somewhere, as well. It shouldn't be hard to get a copy of it."

I'm silent for a few moments. Then, "I didn't think about that. But I'm still not convinced. I'm going to keep looking."

Teresa frowns at me. "I must say that I wish you wouldn't."

"Why?"

"Well, for one thing, you're beginning to look a bit peaky around the edges—like one of those gorgeous consumptives of Rossetti's, if you don't mind my saying so. But it's not your complexion that worries me so much as this strange, yes, *fixation*, like I said before, on some sort of mystery that does not really exist. It's as if you're making up ghosts just to scare yourself, or creating a kind of imaginary friend, like lonely children do? I mean, it's a *novel*, and it's clear enough who wrote it. What I'm trying to say is, I don't think it's quite good for you, dear."

"I think I can decide what's good for me."

"It's just an opinion."

"Fine."

Her eyes drop back to the diary, which she takes from my arms and lays out on the desk again. She turns the pages to examine the writing. "It's a pretty object, though, isn't it? And what a goblin he was, this Tosello. I imagine him as some sort of troll crunching on bones." She sighs. "Still, this business doesn't hold its interest for me the way it used to. And I was *far* worse than you are, more than obsessed. I *lived* here, once. And now, hmmmm . . . I've been thinking of something, somewhat seriously."

"What's that?"

"If my next test comes back clean—you know, I'm still in that danger zone. They don't know what's to become of me yet. If it does come out clean, though, I think I will have to quit my job here. No matter what kind of money they offer me. It's time for me to have a new adventure. Something more forward-looking, not so dusty and musty and old."

I don't say anything to this, but for a moment I see Teresa in the white hospital, closing her eyes as the X-ray machine takes her picture. Then I remember myself lying in a similar blank room, for I've had some experiences with hospitals myself.

"But when you *do* find out that there's nothing there, I want you to tell me," she goes on now, and gently shakes my elbow. "You can tell me how right I am."

"I wouldn't bet on it." I clasp her shoulder. "And besides, you shouldn't worry about me so much."

"And why's that?"

"Because I'm in love with somebody."

She grins at me, laughs. "Well, that's right. You *are*, aren't you? Lucky thing."

With that, she gives me a parting pat and walks out of the library, leaving me with the shadows and fragile histories of the world, and all the mysteries that I think exist.

I sit down at the desk and close Tosello's diary. I feel almost dizzy—saying "I'm in love with somebody" out loud has done something to me, and I would just like to experience it for a while.

I don't mind being alone.

My heart beats and beats.

It is quiet in here, and cool. The brightness and silence of the room and the chill remind me of a hospital, or a cloister. The white walls and plain wood reading desks create no distractions from the sacraments that can take place here, and the book looks so beautiful in this modern space. The leaves are richly colored, dark as honey. The leather crumbles at the touch. I lean down to inhale the eras that come off the pages and imagine I breathe in amber and gold along with the air.

Despite Teresa's advice, I believe a person could find some mysterious yet real thing here, among these books, and totems; inside of this voluptuous silence. A person might even feel her soul in this place, if she sits very still and is very patient. As I sit here, quietly, I think that I can feel mine.

How would I describe it for him? It is made of amber and air and doesn't weigh anything at all. But here, in this room, I can imagine its shape and patched red heart. I would like to paint it for him if I could, that very color, the way it floats and dances. The way it moves toward him even from this distance. It has arms that are reaching out past these walls, down the streets, through all the blue weather and calamitous traffic of Los Angeles, to the shore, and Karl.

AS I DRIVE DOWN the 5 and make my way back to Oceanside, the breeze is tender as suede and the sea burns toward the boutiques, fish restaurants, the scaling motels like green fire. The day before, on the afternoon of Teresa's party, Karl called me at the office and said "we have to talk"—about Claire, and the sex we had last week, and how this has be "resolved." (I did not tell him this, but I plan on "resolving" things with an encore of our previous rendezvous.) On my way to the café where Karl and I will eat dinner tonight, I pass by shop glass dimmed blue by the late light, and lamps that glaze the naked skulls of the off-duty marines knotting their arms around the busts of ecstatic girlfriends. Seeing these women, with their elaborate Friday night coifs like the architecture of wedding cakes and their plummy faces gasping with laughter, I can picture myself here a year ago, or before that in similar towns in Florida and Virginia, clasping onto Karl and trying to fit a month of experience into one or two days' conversation.

It wasn't easy. Sometimes, in the hours after we'd first met at the airport or the dock, when I had already wrapped myself around his handsome body and taken in the small familiar gestures—his large, clam-shaped thumb on my wrist, his close-lipped way of grinning, the way his eyes would close when I told him my yarns, so I could see the blue veins etching his lids—I would begin talking about real estate prices in Los Angeles or he would bring up, say, the idea of my moving to another base, and then it was like winter had gusted into the room. My reaction was always to wrap a fantasy around us, and so I'd make up a Penelope or a Xochiquetzal to bewitch him back to me, but there came a time when this device failed. I found out that stories are like glass, and if you put too much pressure on them, they'll break. Mine began to crack, I think; I didn't feel that old thrumming rush when I told them, and the old ritual stopped working so well for a while.

After we went through one particularly difficult year, when Karl was still in North Carolina and I had just accepted an offer from the Getty, we both decided in a calm discussion to try to see other people, an experiment that seemed to have auspicious possibilities only when considered in its most abstract form. Once the concrete details emerged, the less attractive aspects of this trial became immediately evident—this, when I discovered that my replacement was a woman I had met before at a party, a blonde named Melissa who looked like she'd been carved out of a colossal loaf of Wonder bread and was blessed with a sex appeal that scorched every pituitary within a ten-mile radius. The thought of Karl letting her toss her rehabilitated hair over his naked body sent me into such a panic I could barely spell the obscenities that littered the diary I kept at the time—but then again, I was too busy with my own fling to brush up on my orthography.

James was a molasses-skinned salesman who romanced me with a gusto that I still remember with affection. All his mannerisms had such a delightful novelty I remained happily distracted for a month or two from the shambles I had left behind in North Carolina. One weekend, he drove me up to Santa Barbara so that we might drink champagne by the shore and watch the sun go down. And what a Romeo my suitor seemed, with his white shirt blazing against his tan and his dark hair sweeping away from his face as he lifted the glass in a toast. We ate caviar and salmon along with the Clicquot, while the sun disappeared and the air turned black. As he talked about his mother and gardens he had visited in Germany, I happened to notice that Santa Barbara's weather created perfect conditions for stargazing. I admired the special brilliance of the Dippers, and as he described his childhood I quietly mapped the sky using the informal education in astronomy I'd received in the past ten years. Even later, after we finally went to sleep, the images of the constellations remained vivid in my mind and I dreamt of star nurseries, white dwarfs, and an agile spaceman doing flips and dives through space, then snatching a glittering nova from the sky and placing it, like a diamond, in my hand. When I woke up the next morning I was so depressed I felt like a dead person, especially when I saw that stranger sleeping in my bed.

That night I called Karl and said I had to see him.

I planned to show Karl how much I loved him by taking him as close as I could to the place he loved best. I bought him a ticket to California, then arranged with a company operating out of Palm Springs to take us up in a glider, and when we arrived in the desert it was a sparkling, golden day, with violet mountains and vast stretches of blond sand from which a blue heat shimmered. The white fiberglass plane was to be pulled by a truck down a slope, after which some mystery of aerodynamics would make it float all on its own before our grizzled pilot landed it, safely, on the ground. I had never been in such a contraption before, and it looked so tiny I could barely believe it wouldn't splinter on impact.

Karl put his hand on one wing and squinted into the sunlight. "It'll be just like home."

The captain grinned at him, recognizing the haircut. "Jets?"

He shrugged. "Helicopters." He walked around the glider, touching the nose, peering inside. He was clearly enjoying himself. "This thing could get bumpy." He frowned a little. "I should tell you that the whole digestive thing can sort of come into play here, I don't know if you knew that when you signed us on."

"Ladies *love* it," the captain assured us. "You two'll be nuzzling like Eskimos back there."

"It'll be fine, but it'll be tight," I agreed, then looked up at Karl. "That okay?"

He stared at me. "Yeah, that's okay." He scuffed his shoe on the pavement, and then reached for my hand. "I missed you, you know."

I didn't say anything, and led him into the back, where we cuddled with our knees touching. I hooked my arm inside of Karl's and watched the pilot crawl inside his seat and peer out the dirty windshield. The truck towing the glider began moving, and then the beige landscape began racing past us, faster and faster, until it was below us and we were in the air.

It was beautiful. We were weightless inside the naked weather. The desert spread below us like a bronze prairie that rumpled and rose in our wake. Pocket sandstorms traveled through the plain and I clutched Karl, shouting about the colors in the sky. Thin glades of pink rained through blue oxygen and a mantle of ocher rested over the spines of the surrounding mountains. Clouds like giant dahlias flung mist in our eyes while invisible paws whacked at the glider's wings—I imagined great Dakota beasts breathing below us, like the galing sea serpents drawn in the corners of sixteenth-century maps. The air *was* close inside our carbon-dioxide-trapping plastic cabin, but I ignored any discomfort as Karl put his arm around my shoulder, describing various technical aspects of our flight like wind resistance and the physics of aerodynamics that I forgot as soon as they entered my ears. His face was brightened by a smile I hadn't seen in a long time, and I peered out the window, trying to feel the way he did when he'd hurled himself out of aircraft or imagined rocketing through space. And this wasn't very hard to do. Of course I'd been in planes before, but the insubstantiality of the glider removed the buffer between the body and the tsunamis of wind that pummeled us from all sides. I could very easily fantasize that I was John Glenn or Gordo Cooper hurtling through oblivion past stars, quarks, black holes, and asteroid showers before I crash-landed on Mars.

"Let's give it another shot," Karl yelled. "Let's just stop all this funny business and settle down and have a bunch of kids and bite the bullet."

I tried to answer, but had some trouble with the talking. I wondered if our ride was almost over, as it seemed we had been up for a little bit too long.

It wasn't almost over. The breeze bit its teeth into the glider a few minutes later and shook it the way a dog happily dispatches its squeaking playmates, so that Karl and I were flung propitiously against one another and he began squeezing me to my almost complete delight. Cinematic images of our squirming bodies catapulted toward Earth began to interfere with my ability to spoon, however, and an odd nostalgia also began to influence me. I started to remember each of what I regarded as his less benign professional decisions, which had mysteriously though inexorably led me to embark on this flight, and that film strip playing in my brain—showing now not just the two of us clawing and shrieking through space but also (for some reason) that other unlucky Mexican, Ritchie Valens—inspired me to began listing each of these items in an articulate and didactic scream.

After our pilot finally landed the glider and I recovered in the restroom, Karl and I had our worst fight ever. The sunlight blared down on our faces as we argued and I remember the distinct feeling that the desert was swallowing me up in its sands.

"I can't believe you took that job," he said, about the Getty. "It makes me feel—I don't—without even talking to me about it? I've had this *smashed*-up feeling in me about it ever since you told me. I've got this smashed-up and crashed-up feeling inside me about it."

"I can do things there I can't do anyplace else."

"You can do things there you can't do anyplace else? I *love* you, Sara. I'm talking about how I love you, and about how I want you. But I can't do *this* anyplace else. How am I getting up there from anyplace else?"

"I guess that's it then," I said, too angry to think of whether I meant it.

"Fine then." He started crying. "That's it. That's the big finish. You and me are *good* and over."

He walked away from me toward the building where the pilot worked, and I didn't follow him. I rubbed the muck off my face and glowered out at the view while a strange, quick-pulsing pain began to spread in my chest—I interpreted this as sadness jailed and rattling my ribs. I pressed my hand to my chest and squinted across the tarmac. Karl wound up hitching a ride back to town with an ex-cadet who part-timed at the gliding operation, and the last sight I'd have of him for months was his sheared head bouncing in the cab of a dented red pickup. I watched him recede from me until all I could make out was a spot of blood on the horizon and a few puffs of dust. When he was gone I got into my car and drove home.

6.

After our debacle in the desert, I began my new
life without Karl. I started working at the Getty
and devoted myself to the books waiting for my
attention. They came to me packed in acid-free
coffins, gray-skinned, with cracked backs and warped
faces, often left for dead by heirs with eyes untutored
to the insane care evidenced by some master's
ghostly calligraphy, a gold-dipped edge, a majuscule
trimmed with roses and grotesques. I found them
comforting, as if I were in the company of lovely
dowagers, and I could spend all day and most of my
nights mending them.

It was during these first months that I developed
a reputation as a diligent restorer with few interests
apart from the office.

The clarity of my task mitigated the uncontrollable
weather blowing through me, and I wintered at the
Getty, in this way, for nearly a year. Life outside of the
museum seemed more dangerous; confronted with
the rabbling traffic, the blood-wet evening news, my
unlit bedroom into which I'd enter half-expecting to
see Karl, that rib-rattling pain I'd experienced in the

desert would return. Night after night, I hid out from my mourning by working on my assignments. I'd sit at my desk with gold leaf melting on my fingers and slowly sink to the bottom of a book, which I thought might be the safest place in the world.

One evening that April, though, I discovered that there wasn't any refuge that might shelter me. I had stayed late at the office to work on the fifteenth-century Spanish romance *The Exploits of Esplandian*, which tells the tale of a knight who wanders through savage jungles in search of an Amazon queen of great beauty. The book itself is a subtle stunner, with each leaf of vellum bordered by a thin wisp of burnished gold, somewhat chipped, and the text a magnificent example of the calligraphic arts which flourished under the rule of Ferdinand and Isabella. As I bent down to repair the border with a brush, my hand jerked away from my body and flung strands of the liquid metal, which landed on the recto like another jeweled language. At first I thought we must be having an earthquake, but when the pain began to dilate in my chest I understood that the tremor wasn't outside, but within myself. My hand shuddered, and my body, my mouth and cheeks trembled with a terrible electricity pumping out of my heart as a sweet, sleepy numbness streaked up my arms. I sweated out a cold slick over my skin, the way I (now suddenly) saw my mother sweating, swaying in the kitchen when similar attacks had taken her. I stumbled away from this image of Beatrice and crouched down with my knuckles on the carpet, nearly blind and terrified.

For a while, I was too frightened to go to the doctor. I would make appointments, cancel them. I'd lie in bed nights with my fingers at my throat to feel the pulse, remembering a day during my childhood when I opened the door of my mother's recovery room, only to see a physician strip the sheets off her discolored body and bend down to examine the stitches while she raised her good hand up to her face. I'd remember Karl, too, waist-high in the ocean or reaching for me across his white bed, and often as not these recollections would set the attacks on me again, so I felt the sleepiness and the perspiration, the leaden weight on my chest and shallow breathing. Illness made me lonely and the fear dulled my mind, but eventually I did make it out of my fog and got to the hospital.

I made an appointment to see an athletic blond doctor at the U.S.C. medical center, who tapped on my shoulder blades with her frigid thumbs and monitored my pulse.

"Could be anything at this point," she said, unplugging the stethoscope from her ears.

"It's nerves," I told her. "It's anxiety. I'm depressed."

"Maybe." She squinted down at my chart.

"It's psychosomatic. I broke up with my boyfriend."

"Probably, though the history's not good," she said, then tilted her head at me and smiled. "We'll do some tests. Best to get it checked out, don't you think?"

"Not really," I told her.

But three days later, she sent a tiny camera up my artery to look at my heart. And the news wasn't good. It wasn't a matter of hypochondria or nerves. I had the same heart condition that my mother died from ten years before, which can only be cured by surgery on the cardiac wall—something the doctor wanted to do as soon as possible.

I did phone Karl then, but learned from his answering machine that he was taking a vacation in Hawaii. I left a message, though I immediately decided that was a mistake, and determined it would be better not to answer his return calls. I spent the next day in a dreamy calm state some might have confused for bravery. I don't recall much about my interactions with people during this brief period, although I have a memory of sitting down to an early dinner with my father, Reynaldo, the evening before the surgery. This was at my house in Pasadena, where he would sleep on the sofa that night before driving me to the hospital early the next morning. Dad is a swarthy, thick-bellied powerhouse who normally wouldn't let a hurricane stop him from loving life or making money, but that evening an ashy paleness showed under the warm color of his skin, and he continually fidgeted, patting me with his plump hands or pulling on his mustache. He'd also asked me about Karl once or twice, and seemed to keep jumping up and down to get the phone that kept ringing. Otherwise, he stared at his soup and yammered.

"You're gonna be fine," he'd said, pulling some of the hair out of his head. "You're going to be *okay*. This is no problem. Anybody's got a problem *I* got a problem. My problem is you, eh? You giving me the high blood pressure. My baby girl having heart . . . whatevers? What the hell you call it? Like your mother. They give me any bad news I'll bust 'em in the mouth. They better fix you, is all I've got to say."

"Dad, relax."

"Oh, I'm relaxing. I got *no* worries." Little tears started squeezing out from his left eye, and then the phone rang again and he jumped up to get it. For my part, I closed my eyes and felt as if I could float up to the ceiling, buoyed on my lovely, light white cloud of denial.

Once inside the operating room fourteen hours later, though, everything was different. It was much worse. This was a large, brisk, dove-white chamber, at the center of which stood the light-blasted bed where the subject would rest. The door to the O.R. had a glassed-in window cut into it, which looked out onto the beige hall where smocked physicians occasionally passed by. Masked scientists flanked me, my plastic hair-cap crackled around my skull, and though a nurse bent near and spoke incomprehensible words in a soothing voice, I could not stop seeing my mother lifting her hand to her face while the doctor examined her blue body. I inhaled ammonia and heard the *hump-pump* of the anesthesiologist's equipment as my fingers grasped convulsively under the sheets. Panic sparkled in my brain and I tried to calm down by fixing on the lights in the ceiling, and then at the reflection of a small swaddled girl in the plastic glasses of the nurse. I shifted my eyes beyond her to the door, with its window looking out onto the beige hall.

Inside of that window I now saw Karl.

He was standing very straight, as if at attention, with his stubbled chin crumpled up to support the collapsing weight of his face, though I could see from his moving lips that he was talking to me. I learned afterwards that he found out where I'd be from my father, then took the first available flight from Hawaii so that he might get there in time to tell me that everything would be all right. He held his head in that tough tilt the way they'd trained him to in the Corps, letting me know he'd stand guard there all day all night until I walked out on my feet, and my hands stopped grasping under the sheets anymore. I wasn't shivering as hard. Doctors in smocks stared at him while they passed by, and the security officer who'd kept him out of pre-op tried to kick him out of this hallway too, but he wouldn't even look at them. He stayed there, bringing me through that hell from behind the window, because even though I couldn't hear him I knew what he was telling me and I hung on to those words as hard as I could. Karl. I kept my eyes on him and his moving mouth while they fed the drugs into my I.V. And then everything stopped.

I came through the surgery without any problems. You wouldn't know I'd been a patient to look at me now, except for this scar. One night, too soon after the surgery to make love, he unbuttoned my shirt and laid me out under the lamplight illuminating the cracks and contusions on my body. And I wasn't self-conscious for one second. I didn't mind his seeing the patched map above my breasts because I knew I could never look ugly to him. I folded my arms beneath my head and he kissed all the spots that weren't sore. We both looked at my bruises, talking about them, wondering about what the scar would look like when it healed.

"I feel cracked up," I said. "I don't even feel like it's my body anymore. I don't feel at home in it."

"Well, as to the scar, you'll look fine," he said. "Even in a bikini it won't be a big deal. No one will be able to tell a thing."

"No one but you," I said.

"That's right, no one but me." He hugged up against my side so his knees were tucked under my knees and his belly pressed against my ribs and thigh, and he talked into my hair. "Oh, you *did* scare me, though. You'd better behave yourself from now on and keep out of that hospital. Because I sure can't afford the plane tickets otherwise."

"I'll bet it was expensive."

"Yes it was, you spoiled girl. You've got me on a leash and everything."

"Melissa must have been pretty mad."

"Yeah, well, that's all done now."

I touched his face. "Thank you, Karl."

He was quiet here for a minute, rubbing the palm of his hand against my thigh. He breathed into my hair.

"I'm sorry for our fighting. All I've ever wanted is to keep you safe and happy, Sara. I'm serious, now. I'll do anything to keep you that way."

He kissed my ear, and I tried to comfort us with stories about the heart, then—the wild theories of the ancient Greeks, the fantastic myths made up by the earliest doctors. It didn't work too well, though; everything was still awful and frightening. And so Karl sat up and looked down at me, trying to figure out how to make things better. He began to put his hands on my body.

I closed my eyes and stopped talking.

I've always thought that he put me back together that afternoon—I'd felt shredded and spread apart after the surgery, but when he touched my knee, my shoulder, when he stroked my rib and held my hip something soldered in me. He held my body in his hands for hours. "I love this," he said, circling his fingers around my shoulder, "and I love *this*. I love you here and here." He pressed my thigh, lightly. He pressed his cheek to the flat of my stomach. His palms traveled down my arms and up my back, he rubbed my hands and slid his fingers over my sternum and my collarbone, though still avoiding the bruised area; he smoothed back my hair.

Finally he went to my chest. He raised his hand and cupped it over the scar, above the breast, with such a soft, holding touch. I pressed my hands to the bedsheet. The late-afternoon light came in through the window and brightened his hair and eyes. He murmured his own theories about my heart. His hand stayed over my stitches like a nest; his warm fingers spread lightly over the spot. "I love you here," he said, quietly. And I could feel it, how he turned that mark from a scar into a sign I would never read the same way again.

WHAT HAPPENED NEXT? Time passed, and put us through its giant grinder so that in a handful of seasons we'd rather have a root canal than even say one word to the other, though not once did I think that our problems could crush out that thing between us that made him whisper safety to me through that hospital window, and cup his hand over my heart like a magician palming an egg. Nevertheless, three months ago, when I'd followed him to Oceanside, with its curio shops and cowboy bars and these furloughed marines with breadbox heads, I saw him with his squeeze, the famous Claire. After I heard those danger bells bonging in his voice over the phone, I would have arrived equipped with night goggles and stun guns if that's what it took to track him down, but after only a few hours I spotted the two of them walking down Grandpa O'Connell's street without a shame in the world. She's a redhead, a mighty cute piece of pie that I wouldn't have minded taking a bite out of, especially when I saw how he was draping over her like he'd fainted. But that wasn't the worst part—*that* came when she tilted her head up to him to murmur some Hetairist sidesplitter, so that the man was braying and sputtering with laughter, like he used to when we'd go to Bob's Big Boy to eat ice cream. The next thing I knew, he quieted down, then took his hand and cupped it over the same place he said he'd keep safe for me.

And that's why I'm back here now, in Oceanside once again, to charm him with all of my skills. I am walking to the café where we will eat dinner soon, through the darkening blue winter streets bordered by the motels that beckon illicit lovers to lie inside their tide-soft sheets. It's a busy Friday, which means a boat must have just got in. Marines grasp their girls by the shoulders and escort them past the bazaars selling shells like roses and potions to heal singed skin, to the bars where beer-wielding wives dance. It's the ladies I notice, mostly, humid with cologne and glossy-lipped. A number are Marine Corps dames with cropped hair and sturdy gaits, but they can't compare tonight to the sweethearts who've been waiting too long for some loving from their men. They spill out the bar doors dressed in halter tops and lipstick, so high on sex and reunion they shimmy from the pure joy of it. And I know just what they feel like—like this girl here, lifting up her hair so her lover can admire her neck and kiss the sea mist off it. Or this passionate inamorata drinking from her lover's mouth. Now I watch a woman with long, glistening gold hair run across the street to wrap her arms around a beefy serviceman who lifts her above his head.

I look at her for a moment, then turn away. I feel as if I know that woman but I don't.

Still, she does remind me of someone.

That sailor's bride, the famous Penelope, had similar hair, didn't she? And the web she wove and destroyed every night was also that same color. If I were to snatch her from Homer's poem and drag her out here into the daylight, I wonder what she would do, surrounded by all these other patient ladies and this familiar ocean. I think I might introduce her to another one of her sisters, the constant Ixtacihuatl, a woman who turned herself into a vol-cano out of love for the great warrior Popocatepetl.

And just now, I can feel the edge of a story in me, another one of those poems I like to whisper in his ear. At this minute I have no trouble seeing the wonderful ruckus those girls would cause if they stepped out of their fables and onto this street:

Here, in front of the store selling shells, the two sisters would examine themselves in the shopwindows and they'd be cold and naked, shocked at their own dark thin bodies reflected in the glass. Passersby turn away, cover their eyes, but recognition spreads slowly in the air like a light perfume. Sweethearts now begin weeping at the sight of the shreds of gold shroud still caught in Penelope's fingers, the red mud in Ixtacihuatl's ravaged hair, although they don't know why.

The sisters are also confused.

I won't tell them that their Athens and Tenochtitlán are dead. Or of how Odysseus is tempted by Calypso, how Popocatepetl's body is a now a mountain of rock and fire.

They slip into white robes. Barefoot, they walk down this cold, cold street, gliding past the saloons and trinket shops as if they were on the sure road home. They will sleep on the strand tonight and wake, startled, to the giant sun. They will beg for food on corners and bathe in the ocean. They seem harmless, weak women. But when they cross paths with this girl now lifting her hair to reveal a long white neck, or this bride drinking from her lover's mouth, they hesitate only a moment before touching them with their warm hands, and so inject memory under their skin like a venom.

And they will teach me to touch you like that, Karl.

No one can love you the way I do.

I think you hold my childhood in your hands. I was the only woman who held you, once—on all those nights, on the night after my surgery when you kissed the blue stain on my breast.

The Greeks believed the heart is the seat of intelligence, I told you then. Plato described it as a cushion. Hippocrates as a pyramid. We put a wedding ring on the left hand because they thought the vein of love ran from this finger to the heart.

You cupped your hand over my scar. "I'd say your heart's like a diamond," you told me.

And darling, you were right. When I consider the hot rock of my heart I think you could pluck a diamond from that place. Or it might be a gold web in which I could snare you like a fish.

I see my dark, thin shape in the café's glass window. Recognition spreads through the air like a thin perfume.

You look up.

KARL AND I EAT DINNER by candlelight, which turns the wine inside our glasses into liquid gems. The café has yolk-yellow walls with white molding, and solid pine floors decorated by country rugs. Waiters pivot like ice skaters between the close-set tables while patrons bill and coo, but Karl doesn't seem to notice yet what a romantic spot we're in. His pale face bends over his plate and he stares intently at his uneaten food, the loaf of bread in its basket.

"Last time I saw you," he begins, then shakes his head. "I need to figure this thing out. I need to screw my head back on straight and just get everything cleared up."

"It seems clear enough to me."

"Because I've made promises to somebody. I've bought a ring."

"I think you should calm down." I ignore that business about the ring.

"I'm not exactly excelling at being an honest person, here."

"If you wanted to be honest, then you shouldn't have gotten engaged."

"I met someone who could be with me."

"I've been with you since I was fifteen."

"For a long while before this, you couldn't make time for us. You know it wasn't the first time that's happened, either. And then when I did see you, we'd fight about—I don't know—"

"Karl."

"The same old thing, is what it was."

I look at him and drink my wine until he quiets down again and passes his hand over his eyes.

I tear a clove of bread from the loaf and put it in front of his lips. He plucks it with his fingers and tucks it in his mouth, swallows. Then he lets out a breath.

"I am just not sure about what I'm doing anymore," he says.

"You thought you could *marry* somebody else?"

"I don't know. Yes."

"Well, that was a mistake, wasn't it?"

Karl starts laughing, then stops, and becomes suddenly serious. "All I want to do right now is hug you. Hug and muss you right up. And I don't want to be like that—womanizing's never been my specialty. But when I see you with—" He gestures with his hand. "Your hair down like that. And then you wore that dress the last time." He shakes his head, is quiet for a while. "No, it's not the dress."

I stand up. "Let's get out of here."

"Why?" He looks exhausted. Around us, a waiter flits and hovers, indicating he would like to take our order. "This guy's all hot to serve us up some chicken parmigiana or what-have-you, and I don't know if we should disappoint him."

"Karl, let's go."

"Sara, you tell me, what for?"

I just smile and grab his hand.

"You'll see."

I TAKE HIM TO THE BEACH. Though it's winter, a cloud cover warms the wind up a little, and the ocean greets us just like it did fifteen years ago, with the moonlight flashing and flickering over the waves lying under this long night. Karl stands next to me with his hands in his pockets while the sand collects over the tops of his shoes and he stares out at the small cathedrals the waves make. A fine mist sequins the air above the surf but I slip out of my sandals, take off my glasses, then step onto the lip of the water that opens into this vast, cold mouth where the whales and coral live. On a night like this it isn't hard for me to imagine leading Karl off the sandbank, the water closing in ripples over our heads, as I guide him past the lobster traps and sharp fins, the scattering mercury of minnows, until we reach a soft blue place a world away from the likes of Claire O'Connell.

"I love the ocean" is all I say.

Karl stands in back of me, and when I look over my shoulder his shirt is bright as a pearl in this light. A few hundred yards off a bonfire emits a red halo and the sounds of a guitar can be heard, though no one is in eye's reach.

I smile at him. "Karl, tell me about the sky tonight."

"It's too hazy for much gazing, but I think I can make out my horoscope, and it doesn't look so good."

"Come on."

He walks closer to the water, looks at me for a while. Then he squints, points up. "All right. See up there? That's Ursa Major, with its Mizar and the fainter Alcor."

"Right, I remember that."

"Then there's Ursa Minor, too. The business end of the little bear is your North Star, Polaris."

"Anything else?"

"Not much. But Cassiopeia should show up better in a few months."

"The mother of Andromeda, the chained lady."

"That's right. She's just a fuzzy thing now, but starting in summertime she'll be clear as a dream."

He stops talking, closes his eyes. After a few seconds, he says, "I wish we could just . . . I think it would be great if we could just *stay* here."

"Stay where?"

"Right here, on this beach. With the moon on you like that. Nothing would change. Nothing else would mean anything. I could just stand here, looking at you, all silver and beautiful."

"You usually don't talk like that, about staying in one place." I turn from him and step toward the surf so that the edge of my skirt darkens and floats around my calves. Hiking up my sweater sleeves, I reach down and dip my hands into the water, holding them there until my wrists tingle. I think of pressing my palms, cold and mobile, onto his chest.

"Well." He glances out at the water. "I just got some news—I made a cut in the program. They want to see me for an interview in a month. And if I get it, that'll mean Houston."

I bunch my hands into fists, release them. "That is . . . *great*."

"It's not in the bag yet. They'll do another personality on me, some more medicals."

"I know you'll get it."

"Do you *want* me to, though?"

I don't hesitate. "Yes."

"Because Houston's a big place. There's work there for you. I shouldn't *even be thinking this* with Claire waiting for me back in Pendleton." He is quiet for a second, and then: "But if you're saying—are you telling me that you're ready now?"

I just look at him.

"Because if that's what you are saying, then—"

"Then what?"

"Then I need to know. But otherwise, why even bring me out here? Things are too far along for me to be playing around." He flexes his chin. "And I don't have it in me like I used to."

"Karl, come on." I step out of the ocean and undo my sweater. I throw it on the bank and then kneel in front of him, touching his knees and his thighs. I unhook the buttons on his shirt and slide it off his back; neither of us balks at the weather. And once we're waist-deep, with the water streaming off his shoulders and the chill against my skin, I don't feel nervous anymore. The sea spreads out around us, burning, murmuring, invisible except for the luster sliding off the breakers. I curl around his body and arc my arms up in the sharp air, then dart forward to give him a kiss on the chin.

"What are you doing?" he whispers, his lips colored from the cold. "What are you up to?"

I lead him deeper inside the waves and then roll onto my back to look at the sky. With the water over my ears I can't hear anything but my pulse and my short breath. Karl treads water and cradles me in his hands, and when I turn my head to observe him against the backdrop of the shore, his face half visible in the light, I see that I have lured him a good distance but I feel strong enough to coax him out of sight of those trees waving us back, the sand stretching up to town. Years ago, I read of Luandinha the river spirit who rises from the misty banks of jungle waters to tempt family men from their homes. A beautiful demon dressed in green satin blows into *cachaça* shells and makes a music so powerful the husbands stagger from their beds, muttering an incomprehensible name. When they see the glistening serpent waiting for them on the banks, they follow her without a thought and dive into the water, swimming fast as eels down to her silver boudoir to smoke cigars and caress her feet.

Now I place my palms on Karl's chest and touch my mouth on its blue mark, sliding my lips on the wetness up the collarbone, up the neck, kissing the short hair at his nape.

I begin to tell him the next chapters of Helen's life. I mold the details, omitting some, inventing others, until I've beaten and licked the story into the perfect shape for tonight's setting, and it's sleek as a teardrop I can slip into his ear. He closes his eyes and I describe the floating city of Tenochtitlán, then the ivory-white Vatican with its splendid bowers, the forbidden library, the Raphael rooms. I talk of the juggler's erotic introduction to Petrarch, the great failed feats of Maxixa. Next comes Titian's offer and the leave-taking from the nun in the Pope's gardens— which leads to San Petronio, lit up like a sunset with murals, and the failed attempt on the life of Charles V.

"But as she wandered through Bologna," I say, "surrounded by soldiers, idiot ambassadors, the gold-dripping witnesses to the coronation, she was obsessed with only one thought, which was whether she would see Caterina again."

"Well, does she?" Karl laughs through his chattering teeth.

"You'll have to wait."

I stop talking. We listen to the ocean and our own breathing as we tussle in the water; our bodies press and retreat in the chilled dark. The ritual works. Nothing comes now between the lovely rub of our skin. Looking over his shoulder, I can barely see the shivering trees anymore or the sand as white as washing. I curl my fingers around his inner thigh. I press my tongue to his chest.

He cups his hand on my shoulder.

"Marry me," he says. "Let's get married tonight."

I balance myself in the water, stretching out my arms, and gesture toward the black horizon. "Let's go farther out." I kick my feet through the cold stuff to keep my head up. "Or I could tell you another story."

"No." He floats backwards to find a surefooted place, with his eyes still trained on mine.

A cold snap goes through me, and not from the water. I float toward him and grab his hand. "Come *swim* with me, Karl."

"I'll make you happy. I swear, you won't miss anything."

I dip under the water, rise to the surface again. "I will. But I can't do it yet."

He nods. "I see."

"I'm close to something. I'm close to *finding* something."

"You're close to something." He presses his chin with his thumb and doesn't talk for a long time. Then he says: "Well, I know that whatever it is is really important to you. And I've tried to understand that. I've *been* trying to—why you wouldn't want to be with me after all this time. Be with me permanently. But it's too much for me, I think. It's worn me right out. And the truth of it is,

I'm close to something too. I'm close to somebody I shouldn't take for granted." He tries a smile. "She's all set on a wedding for the fourteenth, in July. It's marked with a big X and everything on her calendar."

I bring my hand to his face, and he reaches up, takes it. He strokes my knuckles with his cold fingers.

"I can't go off with you tonight because of my—" I hesitate here. "Because of my work."

But *work* isn't the right word for it.

I can't marry him yet because if I did, I know I probably wouldn't finish what my mother started more than twenty years ago, when she stole that relic from the museum. I wouldn't excavate this hidden piece of history she believed in so much it made her seem strange, even to me.

Though I can't think of a way of explaining this to Karl so that it might make any sense.

And now his expression changes, in a way that I can't read. "It's really something, how you don't look any different since I first laid eyes on you," he says. "Back when you were just a kid. And me too." His thumb moves back and forth on my palm. "I have every part of you memorized, did I ever you tell that? There've been times, when I'd be stuck someplace on a base, with all these people I didn't know too well—holidays are the worst for that. And if I felt low, there was this thing I'd do to make myself feel better. I'd draw you in my mind. I'd picture you. This swirl of hair here, the pattern of it. The shape of your lip. Your neck, how long it is. Your small little hands. And it would make me feel better, knowing that I had you inside of me like that. It was a real comfort to me." His mouth twists. "That's just something I wanted you to know."

The ocean ripples black between us, and his chest and waist glimmer white above it. A breeze charges the drops on our bodies, blows through my hair, and etches the waves with tiny bright feathers. He presses my hand to his mouth, then rubs the wrist gently with his thumb before letting it go again.

" 'Bye, Sara."

Karl turns and moves toward the bank, struggling through a wave, and I watch as he walks up to the strand and takes up the pants he'd left there. He slips into his clothes and shoes, not bothering to button up the shirt, and only then do I start running up there, too, or trying to, pushing against the pull of the tide. By the time I reach the strand he's far ahead of me, near the trees and the sidewalks that lead into town.

But I can't catch up with him. Because when I've snatched my clothes back on, he's already out of sight. And so I wait for him to come back. I sit on the beach and I wait. I am waiting for you, Karl. I stare at the black air. I watch the red glimmering fire until it snuffs and its smoke matches the fog. And you don't come. Then there's just the green trees shaking their hair and the pale sand and the ocean rushing and whirling and rushing and flooding and roaring louder than I can stand it.

7

The first time Titian saw me naked he nearly went
blind.

I stood on the platform in his wintry studio, waiting
for his command. He nodded and I let my robe drop.
There was one moment when his face shone like a pearl
and then he clapped his hands over his eyes.

"Your darkness," he cried. "Your beauty."

He wore tinted lenses for days after that, and could
only work at night. His assistants, understandably nervous for their own pockets, demanded my removal. My
patron would hear nothing of it.

"Even if I could never paint again it would be worth
it," he confided in me. "But I will paint again. I will
paint you, and then the world will fall to its knees."

These were the men I had fallen in with. Geniuses
and hedonists who thought the globe would be conquered not by war but by a stroke of paint or a drop of
poetry.

Perhaps their dreams sprung from their city's mysterious waters, where they say Venus was born. Or perhaps it was the red tides of wine they drank, or the
witchery of all the courtesans with their shining limbs.

At the age of seventeen I found myself in this land of fantasy.

This was the republic of pleasure.

VENEZIA, LA SERENISSIMA, 1530.

When my patron and I stepped onto the *Piazza San Marco* in the fall and I saw the glittering basilica through a storm of birds, I was enraptured by that city's beauty. I did not discern any dangers in the gold air, or the polished stone churches, or the canals blue as jewels. I did not hear any alarms in the cathedral music that entered me like a passionate spirit, or warning signs in the art so gorgeous it might make one swoon. Nor did I taste any poison in the delicious fare, the small sweet cups of coffee and the garnet wine.

But the perils were there.

I had planned on staying in Venice for a brief holiday, then robbing Titian and making my way to Germany in order to fit Charles V's gory head on my stake. I thought that my only impediments could be soldiers, plague, rape, and famine, and that absent these troubles I would dip my hands in the Emperor's blood in a few short months. Little did I know that my worst enemy was myself. I could not foresee that my hunger for happiness, beauty, and books—those things the Venetians prized above all others—would tempt me from my higher calling.

Although I kept my juggling balls inside a velvet-lined cedar box, my attentions were elsewhere, and I practiced with them very little. I was quite busy with the city's diversions. I became an art lover in Venice. I learned to crave octopus in olive oil and mastered the correct way to taste wine. One night three gorgeous whores read to me from Petrarch, then caressed me until I nearly burst.

I was weak.

I have committed a great crime.

Distracted by luxury, learning, and the most beautiful women in the world (the only exception being my darling Caterina), I would fail my father once again. I stayed in Venice for ten years.

I BECAME A MUSE.

Owing to Titian's ocular difficulties where my nudity was concerned, he bade me to reveal myself to him in stages. Later in the afternoon, after my customary chocolate and bread, then a long bath at the clever hands of an apple-cheeked maid, he would summon me to his studio and place me upon the pedestal where I was to disrobe at his command. He would stand before me, flushed from an artistic ecstasy, and occasionally shout at the harem of courtesans in his employ who milled about the studio in all manner of undress.

"Strip, bellissima!" they would cry at me and then bare their own breasts as an incentive.

"Quiet, you bitches!" he would answer back, perhaps swatting them with his brush or threatening to dock their pay.

But they never did behave. They were cheeky minxes, and somewhat taken with me. The girls rouged their nipples and wore pearls strung around their pink hips. They were strangers to shame. Many were brazen enough to approach me before the Master himself, offering me ripe, rare pears, or gold coins in exchange for even one afternoon in their beds. The most beautiful, and most wealthy, was a fair Spanish girl who stalked the studio like a cat but never approached me in that fashion. A cortigiana onesta by the name of Isabella, she was a favorite of the Ganymedes on account of her cropped hair, boy's leather leggings, and cunning codpiece. Isabella had an attractive air of mystery about her—she was a bookish jade, always reading from her thumbed copy of Ovid's Metamorphoses, and there was a rumor that she still pined for a lost love, a Spanish duchess to whom she had been a handmaiden or somesuch office. Though I could not imagine her in servant's gear, she did have the wit of a woman who had learned to hide her heart. Besides her careers as courtesan and muse, she was also a thief who stole fortunes from the treasures she found about Titian's mansion. On the occasions that he lost his temper and chastised the whores, she liked to place her white hand upon his chest and reprimand them, too.

"I will whip you if you do not obey the Master!" she would roar, and her sisters would turn bright red to contain their laughter. Then, when she withdrew her hand, we would see that she had plucked some jewel from his person, a gold brooch or pearl earring, and she winked at us as she slipped it into her own pocket.

"That's better," my patron would say. And then he would turn his eyes back on me, blinking a little, and command me to reveal one small glory.

"The shoulder," he might say. Or, "the breast." Or, "one knee."

For years, the poor sod could only withstand glimpses of me. Hued muses were not much used in Venice then. To the white eye I was as dazzling as the original Helen and so as dangerous to the artist's health, for that girl did blind the poet Stesichorus. Titian took the fable as a premonition and pursued my form as if I were the sun. He had not painted me yet, instead preferring to spend days without end peering at an elbow; he could gawp for months at my well-turned wrist. My small foot could send him into paroxysms for two full seasons. And so, when I was not eating, reading, gazing upon marvelous art and architecture, or being seduced by harlots who, try as they might, could never erase Caterina from my bruised mind, one would find me in my patron's studio, completely wrapped in sheets except for one naked toe, or one firm buttock, upon which he feasted his slitted eyes.

"I am learning to see," he would say as he stared. "It is as if I had opened my eyes for the first time. Before this a man could never hope to capture night with his brush but you, my dear, are darkness brought to life. Your sinister beauty would cause the flagellants to beat themselves to death, have you any idea? Yours is not simply the absence of light, no, you are what generals and priests fear. Yours is the color of Süleyman's shadow upon this shore, and the color too of the succubus whose smothering is such sweet freedom. Devils and saints would cry at your magnificent berry skin. You are Solomon's wife, you are Lot's wife. You are the terrifying Delilah."

"And you, my patron, are a tremendous lackwit," I would answer. "It surprises me that you have not already died from sheer stupidity. Does not the human animal require some intelligence to survive?"

And so on we went, for years and years. So busy was I savoring the island's pearls—fava beans and olives, oranges with coconut, the girls like fawns, my patron's heart-cracking portraits of the goddess Mary and her uncontrollable Christ, and lest I forget, Venice's famous printings of Ptolemy, the Roman histories, the Odes to Laura, the Confessions, How ardently I longed, O my God, how ardently I longed to fly to you away from earthly things!—so busy was I involved in these careers that I did not understand my other, sharper senses grew duller day by day.

I became distracted by their God. Surrounded by the furniture of this deity, I soon discovered that the dear faces of my idols grew fainter in my mind while my heart continued to hunger after a great Father who might hold my raging soul. These brilliant crosses and lacy temples, the sweet faces of Virgins, Saints, and slim pale Sons seduced my faculties so that I found myself bent in heathen prayer. And questions of theology coincided with questions of art. I knew Charles used the beautiful Mary to drive the sword that killed my father, to steel his subjects against Martin Luther, but I, too, became converted, or confounded. Titian's fame grew as I knew him, and he was knighted by the Crown in 1533, but by that time my soul was too fat and I merely trembled in the audience, and threw away my chance. Still, watching Titian at work, one could not help but think that a higher power moved his brush. My patron may have been an idiot, but I must admit that he was also a genius.

IN 1537 TITIAN took to painting me with such an obsession, such a vengeance, one would think he were a old virgin who had broken into the king's seraglio and was just now seeing the female figure for the first time. Which, in a way, I suppose he was.

I would stand on the pedestal locked in some absurd pose—my arms raised, grapes dripping from my fingers, diamond stars in my hair, diaphanous gilded scarves not concealing my admittedly magnificent delta—while the Master gulped me with his hungry eyes and tried to copy the startling darkness before him.

For a full year, however, he failed. He would wink at his canvases like an imbecilic Cyclops, and then fill his canvas with such gross graffiti of giant-breasted black monsters that were all out of proportion to the human form. I thought it the same phenomenon as when Cortés tried to describe the citizens of Tenochtitlán to his peers—"Animals," he had called us, struggling for his words, "with fire in their eyes and their mouths stained with gore, half-human, half-ape, as bloodthirsty as sharks." The idiot, indeed, seemed to believe these fictions, but perhaps one should not be too hard on a feeble soul like his; or my patron's; it was only that our wondrous bodies strained these men's imaginations too far, and the effect on their eyes and tongues was far more nefarious than mere blindness or silence. We had driven them to the edge of their wits with our perilous beauty. Their faculties were not great enough to hold us. But eventually Titian did surprise me. His eye adjusted, and his genius filled the large spaces I had created. He began to paint me, and successfully now, in these gigantic murals devoted to my splendid nudity, though the goddesses I modeled were not of his old ilk—there were no Danaës in my reper-

toire, no Venuses nor Didos nor Marys. For I
inspired witches of a different sort.

To my enlightened master, I appeared the figurate of
all the dark sinners in Europe's histories. I became Eve,
as well as Lot's bad wife, dusky Medea, heart-arsed
Calypso, also black, fanged Celaeno. Although Titian
did complete several works during this era, among them
the Venus of Urbino and the Presentation of the Virgin
(both using Isabella as a model and each one a personal
favorite), he spent every spare moment devoted to his
new exotic project, which he claimed would crack the art
world open like an egg. Yet despite his blustering, he
was also quite nervous about it, and did not show any of
his paintings of me for nearly a decade. We had already
seen warning signs of the dangers of introducing my
country's attractions to these frail natives—the European constitution was simply too anemic. There were the
cases of Spaniards who, having adopted a diet of our
maize without learning the proper method of cooking it,
were soon poisoned and became as insane as monkeys.
And it had been well publicized that when certain
noble-born ladies had seen our stone (and stolen) gods'
proud and fantastically lengthy penises, they began rubbing themselves with such unabashed agility they
appeared infected with Satan himself.

It was consequently out of a civic responsibility that
Titian kept his masterpieces under wraps, but eventually the ego did rear its slobbering head. In the winter of
1540, he swept into the studio and put the finishing
touches on the mural of Salomé, with all her brilliant
veils.

"I cannot hide these anymore," he cried. "It is a crime against art. A crime against beauty. A crime against humanity!"

And so it was with this moving bit of modesty that the Master announced that he would hold a showing of all the masterpieces that featured me as their star.

THE OPENING TOOK place in March of that year at Titian's own Casa Grande. Although he had dazzled me for years with his spectacular parties, we had never seen a banquet quite like this.

We feasted on roast hen, shrimp in wine, and suckling pig, and he had imported these cunning three-pronged spears with which to stab our meat. It was quite a success. Aretino was there, and the Doge of Venice, and all manner of high-borns and clergy, among them one of the Emperor's favorites, a fish-eyed priest called Leonardi, who apparently had not understood he would be in the company of light women. He blessed himself each time a courtesan burped or bared a breast at table, which we found quite charming. "Look at this silly frog!" a courtesan named Lucia laughed. Then she tweaked him on the nose.

"I am not a frog," Leonardi answered, blushing.

"No, you are not," Isabella said, with a particular edge to her voice that night. "You are a lusty stag, and I desire that you take me this instant, codpiece and all!"

"Oh dear," Leonardi breathed.

"Leave him alone, ladies," Titian said. "Men of the cloth have enough on their minds now without being tortured by whores."

"Does he have a mind?" I asked, then peered into his hairy ear. "I swear I've met shoes more intelligent than this fellow!"

"I am a man of God, and a servant of the Emperor," Leonardi said, fingering the tridents. "The Lord has made me immune to temptations of the flesh and so I am not affected by your taunts nor curses nor your wee pink nipples."

"Too bad," Lucia sighed.

"Leonardi, ignore them," Titian broke in, "and tell us about the Crown's business. Is it true what they say?"

"Yes," the Doge cut in. "Is Charles going to take Barbarossa at Algiers?"

"What is this?" Leonardi asked, holding up the trident.

"A fork, sir," Titian answered. "It's the latest thing."

Leonardi smiled. "How curious."

"Is it true?" the Doge pressed. "I can only hope he crushes the Barbarians considering the humiliation we endured at Prevesa."

"Brother, do not forget the French," Titian sputtered.

"Of course."

"Actually," Leonardi said, "Charles does have his plans. In October he will set sail from Mallorca with Doria. It will be a certain victory. The illustrious Duke of Alba will join him. And the impressive Cortés."

Now I began paying very close attention. Mallorca, Charles, Cortés. With those words, it suddenly occurred to me that I had been here, having some form of this same conversation for ten years, while my father Tlakaelel's body moldered in the bloody dust of Tenochtitlán. Sweat began pouring from my neck.

"What are you staring at, girl?" the Doge barked.

"Nothing, sir." I feigned sudden timidity. "It only interests me to hear geniuses in conversation."

"Well, off with you, stinking harlots," the Doge said. "I have seen enough corruption this year."

The girls bristled, but Titian comforted them with gestures that promised additional pay ahead. He gave the sign and we were all dismissed. Soon we were lodged in Titian's parlor, with several girls taking up a game of penny-prick.

Isabella, however, glowered in a corner, and fingered her copy of the Metamorphoses she had left before on a side table. Her temper seemed especially foul tonight.

I approached her, and quoted what I remembered from that book, from the story of Tiresias:

This love of male and female's a strange business.
Fifty-fifty investment in the madness
Yet she ends up with nine-tenths of the pleasure.

Isabella glanced up. "You know it quite well."

"Yes. My old lover used to read it to me."

"As mine did. A girl I once knew in Spain."

"It's curious that we have the same sorts of memories."

She now shot me a hot look. "What are you doing here, Helen? Why do you let him make you the fool with those portraits?"

"I don't know. I am beginning to wonder if I have lost my head."

"You should leave. This place will ruin you."

"And you?"

"I have my own plans. Venice is dead. A friend of

mine, a witch, has told me a plague will come in ten years."

"I have thought of leaving. Just now. Just now when the Doge spoke of Charles at Mallorca."

"It would be simple to escape, with enough to money to last."

"How?"

She showed me the trident she had palmed, the "fork." "These buffoons do not know what clever devices they invent. I could open Titian's cache now with this small thing."

I sat down on one of Titian's velvet chairs and watched the courtesans play their cards. "I am very sad."

"You must not be. It does not help you."

"My gentle girl, Caterina, was from Spain. When I met her she was a beautiful nun, at the Vatican. She was sent there by the Inquisition. And she loved poetry."

Here, Isabella appeared to have stopped breathing.

"What?"

"I had my heart stolen once, as you may have heard," she said slowly. "My lover's name was Caterina Lucia Gloria á de Carranza."

I became angry. "Are you trying to hurt me? That's impossible!"

She struggled to compose herself, though a tear did slip from her eye. "Apparently not. I was her nurse. A long, long time ago."

Now I felt myself trapped inside some storm. My face was all fire. "You are an insane wretch," I whispered. "This place has poisoned your mind."

But she only took my hand. "If you knew her as I did, then you must have loved her."

I could say nothing.

"And that," she continued, "makes us sisters." She pressed her hand harder to mine. "I will help you out of here, with all the supplies you might need. You are only in danger in Venice."

No, I could not answer her, for the crashing of my heart. All my memories reared their horrible forms and nearly blinded me. But just as I gained back my breath and tried to say something to her that might make sense, events twisted and tangled again.

From the inner chambers of the house, we heard a loud bellowing, as if a bear had just been cut down.

"Hush, Helen," she said. "Something's happened." And here came another roar.

Now we rushed out to find our patron.

IN THE STUDIO *where my portraits hung, we discovered a flock of noblemen and servants fluttering around a lump on the floor, which on closer inspection turned out to be the sack of bones that had been Fra Leonardi just five minutes before. Titian was quite disturbed at the effect his hospitality had on the priest, although my opinion is that the man's ghost was so obviously uncomfortable in its clothes it was looking for even the weakest excuse to make its escape. In any event, the corpse lay there, with a most thrilled expression on its face—the dead man was positively smiling, and I swear one could still glimpse the hint of a concupiscent glint in his bulging eyes. Well, I was not confused, for I'd certainly seen enough versions of that countenance before—on the* faces of gentlemen who emerged from Titian's guest rooms still bearing the stigma of a courtesan's rouge on their fat lips. Moreover, other influences of the Father's erotic curiosities were also evident on the blessed remains.

"Good Lord!" our shy Lucia cried, "look at that horse!"

"What the hell happened?" the Doge yelled above the din, "has he been poisoned?"

"Or strangled perhaps?" Isabella asked.

The Doge now took a sword from his servant and brandished it toward the ceiling. "Murder!"

"I assure you, Prince, no one has been poisoned or strangled in my home," Titian said. "This was a purely natural death."

One of Titian's other guests, a bird-faced royal surgeon by the name of Martelli, nodded. "Natural, I should say."

The Doge turned toward him. "What do you mean?"

"In my medical opinion," Martelli intoned, "the poor man died of an overabundance of lust."

"And how can that be? There were no women here!"

Martelli and Titian cast grave looks at each other.

"I am afraid," Titian said, "it is my genius that killed him." And with that he pointed upwards, to the unveiled murals he had so dramatically displayed for his guests.

The Doge looked where he pointed, thought for a moment, and then nodded. "Ah."

Titian had cleared the studio of everything but the

paintings he had done of me over the past few years. On these walls I was Eve and Salomé and Lot's wife, and every other brand of traitor and harlot contained in the Bible and the Greek myths. I had observed these murals numerous times myself, and never seen anything more than splendor in them. My breasts glowed like pomegranates and my thighs were made of pure nectar. When I looked at the girl posing there, I saw myself as gorgeous as I thought Caterina might have seen me. But then, when Titian pointed an accusing finger at the portraits, I witnessed something else, which was the absolute opposite of true beauty.

I suddenly saw the way they saw me.

I understood that if I were beautiful to them, it was not the beauty of the embrace in the long grass of the Vatican's gardens, or of my darling's fingers touching my lips as she gazed into my eyes. Oh, my delicate sweetheart. Oh, how I yearned for you, for you were a universe apart from this place. In his art I found not the beauty of love, or even of happy rompings in a silk bed. This was the attraction of the brute wilderness, but it was not, as Titian had said, natural, or even me! It was like the twisted reflection of our faces in Cortés's eyes that, in turn, was only the shadow of his own sick passion to kill, plunder, and rape without mercy—and the deadly paintings would serve as God's license to continue those crimes.

Titian, without knowing it, had painted Europe's own portraits, not mine. And now the small crowd looked away from the murals and the corpse, toward me, I suppose expecting that I would burst into flame or show them my horns.

I wished that I could, but I only shrugged. After

that I cast one knowing glance at Isabella and retired to my room.

FOUR NIGHTS LATER I gathered my juggling spheres, then set fire to all ten of those portraits, and all the studies and sketches he had made of me. With Isabella's aid I stole a small bank of Titian's fortune in order to make my escape. I asked her to accompany me, but she shook her head and muttered something about becoming the greatest thief the world had ever seen.

"Well, I hope I shall see you again, great thief or not," I told her.

"And I also, Sister," she said, handing me one of her boy's costumes as a disguise. "Now be off."

I gave her a swift kiss and we parted ways in front of the mansion just now glittering with flame.

I left that Venice of worldly pleasures and its delicacies as soothing as the waters of Lethe. I took one last look at the blue canals, then hired a Moor-smuggler to take me to another dangerous country.

Of course, I had no other destination but Mallorca.

8

Los Angeles seethes outside of my office window tonight. The air is as black as a storm. The city lights burn like a fire.

I wander into one of the darkened galleries, telling the juggler's story to myself. Guards nod at me from their stations. Here are stone figures of Calypso, the bird-legged Sirens, Medea. An incomplete army of the spurned girls Helen represented for Titian.

Medea was a foreigner who wove Jason's beloved a poisoned dress, then drowned her own children in the ocean. And she has a sister as well, though one who wouldn't have been known to Helen, as she wasn't born until after Cortés's siege—that Mexican witch La Llorona, who also drowned her sons in the river to spite a wandering husband.

These are women who grow powerful once their grooms choose other lovers. They possess amazing, transforming passions. They fly through the night on the black wings of their gloom, snatching victims in their claws while millions of people through the centuries scan the skies for even one glimpse of them.

And they turned their tears into something lasting, didn't they? Their sorrow made them into stars.

But I wish I felt nothing.

THE WEEKS PASS and he won't return my calls. The sickening finality of our last conversation seeps into me like a contamination and for ten days I call in sick and stay under the covers. But it doesn't help. I'm as bad off in my dark bed as inside the light and so I return to work—though not the work that I'm assigned. There's almost a hallucinatory quality to it, as I dive into these old books, running away from the image of Karl staggering up the strand, and pursuing at the same time a dark woman down obscure corridors—and I'm almost close enough to touch her shoulder or her long hair, her quick hands and troubled heart.

There are secrets to be found if you just *look*, as my mother once showed me. Everything is stolen but it can be reclaimed. Sometimes, when I stalk these halls at night I imagine I see her perched on top of a stack of antique tomes, filing her long, painted nails, or admiring her reflection in the glass cases protecting the Sirens, or the Aztec codex. Beads click around her throat and wrist. Her hair is plaited into dark braids. *You think you've got a broken heart?* she asks. *Imagine the* putana *who was paid a couple of nickels to pose for this thing. Imagine the countries killed so some rich guy could put this old book in his library. I don't see that written up on the little sign, do I? And if you don't watch out they'll stick you in one of these cages, too.*

It seems like a long time ago when I took on the occupation of liberating stolen books from their sanctuaries, though I didn't then know what weird, rough work it would be.

Still, I keep at it, though with a sinking feeling. I hide in the library and resume my research concerning Helen, sinking into the hush of scholars who have also been given a home by the Getty. I've commandeered a carrel on the second floor of the library, and in the space next to mine there's an expert in Greek who tries to imagine the colors of flowers once strewn at Athena's feet. On my other side there's a Roman scholar who has spent years translating a love poem written to Venus. I think all of us are escaping something. Every morning, after a few sips of coffee and a bit of small talk, each of us retreats with our books, and travels centuries away from this place.

I flee back to the Venetian Republic during the age of the Doge. The most visible women of cinquecento Venice are these same, soft goddesses painted in gigantic portraits by the Master who reigned in this era. In *Danaë*, Titian's heroine reclines against silk sheets, her nakedness accented only by pearl earrings as Zeus descends upon her as a shower of gold. I also study his portrait of Actaeon spying on Diana's plush and forbidden figure. And in a painting that now hangs in the Uffizi, Venus stands on a pedestal, draping a veil against her bare thighs, while cupids and cymbal-playing fairies worship her.

But I also see that Venus was a prostitute who stood in a cold studio, clutching a piece of cloth to her pudenda, while Titian ordered her to pose this way and that. When the workday ended she stepped down, redressed, and collected her *maravedi*. Then she disappeared into the mazy, drowning city.

Hunting Helen through Venice, I now only discover more of these *meretrici*, raising their skirts to reveal white legs. There are no more mentions of her in Fra Tosello's diary, nor any other that I can find, although I bump into many suspicious women wandering the streets, some of them dripping pearls and rubies. Tintoretto painted the famous courtesan Veronica Franco as a plum-cheeked queen wrapped in jewels. Pietro Aretino wrote poems about courtesans' beauty, grace, and infectious corruption. The flavors of their perversions varied. Some of them dressed like boys; others invoked love magic and the Tarot to seduce their more difficult suitors. They were suspected of sleeping with the Devil as well as kings. In 1586 the *meretrice pubblica* Emilia Catena was whipped in Piazza San Marco for witchcraft. Sumptuary laws were taken up by legislators and spies roved the streets. Nevertheless, during Carnival, detachments of courtesans stepped lightly into gondolas, their breasts bared and faces obscured by feathered masks which revealed powdered noses and red, red mouths.

I find all this, but no other records of a dark girl in Titian's employ.

I next turn to Algiers during the Ottoman War, which she claims to have participated in, but there is even less of a trail there. After capturing Tunis, the Emperor, along with the Duke of Alba and Hernán Cortés, sailed to the Algerian coast—then known as the coast of Al Jazirah—to crush Süleyman's famous corsair, Khayr ad-Din. Charles, in his magnificent wig, stood at the prow and commanded his men to capture the territory of Moors. This was a region of Spanish exiles, water, sandstorms, citrus fruit, wine, and the *Quercus suber* tree from which a fine, tough cork may be lifted in layers. Inside the delicate cities of Sinan, shrouded women lifted themselves from prayer rugs at the sounds of musket fire. The Mediterranean glittered off the strange armor of holy soldiers. To the Europeans, each was identical except for the ferocious Khayr ad-Din, plunderer of the coasts of Italy and Rhodes, when a cataract of Turks rushed from the harbor, invoking a sacred sea storm, and defeated the Holy Roman Empire.

It is impossible to find more than a handful of names inside these storms of bodies. And after a while, I realize that it's not all that surprising that I can't recover one apocryphal girl—the whole of Algiers itself disappeared, once. The Phoenicians founded the city, and after the fall of Caesar's empire it was burned off the map for centuries, only to be colonized by the Spaniards in 1511, a handful of years before the torching of Tenochtitlán, and the beginning of my supposed heroine's journey.

FEBRUARY. I AM SURROUNDED by stacks and stacks of books and old maps. At nine o'clock at night, Teresa appears at my desk.

"It looks like you're right," I say. "There's nothing here that proves she lived. It seems silly now. It's much more probable that de Pasamonte wrote the story."

"I didn't say it was silly," she says.

But I push away the book I had been reading. All of it is lies. There was no Caterina, no Maxixa, no Helen.

There was no Aztec juggler, no muse, no assassin.

There was also no wedding with Karl. And I have made a mistake.

Next to me, the Greek scholar continues scribbling about the colors of flowers that floated through the air of Athens during an ancient celebration. I close the books on Venice, Algiers, the Moors' holy war, the courtesans, and begin returning all of the volumes, one by one, back to their shelves.

BY EARLY MARCH, TERESA has begun to do some grudging work on a fifteenth-century copy of Petrarch's *Canzoniere and Trionfi*, illuminated in the vivid style of Girolamo da Cremona, in order to avoid being fired. She hovers over a miniature of the poet romancing his Laura, and applies thin leaves of gold to the book's borders with a steady hand. The gold reflects onto her spare, pale face like a small flame.

"I *really* must quit this job," she says, but keeps at it.

I am not so industrious. *The Conquest* lies on my desk, still scarred, still rotting. I have not touched it for weeks—though she hasn't complained. I examine the glue and the bone folder and the sheets of fine Japanese papers stacked by my elbow. I lift one leaf of the paper and hold it against the light. It is as transparent as a veil or a caul, and I look at her through it.

We are surrounded by such flammable objects, I notice. Not only paper, but also tapestries and the old, fragile costumes. And the gardens of yew trees and indigenous thickets that Mr. Getty would have gawked at. Los Angeles is famous for its brush fires.

As my mother told me years and years ago, we would not be the first victims of that kind of catastrophe.

The famous library of Tenochtitlán was similarly vulnerable, according to legend. I am speaking here of the obscure Amoxcalli, in Nahuatl. Mom described it to me when I was a child, and how could I forget the story? Inside of that shrine had been thousands and thousands of books, each carefully printed on soft amate paper made from boiled and crushed bark fibers. The Aztecs wrote in a way that pleased the eye as much as the tongue, as their letters were not crossed sticks like ours but images of animals, citizens, plants, and gods. A closed eye, for example, symbolized evening; a shield indicated war. A corpse wrapped for burial served as the mark of death, and a scroll issuing from a man's tongue expressed speech.

Tenochtitlán's scholars coded all their secrets with this system— the lost local histories, religious mysteries, wars that ate the bodies of thousands of men whose names evaporated centuries ago. A curious reader, entering the library, must have encountered something much like the great florilegium at Alexandria, or the kaleidoscopic fantasies of Borges.

We might, for example, imagine Bernal Díaz del Castillo there, just after he arrived at Tenochtitlán.

And such daydreaming is dangerous, of course, as it inevitably leads to another story, and stories always need their listeners.

Although later he would be the gorgeously bearded author of the famous *History of the Conquest of New Spain*, in 1520 Bernal Díaz was still Cortés's rough boy hacking his way through the steaming jungle, constantly veering right, and with those fantasies of gold clogging his head. As he followed the general through this alien, absolutely silent city of stone mosques and endless dark bodies, he must have been dazzled by the strangeness of the citizens parting to make a path while locking their painted eyes upon him.

No, not citizens, he would have corrected himself. *Barbarians*, who worshiped blood as he himself worshiped the cross. And he had corrected *them* with his sword. He had watched hundreds die at his feet already and each time understood his holy justification. He understood it now, as he wandered through the invaded city. Their apostasy was visible, he thought, in these temples with their piles of red skulls, and this Lilith he saw wearing infant skin and gold teeth, with dugs bared like a dog's. Satan had reared himself a brood quietly enough here for all these centuries, and without the healthful charges of Christ these people had darkened and become deformed as trees might if deprived of the rays of the sun.

He followed the general through the speechless crowd, past the blood-red gardens and zoos hosting strange beasts and the sacerdotal stone mired in a ground slippery with human offal. He and his cohorts made their way toward Montezuma's coffers, which were rumored to hold all the riches of this infernal Midas.

On the way, however, he became distracted.

He passed one temple that did not appear to serve either murderous or domestic occupations. It was as large as the others, but was not decorated by bone-trinkets, nor did its doorway hold children and nursing women. Instead two men stood before it, wearing a gaudy garb similar to that of the priests, though without the abominable stigmas of human sacrifice. One of them held what appeared to be a bed linen of the finest quality; and from what Bernal Díaz could see, the interior of the temple was shadowy, quiet, utterly familiar in some way, and so, confounding.

He stepped inside. It took him some moments to discover he was in a library, and that this system of cubbyholes contained not linens as he had thought, but scrolls.

The librarian in the gaudy garb approached him, recognizing a reader among Cortés's mad troop. Bernal Díaz watched the man—who had an inky, hawk-boned face, white, white teeth— this man unrolled a sheet bearing wondrous signs and in a deep and sonorous voice began to recite something. A song? No, a poem.

Bernal Díaz somehow understood that this man was reading him a love poem. And that these pictures of goddesses and flowers were words. It was like the moment when the soul enters the child resting in the woman's womb—the moment of the quickening, when the infant may be both loved and damned—he saw in those seconds the soul shining out of the librarian, and the inscrutable genius of this clan who kept their many secrets in this dark, cool house.

General! He cried out. General! (For he knew that he had made a discovery as great as Columbus.)

But it was then that he heard the stamping and roaring, and saw the smoke in the air. His comrades passed by, lugging heavy gold gods. A girl, with her hair on fire, ran through the street. Women screamed, great stone buildings toppled to the ground. Cortés's men had just begun the destruction of Tenochtitlán.

All night, the library burned.

I LOOK AT TERESA now, still bent over the Petrarch, and the gold leaf like a flame in her hand.

"Teresa."

I try to recite this adventure for her, which once was one of my mother's bedtime stories. I think its themes might coincide with Teresa's philosophy. My boss believes that everything should be allowed to crumble into dust but maybe it already did a long time ago. Large as well as small histories show us that these kinds of fires have always made a mockery of archivists, for they have consumed the kings, the courthouses, the markets, as well as the love affairs, my love affair, the mother's. So much goes up in smoke. Though maybe not every annihilation is so bad. At least *that* library retains its mystery, unlike this storehouse for false books, which is a kind of nightmare since nothing changes here, and everything is exactly as it seems.

But then, I find I can't say these things.

She looks up from her work and takes in a breath. She walks over and puts her hand on my moving shoulder.

"Aw, Sara. Losing a man's not the end of the world. You'll be *fine.*"

EVENING. INSIDE MY SMALL South Pasadena house, I wait for my father, Reynaldo, to arrive for dinner. I love my home, having stocked it with private pleasures. Here is my soft Paris chair and my leather sofa and my cherry bookshelves and my books. Here are my small potted gardens, a nineteenth-century English one on the porch, a sixteenth-century tropical one on the patio off my bedroom.

I live by myself. When I am not devastated, I enjoy it here. At night I take long baths perfumed with rose attar and listen to the calamitous happiness of Thelonious Monk and Tito Puente. I grow beautiful flowers, yellow tulips with red tongues flickering through the petals, white orchids with violet lips and marbled genital hollows. I own a gorgeous collection of books. Apart from the signed *El Jardín de Senderos que se Bifurcan*, I have a first edition *Ficciones* I bound myself in amethyst leather, and an expensive facsimile of *Don Quixote* that I like to read while drinking Spanish sherry. I also own an American first of *Mrs. Dalloway*, bought from a high-rent Los Angeles bookstore for a per-ounce price higher than pure heroin's. And the book is a drug. Its pages are ivory-colored and rippled like a wave; it bears the stigmata of Woolf's own signature in her famous purple ink.

But tonight I can't take any interest in my things. I sit on my chair and hold a cold volume in one hand, then get up to make dinner. The sky behind the trees darkens in the kitchen window as I chop onions and grind sesame seeds into a paste in the mortar. Next comes the chiles, the chocolate, and the pieces of turkey, set to simmer on top of the stove for as long as possible.

A fairly conventional dinner, I have to say. When I was a child, my mother and I liked to make my father spectacularly odd meals. We got our ideas out of books—once reading *Candide* like a menu, then doing our best to reconstruct its parrot soups, hummingbird casseroles, and roast monkey-stone pies out of the ethnic food section at Ralph's. When I finished *Emma* there was the quivering blood pudding; after the Tina Modotti show at the museum, fried cactus and meringue skeletons; post-*Shogun* my mother insisted on wearing kimonos and we ate raw Japanese food for a full week.

My father would sit at the table and stare at the masterpiece on his plate, then gawk at the sugar skull grinning at him or the chopsticks in my hair as he tried to make out some inkling of his genes in me.

Beatrice would *roar* with laughter, in a way I didn't see as different until later.

Sometimes I think he still looks at me the way he did then.

I chop the lettuce and artichoke hearts and carrots until his car's headlights paint the kitchen's yellow walls white. I put my knife down, walk to the door. The moment I put my fingers on the doorhandle the bell rings, and then here he is, grinning on my front step: He's tall as a panda, dark, mustachioed, and holding his old guitar made of a polished light wood, in the Spanish style.

"Baby girl!" he cries.

IN THE DINING ROOM, my father devours the turkey mole by tucking large ladles of it expertly under his mustache so that not one of his still-black whiskers is coated by sauce. All of him is dapper—the white silk shirt with the neatly rolled-up sleeves, the khaki slacks with the knife-edge pleats, the luxuriant silvery hair waving back from his head like Ricardo Montalban's in *Fantasy Island*. I, however, am not so stylish tonight, and *he* is not so shy that he will refrain from staring at my coiffure or clothes as he savors his meal.

"Dad," I say, "don't look at me like that."

He flings his hand up. "I can't look at my beautiful baby, with the hair like a broom?"

"My hair's fine. Eat your food."

"A drowned cat's got more pizzazz, okay?"

"Okay. Now, eat."

"*Una muchacha con la cabeza quebrada como su madre, pero mira qué chula, qué preciosa, tan guapa*—if you just put a little lipstick on or something."

"Dad."

"And you're too skinny, too," he goes on, spooning up some more mole and tucking it and shredded lettuce into half a tortilla. As he does this, his rolled-up sleeve slides down his arm, revealing the top section of a scar that's impressed me ever since I was a child. Dad now folds the tortilla into a neat triangle and hands it over to me, causing the sleeve to drop even further, and so showing a greater span of the forearm's blemished flesh, which is not just a white span of scar tissue but also a faint stain of blue.

"I want to see you finish the whole thing, sweetie," he says, about the food on my plate.

My father's nerves never get jangled except where I'm concerned; otherwise, he's of the walk-it-off school of coping with personal problems, or tragedies, as they may be. After my mother died, he only cried in front of me once, and the rest of his grieving took place inside his locked bedroom. Still in the thick of his mourning, he took up single fatherhood without batting an eye, teaching me about menstrual periods, boys, Mexican history, also yelling about gifted programs at P.T.A. meetings and making my lunches as if these were the most natural things in the world. And they were. He'd wake me up at five-thirty in the morning to tame my hair into braids before he went off to work, and I had a home-cooked dinner every night even though he labored more than seventy-hour weeks for his construction business. That white-and-blue scar just now peeking out of his sleeve, though, is the one vestige of the days when my father was not so disciplined. It's the remains of a tattoo in the shape of a fist, which he had removed two decades ago in a barbaric process that left a patch of his brown skin a mottled pink but didn't quite get rid of the faint outlines of a blue thumb.

I reach out now and trace the stigma with my fingers. He looks down and frowns at his arm.

"I'm getting it cleaned up someday. They can do nice things with lasers these days, plastic surgery."

"You just don't like it because it reminds you of what a tough guy you used to be."

"A *dumb* guy, you mean. Not tough. I told you already, the kid who got this thing was a kid with a scrambled brain."

Dad has told me about his early days already, more than once, though the story about the tattoo isn't one that I can tire of.

He got it in the early 60s, when he had only been in the States for less than a year, but already distinguished himself to his employer by the delicate quality of his construction work, and to his fellow jacks by his insubordinate temper. He'd once said that it was *pure dumb stinking pride* that had made him so mad he wanted to bust the head of every man who even looked at him the wrong way. He'd worked with a construction crew of fifty men that was nearly all Anglos, except for two Sudanese and three other Mexicans—all of *them* from Vera Cruz, *not* Chihuahua like him—who knew how to keep out of trouble. They labored on the high-rises springing up in Long Beach—long, rough, dirty days of slamming jackhammers and swinging from scaffolds that resulted in some of the most beautiful buildings the town had ever seen—tall white columns rising through the sea-misty air.

But even with all that good work, Dad had a sour feeling in him. Some of his colleagues didn't mind calling him dirty words or engaging in other hackneyed harassments. There *was* one charitable Arkansas import, an elder statesmen of the site named Lufft who took it upon himself to tuck Dad under his wing. The two men ate their lunch side by side most days, with Lufft sharing his coffee cake and gossiping about the finer points of baseball in mostly unintelligible English, or giving Dad tips on how to survive the construction business. *Keep your head down, is what he said, mostly. When the other men curse me, he said, Don't make a big deal, keep your nose clean and nobody will hurt you. You're a good boy, you stay out of trouble, you remember who you are and everything will be okay, kid, I'll watch over you.* On the other side of the spectrum was a large cowboy named Weathers who liked to gather up a few pals to help him back Dad up against the forklift, then whisper slurs in a singsongy voice until Lufft yelled at him to back off.

Every night Dad would go back to the motel where he lived, then lie down on his little bed and review each insult of the day until he had it fixed in his memory. Within the first season of living in the States these studies had made him absolutely fluent in the abstruse grammar of American profanity, as well as an expert mimic of Weathers's etiquette, as he started to walk around the construction site with his shoulders squared at such an angle they often smacked into his coworkers in a way that didn't seem quite polite or accidental. Lufft tried to have a sit-down with him, catered with a nice piece of his wife's coffee cake, and Dad didn't have any trouble translating his warnings, especially as they were accompanied by slightly too hard, though avuncular, squeezes on the shoulder. But the cautions didn't stop his spit from landing on colleagues' shoes and sleeves, or his glaring back at Weathers, then letting out a low, provoking whistle that must have raised the neck hairs of everyone around.

He might have stayed out of trouble if that girl hadn't showed up, though.

It was an early summer day at their downtown site when the workers spotted a blonde who probably worked as a secretary at a nearby firm, but had been born to pose for tool calendars and the indecent dreams of young men. Weathers and his pals leaned over the scaffolds and yelled down the ways in which they would satisfy her secret longings for the abbreviated sex they were best at. My father then sidled up right by them, feeling the blood beat in his head and his heart cracking like a hammer, and he began to serenade this lady with the vivid lexicon he'd learned from Weathers himself, happily numbering to Miss America the many ways in which he might satisfy himself with her snowy flesh in that torpid, obscene, highly specific and venereal idiom—so the poor thing scrammed away, and Dad rolled in the muck where only white men were allowed.

The entire site went silent. Lufft sat staring at his bologna sandwich while Weathers was so incensed he couldn't even stutter out *spic*, and Dad swaggered from task to task without a hint of remorse in his grinning face. But at the end of the day, after the foreman had left, my father noticed all the men milling around and not going home like they usually did. While he gathered his jacket and lunch box they started crowding around him. They didn't talk much, but stared at him, with the sweat sheeting off their heads, and chewing on their own teeth—especially Weathers, glowering and huffing and gripping onto a shovel that could have taken Dad's skull off. The five other colored men weren't anywhere to be found, though Lufft was. He stood off to the side, shaking his head and muttering to himself, while the mob got thicker around my father and Weathers inched closer to him with that shovel. Just before Dad tried to bolt, Lufft started walking toward them, slow and calm. He went up to Weathers and took that shovel away from him. And then he used it to beat my father unconscious.

Six days after Lufft reminded my father who he was, Dad showed back up at the site, with a face like a smashed ham and some hair missing from his head—and with one other addition, too, which was the blue fist he'd had tattooed on his arm. It wasn't the end of his fighting days. Every night, he kept up his ritual of memorizing every indignity and not a week would go by without his tattoo being reinscribed with another brawl—though he'd learned enough to stay away from Lufft. Despite his fine work, he was fired from that site and seven others, some of which he had to crawl away from, literally, on account of broken bones.

My father never did explain how he went from the boy with a perfect memory to the man sitting at my table tonight. What I do know is that a few years after he married my mother he had a surgeon take off that mark and the grudges along with it, it seems. *Tough it out, baby!* he likes to say these days. *Look on the bright side! Turn a new leaf!* And that good attitude has worked—socially, fiscally, he's a success at his construction business. Every morning the sun comes up he sees nothing but a new day. This is a brown man who controls his own destiny! He doesn't need to look like some hoodlum to prove how strong he is! But as I place my hand over his scar, I'm glad it's still there, and not smoothed over by lasers.

Dad cups his hand over mine and squeezes, shakes his head. And now he cuts off the conversation about the tattoo, so that my reprieve ends.

"So? Why the hell aren't you happy? Tell me and I'll fix it. I got to fix *something*. I'll fix that ponytail of yours for one thing."

"I look fine."

"What, you got the big mope face, you're looking like a slapped rabbit. Okay? I'm being straight with you? You look like a mess with the hair and the sweater. Anybody who sees you can spot a depressed."

"Well, there's nothing I can do about it. Eat your dinner and pretend like I'm fine."

He pats his stomach. " 'Eat your dinner,' she says. 'Eat your dinner.' Well, I ate it and it was *good*, better than all these career ladies I'm dating putting the Birds' Eye in the micro then wanting me to make like they're that Judy Childs, you know?"

"Julia Child."

"Yeah." He laughs. "Yeah, that cooking lady. She could take a tip or two from you, sweetie girl."

"Thanks, Dad."

He pushes back from the table, takes a look around the dining room. "You got a nice place here. I said that before?"

"Yeah."

"Well, it's nice. And I'm just kidding. You look nice. You don't look bad." He pulls on his mustache, peering at me. "No, you do, you look bad. You look so bad I want to beat that kid up."

"You're not beating anybody up."

"I don't know that? He'd kill me. I'll run him over with my car."

"Dad, you love Karl."

"I don't love anybody who makes my daughter cry one little tear, see?"

I stand up, then walk around the table and rub his shoulders. "Let's go to the sofa."

In the living room, he picks up his guitar and strums it for a few seconds before he puts it back down on the sofa and looks up at my shelves.

"Books, books, books," he says, sliding the *Don Quixote* out. "*La* bookworm."

I sit on the sofa. "How's work?"

"How's work. Work's fine. I got this contract in Pacoima and I got that contract in San Diego and I got one in the San Fernando Valley."

"That sounds good."

"Yeah, it's good." He's not thinking about what he's saying. He's looking at my copy of *Don Quixote*, and now he holds it up for me to see. "Your problem? You want me to tell you?"

"No."

"Your problem I think is books like this. With the brains in the clouds. Your mother loved this book."

"I remember."

He lets out a big sigh. "Your mother was crackers. She was a good woman and I loved her, and I wish she was here but she's not and we can say what the truth is. She was bananas and when I see it in you it makes me crazy, okay?"

"I'm not going bananas, Dad."

"You are. Look at your fucking clothes!" My father's face reddens and puffs out, and I know it's because he becomes very tense when he doesn't think I'm in control.

He comes over and gives me a too tight hug, so that my face jams against his chest. "Look. I don't mean to swear at you. You're a lady, I respect you, I love you. I just want you to keep your brains in your head."

I mutter into his chest, "I *have* my—brains in my head."

"Nah, they're all scrambled, too. The problem is, you think too much. Uh? I know, I used to think things all the time. *Me entiendes, loca*? When somebody gave me trouble, somebody hurts me, I was like a stupid and kept it all *here* in the stomach. 'Ooo, am I mad,' I would say. Or, 'Oh, I want to cry. The whole world hates me. Boo-hoo-hoo. Ya-ya-ya.' But then! I got more intelligent. I put my eyes on other things. I worked, I worked. I keep my mouth shut. I push and push. I thought, forget them, man! I'm going to make this mine. And then, see? When I look at you, I think, well, my baby's got it already. Everything here, it's yours. It's your, what's it called." He snaps with his free hand.

We've probably had a variation on this conversation just under two hundred times before, and I know just what he's going to say.

"Birthright."

He nods. "Yes! Birthright. It's your birthright. You're born here, *wham*. Everything for you. Your problems are tiny problems and you have got to just tough it out. All you've got to do is close your eyes on the bad. But instead here you are running around like a jackass with that hair!"

He lets me go and I put my hands on his face and look at him. I have Beatrice's bones but his coloring and his chin, with its little cleft. I kiss him on the cheek.

"I just want you to be okay, okay?" he says, gently pinching my bicep.

"Okay."

"Because your mom, you know. She'd look at things and want it all to be different."

"I know."

"Being her was no picnic."

I nod, then go over to his guitar.

"To be honest," he goes on, "being married was also not always a picnic. Okay? She was an unhappy lady sometimes. A funny kind of person, and I don't know why. I don't know why she couldn't make it better like I did. She was a stubborn girl. A beautiful girl." He leans up on my bookshelves, and squeezes a hand into his slacks pocket. "Sometimes I think, what if she lived? How would she be? Would she be all right? In the head? You know, I hope so. But I'm not sure, speaking the truth. And that's how I see you going along. I think maybe you've got too much of her in you, and not just the good things."

"Dad, stop worrying."

"What, all my life is worrying. The day I had you I started worrying. The day you started school I worried. I worried when you rode a bike. I worried when you graduated from college. Let's not talk about the day I'll stop worrying, huh?"

I pick up his guitar and hand it to him. "Come on, enough of all that."

He takes it, and finally laughs. "Exactly! See what I'm saying? Get a little spring in your step!"

Although my father is a practical man he does have a weakness for good music, and possesses a talent for playing the guitar with a delicacy and emotion that surprises most people who don't know him that well. He likes to say that he's pure Indian down to the bones except for his hands, which are small, almost feminine, and agile. He calls them Spanish hands, because they're perfect for playing the flamenco, and I've been listening to his serenades since I was a child.

He sits on the sofa and has just started strumming a few chords when he stops and looks at me.

"You know, you remind me of the nice things about your mother too. I don't want to just talk about the bad."

"Like what?"

"Oh, let's see—when she was happy? She was smiling, dancing. Twinkly toes. And she loves you *very* much, you remember that. Always kissing, hugging."

"Yes."

"But then, the next minute, she would go upside-down, like when she stole that thing from the museum. Christ! She was always mad. Always with the moods. When I was young, we had that in common."

"But not anymore."

"No—damn, if I was still trying to pick the fights with the ding-dongs who give me crossed eyes I'd never have time to make any money."

"What changed your mind?"

"What do you mean what changed my mind? *I* changed my own mind."

"Why?"

"Why?" He shrugs. "Survival of the species, baby." He keeps his head down and appears to think about this for a few seconds longer. His fingers begin spinning a soft, complicated piece of music. Then he says, "Nah, that's not it."

"So then what?"

He looks at me, very clearly, very seriously, and full of love.

"Baby girl, I changed 'cause we had you."

His fingers begin working their magic and the music spills out of the guitar like a dream. My father's flamenco says soft things that he can't, and it helps. After a while my sadness lifts.

He makes the moment last by playing for a long, long time, as many songs as I like.

AFTER DAD LEAVES, a dreamy quiet seeps back into the house and my previous feelings come roaring back, making me less festive. A wind breaks up the trees off the lawn outside so shadows spin and flicker on my study's walls. I wander about for a bit, picking up a vase, plumping a pillow, then sit at my desk and examine my rotting book, which I (breaking firm Getty policy) smuggled from the library earlier in the afternoon.

This is what else is on my desk besides *The Conquest:* A fountain pen, an inkwell, a candle in its stick, and a box of matches.

I sit here until the night deepens, thinking in the dark.

I guess I shouldn't be surprised that this is an apocryphal book, and that it's the lie that everyone believes. Since before *Othello* white geniuses have been dressing in drag. William Shakespeare himself probably dyed his skin to play the tragic Moor or tucked up his privates to act the part of Portia.

Though it does make me wonder. Who was right? My mother or my father? I'd always shrugged off his confidence in "birthrights"—that is, the right to all of *this*, everything I can touch, see, hear, taste, or smell. I thought, like *her*, that my real inheritance was more difficult to discern, as it had been burned and buried hundreds of years ago, and could only be lifted into the light with a lot of hard work and luck.

But if he was onto something, and this is my birthright, then I don't want it.

Just what have I been restoring all these years, anyway?

All the riches of the ancients are poured into the museum like honey. And Jean Paul Getty, once walking through the halls of his mansion and examining his various sculptures, jewels, the diaries of deposed kings, the calendars of water-worshipers, had access to the recovered memories of a great world because of his fabulous wealth.

We should recall, however, the day when his money was called upon for another purpose.

In November of 1973, Getty's grandson, a drug addict named Jean Paul III, was betrayed by an associate and kidnapped in Italy. Through a series of notes and phone calls, his ransomers gave their demand, which was fifteen million dollars in exchange for the life of the boy.

Getty, secluded at his mansion in Surrey, refused.

The newspapers clamored for a comment, though Getty remained ensconced in his mansion, looking over his paperwork, dressed in an impeccable suit out of which rose his large, withered head. He was not troubled at all, being convinced that his grandson had orchestrated an elaborate fraud in order to steal drug funds.

He maintained this belief until the boy's severed ear was sent to him by his kidnappers in the mail.

Getty did pay then.

If I told Dad that story, he'd shrug it off in a second and say that "Getty" was just another word for the check that pays my rent. But I know it's also the man in whose name I work.

If my mom were alive now, and I told her what I've found out, wouldn't she be disappointed? She'd say this hunk of vellum isn't valuable enough to restore, let alone steal. She'd argue it wouldn't even be worth the postage to send it back to its original owners. Then maybe she'd tell me that story about libraries and arson again.

Now, thinking of her, I pick up the matches on my desk and strike one. A scent of sulfur charges the air. A church's light glimmers around the room, onto the scarred, false book, which looks as delicate as a grandmother's hand. And I do admit that a moment comes when I consider allowing the fire to eat the boards and lick the leaves black to obliterate the thing that kept me from Karl (which is only myself, only my own mistake). I raise the match, the little flame blazes. But I just light the candle. My father can rest assured. I am incurable. I have problems with nostalgia but my imagination immunizes me from insanity. And though it's tempting, I could never do that to a book.

PART *three*

9

Two months after I watched Karl struggle through the waves and make his way up toward the shore, I get up early in the morning, put on some jeans and a sweater, then climb into my car and sit in the driveway for more than an hour. The neighbors jaunting out of their doors and into their cars shoot me odd looks before they drive off, perhaps because of my frazzled expression or my frozen posture behind the wheel. What they don't know is that I have had a shock to my system. I have put my finger in the socket. I'd always thought the lump of mud we've termed reality was an ocean deeper than surface, and that some secret knowledge would glimmer at me down in the murky depths if I just looked hard enough (or told enough stories). Well, I've looked hard now, and I believe my eyes.

Where *do* ragged souls go to have their visions? From my previous reading, I'd say the desert and the end of the world, which are the countries of the dark, exotic unknown.

The only problem is, I live in Los Angeles, Califor-nia, which is the desert, and is the last stop in the world. And on account of being Mexican, I already am the dark, exotic unknown, and know how ordinary it is.

So this morning, I cut my losses and flee as far to the ends of the earth as I can. Which isn't that far at all.

Once again I travel to the beach.

I scoot out there doing about twenty over the speed limit the whole way, until I reach the region of bikinis, shoppers, cops, and schizophrenics, where the spray rustles the burnt leaves of the palm trees gracing the boardwalk like tall tattered rajahs. Normally, with all the commotion, a Southern California beach wouldn't be the most contemplative place, but it's still cold in Santa Monica and so the strand is mostly deserted, and what with the clouds and mist it looks as barren and clean as I feel inside. Tromping toward the shore until I find a flat spot, I lie down on the gelid sand, shivering into my jacket, and consider the scene from my new perspective. I listen to the birds caw as they rip apart some livid food. I gaze up at the electromagnetic waves vibrating turquoise in what we deem the sky and consider the god-drenched dreams we have of that blank place. I stay here for a long, long time, so that the grains make their way up into remote crannies and I draw stares from lime-haired surfers with rubber legs. I observe the ocean eat the world and the blissfully ignorant child building castles at the lip of the water. I watch a stooped octogenarian push his metal detector through the sand. He's dressed in neon orange shorts with hairy fringe and a reclaimed T-shirt that calls upon the rabble to RAGE AGAINST THE MACHINE. There's an expression on his face that says he thinks he'll discover the Kohinoor diamond in the clutches of a crab.

"Find anything?" I ask him.

"Not quite yet, Missie," he says.

"And you won't."

"Well, ah, I found here a Seiko watch, and I found sixty bucks in nickels and I got a Tommy Hilfiger sweater this year already.".

I laugh. "What'd I tell you?"

The old salt dismisses me with a grumble and wanders off.

I lean back in the sand and listen to the waves, wondering if history and love aren't any different from the fribble that man collects. The measure of either history or love could be me, or a corncob, or the Treaty of Guadalupe Hidalgo, or a Seiko, or a redhead named Claire, because they're only empty frames upon which pure subject transforms pure object into same, like in the stories my mother used to tell me about the magic bag of Ali Baba which remains empty until its owner develops some ludicrous desire.

But I should not have thought of that—because now, as the mist travels up from the sea like a ghost, I am thinking of her again and of the tales she regaled me with that year she was in the hospital.

According to the doctor, my mother's first stroke was a small one, though it was strong enough to warp and weaken her left hand. In the hospital, her face and hair glowed dark against the sheets, and she had me help her apply the brick lipstick and purple eyeshadow that were the hallmarks of her beauty.

Come here, baby, she'd whisper to me when I finished, I'll tell you a story.

I would bend toward her, through the waves of rubbing alcohol and medicine, until I reached the tender atmosphere of her skin. Any fear I had dissolved in the heat of her tales—in those last months her storytelling reached a hot, scary pitch and she told the most fevered rumors of war and magic I have ever heard. With her dark face blazing against the pillow, she recounted in her roughened voice the tale of the devil Malinche who led General Cortés up to the highest cliff in the land and offered him the entire golden country if he would only worship her on his knees. She murmured again of the burned Aztec libraries, one of which held the only copy of the *Lauh al-Mahfuz*, the Tablet of Life written of in the Qur'an, and that God is now lost without. She also whispered to me the confessions of Xochiquetzal, the flower goddess who ate the forbidden fruit of knowledge and blinded herself when that wisdom revealed that she had slept with her mother and killed her own father—and of La Llorona, the great witch who drowned her infant sons in the river as repayment for her husband's infidelity with Glauce, the daughter of Creon.

My father would sit in the chair next to mine, trying to divert her attention to different subjects, or attempting to make jokes, until he finally stopped and listened to her hallucinations, though while grinding his hands into fists.

It was not easy on him, those last seasons, as her strange flights contradicted his keep-your-feet-on-the-floor philosophies he believed, and still believes, are necessary in order to survive. There were times he became so disturbed at her freaks he threw up his arms and walked out of the room. It baffled him how she would talk for an entire hour and then stop abruptly to stare at him, strange and silent; she might begin arguing with him, or she could cry or smile. He would walk outside to argue with the doctors and then weep out of our sight. He would go to the gift shop to buy her magazines, flowers, perfume, which she did not want.

But I wouldn't have left that bedside for anything.

I've heard people say they forget the faces of their most loved dead, though my powers of recollection grow stronger every day. I can not only carve out the shape of her cheekbone from this sand, nearly hear her burnt-sugar voice, and summon the details of her surprising, miscegenating genius, but as I sit among the ocean's bric-a-brac and scavengers, I can now fully reassemble, too, all the nested, crazy pain she could never seem to do without. I remember everything in the time before the hospital—the crying jags in the evenings and the unmetabolizable *menudo* breakfasts served to me in bed the next morning as indemnity; her distrust of strangers; her hot, close embraces in the hallways of our house, the shaking of her hands, and the hours writing, writing, writing *something* down at her little desk in her bedroom, though I'll never know what it was, as all those papers were shredded and burned. There were the days she wouldn't go out; she expressed her nostalgia for Mexico by pretending not to know our neighbors' names; I remember the evening she read *Don Quixote* under the lamplight, and crossed out the last line—*my sole aim has been to arouse men's scorn for the false and absurd stories of knight-errantry—* with the furious ripping of her pen. And I can see the anachronistic anger cresting her face in the minute before she stole that relic from the museum, then the sublime, selective deafness later when the police pounded on the door.

A candy wrapper blows by my feet, the last vestige of a Marsbar treat long ago digested and done with. I can't see the surfers anymore; the sand makes its intrepid way up my legs. The Karlbereft breakers pulse and withdraw, tumbling in their green cups glinting shells and shattered amber beer bottles, bits of sunken yachts and smithereened fish—and I know that if I ever want to get a good look at mystery again, and not just eyeball these odds-and-ends and the trash and yellowed remains of the day, I'll have to admit my mother's problems into a new reading of her stories, and into a new translation, too, of the way I've spent these past ten years.

TWO DAYS LATER I am back in the office, working across from Teresa. Her spicy sandalwood-and-lilac perfume fills the office, and the insistent strains of Beethoven reach us from a distant radio. I am slicing a sheet of Japanese paper with an X-acto knife to fit a leaf of *The Conquest*. An aggressive mold eats at the last third of the folio and suffocates whole paragraphs of text so that they look more like hieroglyphics than vernacular Spanish. The Japanese paper, which is called kozo, is a distillation of white silky fibers, like a thick, plush web. I attach a scrim to the page I'm restoring, using a light glue, and it nearly disappears into the vellum.

Under the film, I can just make out the phrases I will copy in my handmade ink. They glimmer at me from beneath the corruption, waiting to be released. And we are lucky—the words are still decipherable so I will not have to do any guesswork.

"How goes it over there?" Teresa asks. "I'm perfectly bored." She's sitting at her cluttered desk and paging through an Italian Renaissance missal, which boasts Giorgio d'Alemagna's rich illuminations of gold demons attacking a kneeling St. David. Her hair's grown longer now, and curlier, and she can't stop touching it.

"Fine."

"I meant to ask you—have you talked to Karl again?"

"What do you think?"

"I take that as a somewhat hostile *no*. When is he getting married to that girl?"

"Four months."

"You *seem* to be taking it better, I think. Yes? Or no? Or are you just very quietly going bats?"

I bend down and blow on the glued kozo. "Do we have to talk about this?"

"Well, let's talk about *something*."

"I'm just concentrating on this thing so I can finish."

"This 'thing,' eh? Sounds as if you're getting sick of it."

"I'm ready to be done with it, that's for sure."

"And to think that for months and months that's all you could talk about."

I shrug. "Not anymore."

She cocks her head at me. "If you don't start cheering up I'm going to have to *spank* you, Sara."

But I don't say anything to that, and continue working for a few more minutes in the silence.

And then: "Did you ever catalogue it?"

"Yes, I did," I sigh.

"Under de Pasamonte?"

"Just like you told me to."

She furrows her brow down at her work. "Well, I suppose it's for the best."

"I hope so. You've been telling me to do it for about a year!"

She laughs. "Yes, you're right." She puts the text block down on her desk, then leans back and looks out the window. The season starts early here and the gardens flush with red and blue. "That's what I told you, all right." She runs her hand through her hair, so the curls pop through her fingers. Her eyes are about the same color as the violets outside, and she squints them at the garden. "It's a pretty day, isn't it?"

"It's fine."

"You know, I've been thinking—"

"Mmmmmmm?"

"It's because of you and that silly book. I think you might have persuaded me of something—at least partially."

"What's that?"

"Well, I've already told you my thoughts on this place, this *job*. The whole idea of this profession, which I now simply object to. The almost morbid fussing about with these objects. The ghastly amounts of money we spend on these *things*. But now"—she tilts her head at me, crinkling her eyes—"when I look at you, I think, perhaps it *is* a worthwhile occupation. Not for all, obviously, not for me. But for some, it is *not* ridiculous."

I shake my head. "No. You were right the first time."

"How's that?"

"That what we do is ridiculous. That what we're doing here is totally ludicrous and irrelevant."

She contemplates me for a moment. "Oh my, you are depressed, aren't you?"

I continue blowing on the kozo and ignore that.

"I know what might cheer you up. Let me tell you something that happened to me once—*no, stop* wrinkling your nose like that. Actually, the story's not about me, exactly, but my grandmother, Alice. A lovely woman. A *reader*, more specifically, you would have loved her."

I look up from my book.

"I used to visit her all the time when I was a child," Teresa continues, "back in Boston, which as you know is where I grew up. And Granny Alice was blind—not completely, though all she could see was the color yellow with some dark patches moving through it. She used to *love* me to come to her house and read to her. She had this library, with these lovely floor-to-ceiling bookshelves stuffed completely with books. It was her second collection, she'd lost the first one in the Depression. A marvel the first one was, she used to say. Filled with first editions and other treasures. But her new one was almost as fine—it was splendid to me, anyhow." Teresa raises her bronze eyebrows for emphasis. "There was this one particular day when I came over—I pulled out a book of Emerson and I started reading it out loud. And you know how insane he is. I read out . . . I still remember . . . *A man of thought must feel the thought that is parent to the universe.* Have you ever come across that tidbit?"

"No, I was never much for Emerson."

"I agree absolutely, I was always more of a Byron girl, or Dickinson. In any event, I read that out, and I asked my grandmother what it meant.

"She smiled at me and reached out for the book. She ran her fingers over it, discussing its binding and what she thought Emerson might be saying. But I can't recall anything she told me. What I do remember is how on the cover there was this intaglio of Ralph Waldo's face—and he looked like an old sheepdog, some sort of hoary wolfhound. My grandmother began tracing that face with her fingers.

"And right then, I thought of how she'd lost her library again. First from the Depression, now from her blindness—except that the binding, the book as a physical thing, wasn't lost to her. She could still connect with it through touch."

I have kozo and glue stuck to my forearm, and I start brushing it off. "I don't think I understand what you're telling me."

Teresa clasps both her hands at the back of her head. "It's just, that afternoon's what got me started in this business. I always had a fascination with bindings after I saw her touch the book. But now when I think about that day, I see it differently than I used to. I see how even if nothing in those books was real—I *still* haven't a clue what Emerson meant—it helped her. It refreshed her, it *fed* her somehow." She purses her mouth. "People need a kind of context, it seems."

I continue rubbing my forearm to get the glue and paper off. "Before, you said I was fixated. Now I'm not."

She nods. "Yes, you do tend to jump a bit too much into your interests. And a large part of me still thinks it would be better if that 'thing,' as you now call it, simply fell to pieces. That hunk of paper should be moldering in this crypt, *not* a bright if somewhat strange girl like you. Sometimes I've fantasized, to tell you the truth, about throwing it out the window and letting it rot under the rosebushes—then perhaps you'd spend more time on fun, on *life. You* know: getting drunk, going to the beach—or better yet, wasting whole afternoons on perverse adventures with your sailor."

"But?"

Teresa smiles at me again. "But perhaps a little context wouldn't hurt you, either. You *have* gone off the deep end, haven't you?"

I blink down at the folio. The script underneath the murk looks like a message written on the floor of the ocean. The patched part of the leaf shines like healed skin.

"You might be right," I admit, and try to get back to work.

I don't, though. My hand rests on the page, and the words here are sometimes blurred, gnarled by age, too pale.

But I can read them. I can't help but read them. Here is the girl on the galleon again. Here is the master juggler dragging the moon from the sky. And here is Caterina quoting those passages from Petrarch to her happy, outcast lover.

THREE MORNINGS LATER, I begin looking into the life of Padre Miguel Santiago de Pasamonte, author of the famous works *El Santo de España, Las Tres Furias, La Noche Triste,* and the untitled work I call *La Conquista*—or, *The Conquest.* There is a great amount of secondary information to research. In the Getty alone one will find three entire shelves devoted to criticism of his works, and two university libraries in Los Angeles own well-endowed de Pasamonte collections. Though few hard facts have been gathered about the life of the novelist and theologian, the dearth hasn't deterred an army of academics from excavating the mind that invented the notorious blood-starved monsters, deities and diabolic soldiers, sadistic bishops, and the bacchic frenzies at which limbs soaked in sweat and wine seem the indistinguishable members of some giant, groping beast. In these fantasies, certain scholars have found what they think are the last shudders of the gothic. Others, also citing Dante's *Inferno*, speak of the inklings of modern horror. All agree that like Dante, or Carroll, or Poe, de Pasamonte possessed a fevered imagination.

For example, in one of his most famous works, *La Noche Triste*, he writes of an unnamed deity who destroys a peaceful republic with a series of curses. In this novel, the god murders the sons and fathers of the kingdom and then takes all the widows as his wives after promising them redemption. In the infernal marriage bed, breasts gleam under dark stars, and lips kiss glimmering skin the women find as cold as ice. When the ravaged brides finally unfurl themselves from their groom, they look up to see a bright light, which is not gentle, but scorching, and burns everything it touches. Only then do the doxies know that they have not been delivered to heaven as they supposed, but a far different place made of heat and tears . . .

Now, *who* would write something like that? And why?

I traipse back to the Getty stacks and tuck myself back into my research. I check out every book we have on the novelist, and enclose myself in a small tower of volumes, armed with a pen and a fresh tablet of paper. I have only one query guiding me, which is to fathom how a man like Miguel de Pasamonte could write such a convincing masquerade as *The Conquest*.

While reading up on that question in the hundred or so pounds of cheese-smelling texts I piled on my desk, I learn a few other things that are interesting enough.

Scholars agree that de Pasamonte finished his first novel, *Las Tres Furias*, in 1560, and, as with all his novels, it was intended only for private circulation. They also agree that he soon lost control of his readership. In the fall of 1561, a Spanish noblewoman named Hildegard Fernández read a pirated edition of *Las Tres Furias*—it is a story about three Furies who wreak havoc on the Vatican—and some days later was found naked and screaming about devils as she ran up and down the banks of the Tagus. A few weeks after that, over two hundred copies of the novel had been printed for the Inquisition's investigators alone, and the resulting attention made the novel's influence spread far more than it would have otherwise. Within the year thousands of Spaniards purchased bootleg editions, and many readers were contaminated like Doña Fernández. The High Inquisitor received reports that covens were cropping up in the forests outside of Madrid, where aristocratic ladies were transformed into the devil's bitches and sacrificed infants in his honor. At least a dozen literate wives slaughtered their husbands in their beds; men began to carry charms to ward off this new plague of witches. In '63 a fantastic riot convulsed the street where booksellers turned up with the bootlegs, and at least ten patricians were killed in the mêlée.

Official reproval was swift, but by the time the Crown had notice of de Pasamonte's transgression he had already disappeared. The Holy Brotherhood (this was the King's police), charging to de Pasamonte's monastery in Cáceres on May twenty-fifth, 1561, broke into the priest's cell (according to court records) only to find one *"swarthy hunchback of a maid committing herself to the Virgin Mother thru a quite piteous display of groaning & prayer uttered in an incomprehensible babble. Interrogation revealed the beldame to be clearly feeble in mind & spirit and evidence of the Heretik's whereabouts otherwise undiscoverable. One stallion missing from the monastery stable apparently used in flight. Heretik's cell contained no other residue of interest but many books & papers hereby dedicated to the care of His Holy Inquisitor who acts solely in the name of the Lord our God . . ."*

Many of the "books & papers" were burned on sight, although some of the original works of de Pasamonte were saved for investigators. Due to the public insurrections catalyzed by *Las Tres Furias*, the Inquisitor approved over 50,000 reales be spent on de Pasamonte's arrest and the arrest of his lover, the bluestocking Sofía Suárez—but she had disappeared from Spain along with the monk. During the manhunt, which would last a full twenty years, the Crown arrested several innocents, and overeager constables killed at least three ersatz de Pasamontes. Yet he was never found. There are some reports of de Pasamonte sightings in Morocco, Turkey, Italy, and even New Spain, but most of these are probably apocryphal—something akin to Elvis sightings today. The failure was a tremendous humiliation for the Holy Brotherhood, but we should also remember that the investigation proceeded under insurmountable conditions.

One of the Brotherhood's biggest obstacles was de Pasamonte's trick of disappearing as soon as he doffed his robes. Without his monk's garb, no one was quite sure what the man looked like. A few biographers think that he made an escape with the help of an underground, while others speculate that he was killed by a highway robber (Spain was riddled with them at the time), then buried in an undisclosed location. But the most popular scholarly conjecture is that the monk simply put on a layman's uniform—a farmer's gear, perhaps? a beggar's rags?—and then walked out of the country under the very noses of his accusers.

"EVERYONE'S GOT TO EAT LUNCH," Teresa says, glaring at me over the tops of the books on my desk.

"I'm not hungry," I answer.

"I've brought cheese and ham and this fantastic Italian bread. And iced tea with lemon in it."

I look up. "What's today?"

"The thirtieth." She shakes her head. "*March* thirtieth?"

"I know what month it is."

"You haven't come up for air in I don't know how long."

"This is interesting."

"You're pale and you've lost more weight." She cranes her neck to peer past the hedge of books. "What *are* you looking for?"

"I'll know it when I find it. I think."

"Well, you must eat *something*." She puts bread and the ham and the tea on a clear spot on my desk. "And at least you're not depressed anymore."

"I don't know about that."

"Are you, then?"

I shrug. "I'm busy."

I break off a piece of bread and put it into my mouth. Teresa looms in front of me like a stern mother who disapproves of my obsessive tendencies. I don't tell her how right she is, that I do need this context, and that this is the happiest place for me right now. I don't tell her Karl will marry Claire in one hundred and four days.

I bend my head back down and return to my book.

THE NOVELIST'S PHYSICAL appearance remains a mystery. A number of annalists, using a kind of protophrenology, talk of his erotomaniac's skull conformations—the sneering lips, the cock-eyes, sinister complexion, and delicate nose. Yet as these depictions are mostly all second- or thirdhand, and are warped by Renaissance pathologies, they have little credibility for the modern biographer. Some of the noblewomen driven to the brink of insanity by his books speak of having visions where he appears to them as a hand-some blond man with dark, burning blue eyes and an astronomical member, but these descriptions too, should be disregarded. The only tempered account I find of de Pasamonte's person stems from a diary entry written by one François Amyot, a mid-sixteenth-century dilettante, who (if the report can be believed) describes meeting a well-educated pilgrim traveling, like himself, in Turkey during the year 1571:

> I knew the man to be civilized as I overheard him speak in both Latin and Spanish to his female companion. This, despite his dress, which resembled that of the Berber, with the skull-cloth and ugly cotton gown worn by the infidel. Nor was the man quite *clean*, I may say. Nevertheless I was so starved for intelligent companionship I approached him and introduced myself. He seemed immediately interested by the books he saw me carrying, and I agreed to exchange some of my library for his. When I asked him his name, he did not answer at once, but turned his shrouded head toward me so that I could see the most amazing set of fiery eyes, which seemed to have absorbed much of the madness of this desert. He stared at me, I swear, for nearly a minute without blinking, and I understood then that I was in the presence of a holy man, a lunatic, or both. Let it simply be known that I have never been so frightened as I was then, for he was clearly a person of extraordinary power, and I believed that if I insulted him he would have commended me to Hell then and there.
>
> "My name is de Pasamonte," he said.

Although the record of de Pasamonte's bearing is less than scanty, there is more information about his personal background. Church documents reveal that he joined the clergy in 1558, when he was in his late thirties, after having a nervous breakdown in his native Barcelona. His Inquisition dossier contains some contradictions on the date and place of his birth, but the weight of evidence indicates that he was born in that city in 1520, was the son of a watchmaker, and had been apprenticed for some years as a scribe (a waning occupation, on account of the invention of movable type) before he entered the pastorate. He was fluent in six or seven languages, including Latin, Greek, Spanish, Italian, and German, and when he was not ministering to the poor or helping other novices in their studies, he enjoyed writing his own translations of the classics, such as the *Iliad* and Augustine's *Confessions*. In all, he seemed an ideal monk, and was acknowledged as a considerable asset by his superiors at his monastery in Cáceres, as he was not filled with the troublesome passion that often plagued the younger initiates. Moreover, such late affiliations were not that rare in sixteenth-century Europe, when a number of men and women who found the pressures of family and livelihood unbearable escaped to the Church. It is unknown whether de Pasamonte left a wife or children in Barcelona, or what caused his breakdown, though his superiors believed that he was a sexless creature, describing him to Inquisition officials as a person who had "devoted his ardor to God."

Imagine their shock, then, when the scandal broke.

It was the novels, with their blow-by-blow accounts of sex and witchcraft and pagan religions, which first took the clergy by surprise. But the discovery of de Pasamonte's clandestine affiliations was almost as devastating. Despite the pall that the Inquisition cast over the intellectual circles of Europe, lively salons devoted to the literary and the concupiscent managed to survive in the parlors of adventurous nobles. Titian's own vibrant household is just one example of such a confederation, and readers of Casanova's *History of My Life* will see similar outlawed debauchees flourishing almost two hundred years later in Venice and Paris.

It turns out that de Pasamonte's companions, who met in a mansion on the outskirts of Cáceres, constituted one of the most celebrated cliques of the era. But unlike the salons of Titian and others of his mold, many of the active participants were highly educated women.

Paging through these histories, I enter a luxe drawing room adorned with tapestries and paintings and lit by thin beeswax tapers that lend the air a golden glow. Ladies spread their bejeweled farthingales out on French chairs and debate men of rank. In the corners lovers may be found whispering Italian poetry in each other's ears or feeding one another pomegranate seeds from the cups of their hands. Bowls of shining fruit and wine wait on tables. A drunk madrigal begins singing. Books are everywhere—on the side tables, on the chaise longue, and on the bed in the center of the room where the salon's hostess lounges, wearing nothing but pearls. She invites a comely friend to lie by her side, and as she begins caressing her, de Pasamonte enters through the door. She turns her head toward her lover and waves hello.

This woman is the famous Sofía Suárez.

10

Mallorca, October 1541.

After I escaped from the tempting clutches of Venice, I was so emboldened that during the months it took to reach this island, from which Charles V would launch his battle against Süleyman the Great, I imagined that my homicide of the Emperor would be as effortless as the murder of Fra Leonardi. Although the trip was arduous—the foul Moor-smuggler who provided me passage tried to sell me to a German, and his carrack was attacked by pirates, besides—I refreshed myself with fantasies of how I would skewer Charles's soft body with my obsidian knife, or pop his head off between my knees before his royal soldiers sent me to the fabulous House of Death. But when I finally arrived on Mallorca's sandy banks on the very day His Highness was to set sail for Al Jazirah, I discovered that an assassination of an emperor is a much more difficult chore than a girl might suppose.

For one thing, I could not find him.

At the port there were galleons as far as my eye could see, each to be filled with this gargantuan rabble of sailors and stumbling livestock whose combined fly-rich stink could send any person with a refined palate to an early grave. I struggled through this crowd, searching for any sign of that frog-jawed bastard; though I was dressed in Isabella's lad's costume, and no one had questioned my status as a hobbledehoy, I was still quite frightened that the color of my skin would fetch me a quick killing before I could board Charles's ship and chop off his head. Moors (which those dunces took me for), in particular the Mudéjares, were being executed upon the silly whims of the Christians, which did not bode well for my survival or employment. Nevertheless, I soon made the happy observation that when labor was so badly needed my darkness would be all but ignored.

I stood in front of this fleet of magnificent galleons, built out of cedar and with their sails like the folded white wings of one of Titian's giant angels. As I was straight-backed and ably muscled the ships' various commanders all attempted to wave me on. Still, I moved past hunchbacks and toothless destitutes, as well as sailors built so large and fine my friends back in Venice would have admitted them to their beds for no charge at all. I saw impressively scar-faced captains bellowing at cows, and mere slips of boys begging sailors to smuggle them onto the ships. I even saw the famous Duke of Alba with his giant feathered hat (I recalled his pictures from the Newes). But there was no Charles to be found.

After several hours of rummaging through this pile of men who were now nearly all assigned to their ships, I spotted one commander in front of a smaller galleon called the Santa Marta. He was a wizened little man, and wore a small gold charm around his neck supporting a noggin like battered gray stone except for two burning eyes that fastened on me. Even with all the damage he had endured, I recognized Cortés immediately. And I could see from the rolling and protruding of those burning eyes that he discerned me—or, at least, my race. I considered taking this second best and running at him with my blade, and I would have whispered an ancient curse in his ear as his filthy shade departed its weak home. But then his life was saved.

I heard a shout and turned, only to see Charles with all his fantastic ugliness adorned in blood-red clothes, with precious gold in his helmet, gold in his sword, gold in his baldric, gold in his rotten teeth, as he stood on the prow of Andrea Doria's galleon, which was even now setting sail.

I did not wait even long enough to take one breath. I flew to that ship like a quick light thing. I stepped on board and clung onto the rails as the galleon crested Neptune's broad dark back.

And now, I thought, the King is mine.

I was always a confident girl.

STILL, ON OUR EIGHTH DAY OUT, I had not yet discovered myself bending over Charles's blood-mizzled body as I would have liked. I glimpsed our benighted leader sometimes as he made his way past the galley intoning his illiterate orders out of that pelican's chin, or scanning the garnet ocean with his small greedy eyes. I could not get within arm's length of the man, as he was hedged by guards who would snuff me before I could do so much as pull his hideous nose. These were tall, thick soldiers, the strongest and smartest of which was General Miguel Valenzuela, a handsome blue-eyed Spaniard who was as notorious for his Olympian whoring as he was for his successes as a Turk-killer. He wore a medal of St. James, cast in gold, which had been bestowed by Charles himself after Süleyman the Great's reversal at Tunis. But his more impressive trophies were the six Chaldean concubines he stole from the harem of the infamous Khayr ad-Din, also known as the great Barbarossa. The girls, whom he'd installed in his personal seraglio in Aragón, were all soft as rain and blessed with the nimblest lips in the world.

It was enough to make even the strongest knee buckle, I think.

But then again, these were only stories that I'd been told. I cannot verify if the legends were true. Though they did entertain me in that dark, dank place, as I found myself elbow-high in offal soup or lamb kidneys or wriggling snappers.

Yes, those bloody bastards had made me into a cook!

Me, an assassin, a Muse, and a world-class juggler, a cook!

Or, to be more precise, they made me into the royal saucier. My specialties were relishes and sauces and chile-fired minestrones and oh, such delicious chutneys and these simply fantastic marinades.

THE TRUTH IS, I preferred the culinary arts to killing and, behind love and juggling, discovered that cooking was my third-favorite occupation. My duty has always been threatened by my heart and my tongue. Once I discovered that Charles's corpse would be a more difficult prize to obtain than I thought, I spent more than a month scheming on how to break through his shield of men just long enough to insert my dagger into his gut.

And in the meantime, I cooked.

If the Virgin Mary or even Beelzebub himself were given a wooden spoon and a bag of spice, they could not have done much better than I. I turned turbot into a delicacy as sweet as angel's tears; I transformed beef stew and a few handfuls of dried celery into Zeus's own ambrosia. The sailors reeled at every meal, and such orgasmic exclamations could be heard from the dining hall that I'm sure they frightened even the fish. A few weeks into my success I recalled that in Tenochtitlán, before the deluge came, our feasts had been similarly antic. Our royal chef, a genius though temperamental witch doctor by the name of Toteoci, concocted dishes that inspired revels lasting for up to ten days. Toteoci had, though, a rather shoddy habit of cursing his fare when he was in bad temper—such as the time when he was spurned by one of Montezuma's wives, and turned her into a repulsive hairless dog with gigantic eyes that always seemed somewhat confused. (He was sacrificed the very next day.)

Despite the bad end of poor Toteoci, one night it came to me that I might be able to achieve my objective by doing the same thing. I could curse my food and turn these unholy buggers into peacocks, or apes, or I could drive them all mad.

It was this last option that I chose.

I determined to do to Charles what he had done to me, which is make him, as well as his men, feel the torture of all their trapped passions. Sometimes at night I felt my family's spirits and kisses so keenly it seemed my body might burn out like a fire without air. And sometimes, too, I saw myself as I might have been, with all my love intact, and the image of that woman's face was so candid it nearly killed me.

It was decided, then.

The crime was to occur on October the second, when the head cook placed an Andalusian fried beef dish on the menu, and ordered me to compose an accompanying sauce. In the morning, the cook proceeded to the kitchen stable, then emerged a few hours later, covered with blood and bearing ribs and chops from a few fat cows, all the while complaining about the difficulty of keeping those nervous beasts stored in their pens. I elected to fashion a delicate partner for the meat, which was a Spanish-flavored broth in which my curse would swim.

Into a beef bouillon, I scattered the red stigmas of saffron, which stained the soup a heart color and scented the air with the breath of beautiful lost lovers. Next came garlic and onions, reeking of tears, and virgin olive oil to remind diners of their untouched ardors. Lemon juice would blind the senses to all but the most intense satisfactions, leeks would confound logic; red pimientos are known to inflame even the most phlegmatic natures.

And to top off this brew, I added the final spell, which was to place my mouth at its very surface and whisper into it a secret and potentially lethal charge: "Listen to your heart." While I did this, a few drops did find their way to my lips, and I ingested some of the elixir before I wiped the remainder off. But I will say it tasted the way a rainbow might, or the lips of a never-forgotten amour.

Then dinner was served.

At the first collective bite, I saw nothing, and my hopes fell. But then came the next bite, and the next, and after that an eerie, full silence fell over the hall. Sailors, with their spoons still to their mouths, stared into the spinning distance with the distracted expressions of stone pharaohs. Some of them began moving their lips, and then shifting about in their seats with an unchecked violence, as if they were arguing with private ghosts. The Emperor was similarly touched. He blinked up at the ceiling, and a tear rolled down his cheek. His face was absolutely white.

Now General Valenzuela, that Herculean whorer, stepped back from his bench. His face was the color of fire, and contorted into the shapes a mute makes when trying to speak. He attempted to calm himself several times, by pulling down his jacket, fiddling with his St. James medal, and clearing his throat. But it was to no avail. As if he were a sleepwalker, he staggered to one of the far eating benches, where a gorgeous boy-sailor, a mere swabby, sat. Valenzuela swayed above him, beating at his own chest with thick fists so that one might think he was about to slay the boy or himself.

Then the general, this most manly of men, and one of the most feared, pulled the boy to his feet by the shoulders and gave him a passionate kiss.

After that, all hell broke loose.

Everywhere one looked, men were stark raving mad or locked in torrid embraces. One hulky lieutenant with the face of an ox wept at the knees of an African oarsman-slave, who soothed his friend by giving him a kiss on each eyelid. Another commander ran his fingers through a fellow general's red hair, and sang to him the most ardent lyrics from *Orlando Furioso*. Elsewhere, slaves plunged blades through the tender bellies of their masters and mariners shambled about calling for their mothers, or even hurling themselves into the ocean to live with the whales. The head cook began eating everything in sight. Charles's valet ripped the costume off his employer's shoulders and began prancing about like an emperor manqué.

And the great man himself?

I lurched toward him, grasping weakly at my blade and blinking through the haze. He was still at the same bench, white as death and weeping. In my own pain I forced myself to sit next to him and began hexing the Crown and the Crown's children in my old, eloquent, and just-now-remembered tongue. But he did not appear to hear me or my evil tone. Instead, he gazed into my eyes directly, grasped my hand, and spoke.

"I miss my wife so very much," he said. "My angel, my only heart, lost two years ago in childbed. She was the only person who understood me, and I would give up my kingdom for even one sweet kiss from her now."

I had expected anything but this from the filthy dog. The less human he was to me the stronger I would be. And my nerve did flee me once again, for I had poisoned myself with my own brew. My breast was filled to cracking with passion for my darling, darling girl, and I had the urge to follow my heart to the edge of the ship and beyond, which was the closest I could be to her.

I dragged myself out of that place, and toward the outside deck, toward the sea, which was so blue it might be a hallucination of the sky, except for the warships littering the waves. This was when I heard the baa-aaing and the lowing, and I turned my head to see the livestock poking their huge heads out of the unhasped kitchen stable doors and calling to their neighbor.

For in the ocean's distance I now witnessed a bay-colored cow swimming toward the emerald coast of Al Jazirah, which just now glimmered in the distance, as if it might be the surest way home.

I thought, poor poor cow, poor girl, lost in that cold bed.

I watched until the sky blushed a darker blue and she disappeared.

I TRIED TO PRAY to God-the-gods that night, while I examined the black, star-scripted bowl of the world. But why should He care about me when He permits this cow to helplessly drown? When they permit thousands to die in their dishonored blood?

I tried to see God that night, in the plain face of the world, apart from the splendid architecture of lies and even the love words of Caterina and my dear father.

I tried to understand myself and what I would do, here, against the chilled black wind which would strip all the other voices away.

But I could not.

Messages were everywhere I looked. Codes that were whispered years ago entered my ears. The sky was not a naked black shield that might protect me, but instead, the stars overhead made strange letters that spelled out my father's ancient command.

If I could be what I choose, it would only be love, but I could not choose.

Thus, in earnest, I prepared to kill the King.

THE NEXT NIGHT, when the potion had worn off and I was strong again, I girded my heart as my father had instructed me to do. I took all my memories and wove them into the strongest cambric, then twined them so tightly around my soul no question could pop out. It was a beautiful windless evening, and warmer than it had been before, with the vast black pages of the sky and the sea printed with twinned and twinkling words, warnings. The other galleons surrounded us like dark guards; I spied Cortés's *Santa Marta* floating nearby, and the sight of that foul ship gave me strength.

I had murder on my tongue then, yes. I was prepared. I had murder in my eyes and in my boiling blood. I remembered my father again and locked myself inside his last wish.

I rose from my pallet in the deep and silent night. I put my blade between my teeth, and began to soft-step over the decks, not making as much noise as a caterpillar on a leaf. The decks were newly washed of the blood that had run during the massacre in the eating hall, and in the ensuing day there had been at least four executions, but I had not taken any notice of these events. I now crept past black portholes through which I could hear the indelicate music of sleeping sailors, and some lighted ones where sinners hunched over liquor and cards, muttering about bringing Berber heads home as prizes.

I floated by them like a shade, toward the lighted

hall where the Emperor slept surrounded by his wardens—such as this one guard in front of the palace, a strong boy bearing a gleaming cutlass he must have won for bravery in war. I crouched in the shadows, examining him by the light of the moon, and made out his flossy blond beard and intelligent eyes. He must have sensed me, for he turned and would not have waited another moment to slice my life away except that I rose from the shadows and startled him by baring my breasts before his sword—an old wicked trick!

The sad boy did hesitate then, and I stabbed him without mercy and without one sound. He fell to the floor, bleeding black. I extracted my weapon so as to continue my journey, but at that second I heard something in the water, a bump and splash, and I peered over the rail.

There I saw a beast moving inside the glinting lap of the ocean, and, insanely, I thought it might be the cow come back. It took deadly minutes for my eyes to make out the shape of a small boat, which was filled with men.

These were Turks, sent on a suicide expedition with the same object as mine.

But by the time I understood this the pirates had me in their tight hands. One of them was breathing into my face, and looking at me with his tilted eyes.

Eyes I recognized.

"Maxixa!" I whispered, for it was he.

"Daughter?"

"I have blood on me Maxixa! I killed a boy!"

He quieted me with a hard hand on my mouth. A small army of Turks loomed at his back. "You must leave this ship, daughter, there is nothing but death here." He did not ask me how I had arrived at this place and instead squeezed me until I calmed. "Where is the savage?"

I pointed in the direction of Charles's chambers, and pointed also to the Santa Marta and told him how Cortés slept there.

"The animal will pay, as will his ruler," Maxixa said, and this is when I heard the exhaustion and agony in him. "I have waited years for this moment, and am not surprised to see you here. You should witness this trial. And although I hope you will survive it, it does not matter. Do you know, daughter, that we are dying? That our world is dead? This ocean beneath us is nothing but a grave to me. This air is a light coffin which I am desperate to enter so it will stop this terrible haunting. Our fathers continue to visit me, you see. They have instructed me quite wisely in the ways of the underworld and I have never been more skilled in my life. My art runs in me as fluent as breath. Do you remember the days when I used to summon the moon? What gentle trifling that was. What joy. But now the joy is gone and I am only an instrument of wrath."

He was standing before me, with his hands on my shoulders, and his face was a twisted reflection of pain. He had also spoken too loudly, and in our native tongue, so that a few Spaniards were just now making their way over to us.

"Beware," Maxixa said to me, and pointed at the boat in which he had traveled here. "Escape, my lovely daughter."

And those were his last words to me, as the waves now began to rise out of the mirror of the water, and the wind started to dance and howl over the men's yelling.

The Spaniards had seen my dead blond boy and let

out a call of alarm. Whites and blacks battled hard on the decks with their shining, dripping blades, with the Turks fatally outnumbered but still protecting their charge. Maxixa unclasped my hand and walked through the hurling bodies to the ship's edge, speaking to the sea in our perfect language, a tongue alien to these ears but which the waves appeared to understand, as they leapt to him as faithfully as dogs. The sky gathered like a fist holding fire, and screaming Maxixa was robed in light, swathed in this thin midnight sun, which cracked Heaven open so that the gods could hear his brutal prayer.

He then removed one silver orb from his pocket, one of the old juggling spheres that had failed him so terribly at the Vatican, but which did not decline his will now.

He threw the orb into the ocean, and after that the sky became the sea, and the sea was a monster.

Great black shapes of water with awful faces rose before the ship and shook it in their killing hands. One of these devils crushed Maxixa in its liquid mouth. Men were shredded by the sea's fingers, while fire-crowned Christ or Peter wept other storms. I was a small speck inside the great lake of God's eye but luck or clemency plucked me out. I dove to the small boat shivering in the ocean, cut the rope, and rode a giant wave made of cold and the roaring of ghosts. All was storm. Seawater filled my eyes and mouth. Lightning illuminated salt serpents, which bit into ships with their clear fangs, until one of them turned its ice eyes upon me and swallowed me into its belly.

And so the storm raged and raged, as it drowned me and pushed me to the shore.

One hundred and fifty galleons were lost that night.
I nearly died.

But by some stroke I woke the next morning, with my cheek tucked into the whitest sand, and a gorgeous sun streaming heat onto my body. Broken bits of ships had also washed up, along with a few pale, staring men, and the crushed Santa Marta, in front of which Cortés now defended himself against a new army of black soldiers and their French friends. A curious Turk bent over me, and laughed when I rolled my eyes toward his face. Noting my coloring, he spoke nonsense words to me and wiped the blood away from my many wounds instead of increasing them.

I stood up and saw the emerald coast. Here were palms like tall, wild-haired women and mountains reminiscent of my old goddess, the princess. A carpet of amber crystals caressed my feet. I watched with a stunned nonchalance Cortés's to-ings and fro-ings with his enemies, but was so numbed I did not care how it turned out. I think I may have collapsed then. My friend summoned his servants and placed me on a palanquin made of hide and bells. Accompanied by this strange symphony and the sound of pounding feet, they took me away from the water, past the palms, toward the mountains, into the dove-white labyrinth they called the Casbah.

And so began my years in Al Jazirah.

11

I found myself in this perfumed oasis of pirates, where women hid in their homes and men, returning from wars filthy with their victims' blood, would collapse on prayer rugs and happily succumb to their king's strict laws like boys desperate for their fathers' loving correction.

Are people no different the world over?

The battle had gone well for the Turks. Although Maxixa died and Cortés somehow escaped with his life, many of the Europeans suffered extraordinary deaths, either by the chilled hands of the sea or the hot ones of these men. Charles fled to the safety of Cartagena, then Valladolid—though it did not take a prophet to see his future surrender of the Ottoman Empire, or his acquittal of Burgundy with the Treaty of Crépy.

These Turks now gave a nice piece of the credit to Maxixa, which in turn made them favor me, as they thought us blood-brother and -sister (I had been completely nude when I washed onto their shore). Despite my revealed sex, they did not seek to strap me to the kitchen or the bed, as they believed me a great magician like my brother, and so a good asset to their army.

On my fifteenth day there, after I had spent those weeks shivering and hallucinating flossy-bearded ghosts from a fever, I recovered from my illness and was compelled to appear before Khayr ad-Din, the famous Barbarossa. I must admit that the tales of the Venetians had polluted my mind, so I imagined him as a hoofed Satan, all horns and claws, bolting innocents into his reeking maw.

But he was just a man, exhausted and quite handsome with the luxurious red beard he caressed with his ringed fingers. He sat on his carved throne surrounded by gilded pillows and slaves decorated with silver veils and diamonds in their navels.

"If your fine brother had returned from the sea, I would now name him second corsair, and give him sufficient wives and gold to fill three palaces," he told me, in perfect Spanish. "And yet, your brother, whom I called my brother, was less curious of jewels than he was of the treasures he could command from the stars. Though he was a pagan, the God of Abraham blessed him with such craft we knew him to be a weapon designed for our holy ends. And we have reason to believe you have inherited those same arts. Are we correct?"

"I am a mere prankster, my Lord," I said. "No better than a clown."

"We take that as an admission of power."

"If you like."

"Out of deference to your brother, I will ask you to join us, and not command you to do so. I will grant you any wish as payment for his services."

"I will not join if you ask or command, my Lord."

"Do not offend this corsair, woman, I warn you."

"Perhaps offense will grant me the sleep I crave."

"You are mad, then."

"Oh, I see demons and such monsters I am surprised I have not gone blind."

"I will give you more wealth than your dead country surrendered if you join us. Any pleasure you request will be administered by the softest or hardest hands you might desire. You will win such authority hundreds will quail at your feet."

"I have no interest in these things, sir."

Barbarossa now stared at me, and stroked his glossy beard.

"You said you would grant me any wish I had," I said.

"Yes."

"Well, I have only one wish. And that is to be left alone."

He twisted his mouth, but nodded. "Let it be done, then."

And it was. Barbarossa, who would only live for another five years, was as good as his word. I was as free as a man, and like other fabled adventurers, I wandered that oasis attempting to cleanse my sickness in the sparkling waters and scorching sands.

But for a long time I was lost in that desert.

With an unprecedented vigor I scrubbed my brain free of the past, but found that my father's counsel in favor of recollection had been correct, for instead of wiping my memories away I had only polished them with every stroke so they gleamed and glittered like a sharp knife.

Then that knife cut my last rope, and I was unmoored.

I RETURNED TO JUGGLING *to make my living, and stayed among the Turks who helped me discern beauty in places I had never looked, nor imagined, before. I saw grace not only in the blue bay or the white city like an echo of Heaven or the leopard eyes gazing above veils, but also in Africa's giant spare faces of rock, pale as the vast sky, and the endless temperamental charts of sand beyond the city's lawn. Al-Jazirah was built for the satisfaction of that region's famous marauders, and in the fair heart of their Casbah one might find every variety of bright pleasure—philosophical arguments, poetry, Italian gold, music, marriage, the sugar-dusted pigeon pie succulent with orange-flower water, almonds, saffron.*

But I turned away from these things, and away from myself, toward those sheer faces of rock and sand and the bay's long dream of water. I wanted to know myself anew against this blank space. I wanted myself to become as blank as the rock above the water. And my heart as clear as water, and as harmless. I would scrub myself a new skin on this harsh carpet of rock. I would need and be nothing.

I abandoned all luxuries except for nature. To survive I buffooned for the amusement of pirates and their jewel-glittering kith. As they knew me to be Maxixa's kindred I was in great demand and would have been paid a king's share, but all I asked for was a drum of water to cool my throat and a few handfuls of food. Then, when my thirst was slaked and the monster in my belly quieted, I would stand before them, thin as a weed, dressed in little better than rags, and astound them by defying the laws of the air. Strangely enough, my circus gifts had strengthened though my other faculties had suf-

fered the opposite fate. My employers would throw their heaviest and most deadly treasures at me, yelling with glee, and I could spin them all toward heaven as if they were mere mist. Scimitars sharper than lion's claws were mild toys in my hands, as well as snakes and, my favorite, gold torches, which would fill the rooms with a magnificent sparkle as if the stars had just flown in through the window.

Between performances I preferred to retreat from the city, and travel with bands of nomads to the desert where I might sleep in the bed of the sand and drink from sacred wells. I would lie perfectly flat on the dunes and try to imagine a pure future, which I thought might look like the sky or the desert rock—empty, faceless, naked of a name, as I hoped I would be, too, someday. I began to see myself as perfectly free, as free as the dead! For the dead have no names. As this rock had no name, and no language.

Eating a small supper of locusts mashed with dates one night, I stared at the endless velvet space above me, which was so empty and cool, like breath, like the most blessed absence, that I found myself in a state of flawless peace.

And there was the early silent morning after a sandstorm, when the nonstop stretch of desert was absolutely smooth, and the cream sky, just now brightening, was its exact same color—a landscape so seamless not even the horizon scarred it—and I understood myself to stand that second within a charmed void so powerful it might erase me, and I was not afraid.

And if sometimes I saw Quetzalcoatl's strange face staring at me from the rock cliffs, and Caterina dancing with the flossy-bearded boy above the sand, and if I once heard the clouds serenading me with a fantastic version of Desprez's Hercules dux Ferrarie, complete with lutes and castratos, I simply tried to ignore it.

But, of course, I had gone perfectly mad. I was no different than the whites who lost their minds at their first sight of our jungle, or from their flawed diet of our maize. And I do not blame them anymore for their lapse of judgment, as I used to. This state I encountered was the ultimate solace, as there was no feeling in it, nor any recollection, nor any sadness. It was a balm for my bloody heart. For there in the desert, I had found the secret, and horrible, answer to dread: I had discovered the consolations of nobody, nowhere, and nothing.

AFTER FIFTEEN YEARS of this trance, I was called upon to perform for a pirate who had recently joined Süleyman's ranks, and who compensated for his novice status by leading a campaign against Naples as famous for its brutality as for its fiscal triumphs. He called himself Ibn-Idrisi, and those who had seen him often commented upon his magnificent battle scar, which stretched from his eye to his chin, as well as his incredible prowess with women. Although he was known to have once snapped a Venetian's neck with his thumb, legend had it he owned the softest lover's hands on the continent, and the only person who owned more wives than this Berber was Süleyman the Great himself.

As was my custom, I came immediately when called, as I had no other obligations, and soon found myself within the walls of a gold-flooded palace, more splendid than any of the mansions I had seen in Venice.

Gorgeous women peeked at me from behind pierced ivory walls; hallway chairs were made of ebony and carved elephant tusks; sandalwood- and hemp-scented rooms were silent except for the whisper of gold bells on concubines' ankles. A stout butler, robed all in white, led me to the fabled man's boudoir, which was hung with all manner of gilded curtains and chandeliers, and boasted besides a gigantic red bed upon which lay thirteen girls of incomparable beauty. As well, there was a chair and small desk at the far end of the room—ebony and tusk again—and this is where the sea baron sat, dressed in a maroon and silver coat. From my vantage, I could barely make out his face except for the long scar on his cheek, as he was turned away from me and signing various papers.

The girls now began whispering and giggling at my dazzlement, so that I remembered my manners. I bowed deeply before them, and did not even try to peer up their dresses.

"You are the buffoon?" Ibn-Idrisi now asked, his head still bent.

"Yes, sir."

"My dear wives have been complaining about a lack of entertainment. I hope you will be able to amuse them. You come highly recommended."

There was something in his voice which I found familiar, and quite wonderful. It put me immediately at ease. "I will do my best, my Lord."

Ibn-Idrisi now stiffened in his chair, and stared down at the page. Only then did he look up, and I saw that he was familiar to me, and wonderful, and that he was not even a he at all.

He was a she!

And she was my sister!!

The great Ibn-Idrisi was none other than my old friend, the Spaniard Isabella, dressed in another one of her marvelous costumes and with her face cut in half by that rough scar that nearly obscured her beauty.

But still, I did recognize her. She was smiling at me as if these years had never passed at all.

"Out!" she commanded, snapping her fingers, and all the wives scattered.

Now we embraced and laughed our questions into each other's neck, weeping some as well. I quickly told her my tale, and she told me hers.

"Oh darling, I am the most fabulous pirate!" she cried. "I am the most feared man on the seas, if you can believe it. None of my new brothers even suspect. After I sailed here, all I had to do was chop off a few heads and the fellows couldn't even imagine the sex under my pants. 'Oh, the mighty Ibn-Idrisi,' they call me. 'Oh, Señor Ibn-Idrisi, how fantastically terrible you are!' Well, certainly Venice trained me to be a killer, but after I received the scar, my lot only improved. And of course I have my wives in such a Heaven of jewelry and orgasms they wouldn't breathe a word of it."

"So you've done everything they say?" I asked.

"Yes, it turns out I have quite the bandit's talent."

"I have found that I do not."

"What do you mean?"

"I killed a man, Isabella, and he haunts me. Here, in this desert!"

She grasped me by the shoulders. "Long ago I told you not to think of those things, my dear. You must be more pragmatic, my sister. And as your sister, I will let you know that you look like the walking dead. Have you seen a mirror?"

"I have no interest in what I might find in a mirror."

"You may stay here with me as long as you like. Forever, if you wish. I will give you a staff of wives, and I will build you a house so we can live side by side."

"I do not want a wife. I only miss Caterina."

And when I said that name, her face paled to an awful color.

"It is better not to," she said, very seriously. "It is better not to think of her if you can."

"Why?"

"I still have spies in Europe, and they tell me she has become an interest of the Inquisition on account of certain 'blasphemies.' "

I only stared at Isabella and could not speak.

"She is imprisoned, Helen. In the Vatican."

I looked into my old friend's eyes, and felt the gratitude I had before, when she helped me escape from that cesspool of Venice. With her aid my life turned one more time, for at her tidings it was as if I woke up again, after all those long years of sleep.

FOUR DAYS LATER, I found myself furnished with enough of Isabella's wealth to make a safe journey back to Europe. She, however, would not join me.

"That is no world for me," she said. "That place will kill me."

So there was no persuading her, no matter how many times I begged. On October 14, 1556, I waved good-bye to Isabella, who remained on the shore, after forcing upon me an additional, and rather gigantic, fortune of gold and jewels. This generous sister of mine— I think that is the last time I will ever see her face, though it does not fade even with all the years.

Now I turned my eyes back toward Rome, the place I had been brought to as a slave nearly twenty years before. The place where I had fallen in love.

Caterina.

How I longed for you, my wife, as I sailed back over those dangerous waters. Oh my heart, how I longed to see you safe in my arms.

12.

The fourteenth of April, six o'clock at night. I am sitting at my cubicle in the Getty library and examining a collection of very old, fragile papers, which are the originals of Sofía Suárez's letters we purchased from a collector in Spain. They were hastily bound in silk and the fabric pulls away from the boards, between which the letters lie slightly crumpled. They're printed on ancient-looking linen stock, brown with age, and so delicate scholars must wear white gloves before touching them (though I am not).

My hand is almost the same color as these pages, and I turn each leaf very carefully. They look like moths' wings.

JUNE 3, 1559

Did I not tell you apricots were known to be the most magnificent aphrodisiac, you silly duck? My sweet Pasamonte, how strong you were the other night, I nearly fainted at your tricks! Let ME be the man for once, my jewel! For brutes like you do have the advantage, I must say. If you would give

me leave, I would dress like a knight, with my sharp
sharp sword, and ravish you as if you were an inno-
cent bride. . . .

Born in Aragón, Spain (most think), Sofía Suárez was a culti-
vated temptress of independent means who imported the most
delectable banned books and exotic foods for each of her soirées.
No one knows from whom she received her funds and her family
line has been lost for centuries, though her mysterious past is fra-
grant with rumors of some blasphemy, which drove her from her
home to a mansion outside of Cáceres. She was, moreover, well
known for her sensational atheism despite the religious calling of
her lover. Her *salonistes* studied pagan philosophy and the sci-
ences. They read Cicero, Epicurus, Machiavelli, Copernicus, and
Fra Bartolomé de las Casas. She was a generous patroness of the
arts and a legendary correspondent—this surviving body of her
letters amounts to almost one thousand pages.

But she will still be better remembered for her erotic life.

The face in her famous portrait does seem to belong to a pleasure seeker. I've found it in a book. (Outside my window, weeks
pass, but I am tucked safely inside the sixteenth century.) She had
wide clear eyes and ample hair, which was blond like her skin,
and a small wicked mouth curled in such a knowing way you must
believe it has been kissed ten thousand times. And she admits to
being kissed more times than that in her letters, which reveal her
carnivorous and experimental appetites. There are the sex
games—for example, her talk of virgins and swords, over which
titillated scholars have spilled much ink. She had also, it seems,
more than one lover.

How she met de Pasamonte remains a riddle, although from her
correspondence it sounds as if they had known each other almost

all their lives. She writes of his "charm and grace and genius." Of his "compassion" and "bravery." She even writes that he saved her life (a topic of much speculation). She says he *was* her life. *Of all the people I might ever meet,* she writes on December 12, 1559, *I would never encounter anyone else such as you. You contain my heart and all its contents, my beloved. Each drop of my soul is a pearl in your tender hand. I do not think that the sun of Egypt could burn as hot as my passion for your skin. Nor rubies or emeralds, my dear, contain as much color as my spirit takes on when you smile. When I see you next, make me shudder once more in your arms. Do not ever leave me again. Before you I thought the future a wicked joker but I know now there is no future but my gentle Pasamonte. I love only you.*

As I read these testimonies, it seems to me no great surprise that de Pasamonte would risk everything to visit his mistress and her forbidden circle. There are no known letters of his, and so we can only guess what he thought of their arrangement or of his paramour's extracurricular interests.

I am speaking here about Suárez's other lover.

Although only a few of Suárez's letters to de Pasamonte survive, about one-quarter of the epistles in the collection are to an unnamed woman whom biographers have named "the dark girl," after Suárez's own rapturous celebration of her features. When I reach the middle of the correspondence, I find: *My perfect girl, yesterday, when I woke up next to your rose-dark body I thought myself in a dream. Your hair is still the same shade as sleep and your eyes the tender umber of the woods. When I bade you to dress in that pink gown, did not our peers gasp at your beauty? I was so proud to call you mine as you sauntered through the room dazzling them with your wit and command of Italian—what a laugh we had when you murdered that Buosa Mascheroni's ego! But this is not why I love you, my dear. No, I give you my love because you are the most excellent friend I have ever met. You are a fearless person. I depend upon no one else.*

IT IS LATE AT NIGHT now, and I am more than halfway through the correspondence. Page after brittle page only yields more confusion.

We can't be sure if de Pasamonte knew of Suárez's infidelity, and if he did, how he responded. But certainly she did love this girl with an affection that matched the one she felt for the priest. The details of how she negotiated her heart and time between the two become more obscure when we consider that Suárez probably escaped Spain with de Pasamonte after word of the novels reached the Inquisitor. What became of the dark girl remains a mystery—though some speculate that she escaped with the pair. The only sure fact I've learned is that in the 1550s and 1560s, Sofía Suárez was in love with two people, and wrote them both intense, romantic letters.

But this still doesn't answer my central question.

Who was this man de Pasamonte?

I THINK I COULD SPEND one hundred years pursuing the truth hidden here, if I had health enough, and time. In this library. In this carrel, with its steel lamp. Sometimes I glance up from my books and see specters around me, people who seem less real than the dark-blooded creatures struggling inside these pages. It helps me, somehow, and I know that this is some kind of *evidence*— though of what I can't be sure. But I feel better here, swimming in these books and moving farther and farther from the shore to some other green place. I am looking for someone—though who it is, exactly, I'm not sure.

STILL, DESPITE ALL my efforts, another influence does inter- fere, and continues to remind me what century I live in. My father.

"You going to spend forever in that cave? There's more to life than work, you know. I read once in the paper about a professor guy who was working on the life of Jefferson, okay? And this guy, he spends so much time in the library, he didn't have any buddies, no girlfriend, no nobody. One day, an earthquake comes, and he gets buried under five tons of books. But since he doesn't have any friends, no one remembers about him, and he's smashed there under the encyclopedias for like a week. He almost died! Is that what you want?"

"Dad."

"Come *on*. Take a break. Don't you want to see your old man?"

"Of course I do."

MAY 17, LONG BEACH.

My father and I sit in his dining room, preparing to eat Moroccan pigeon pie at an old oak table with carved lion's feet that's been in the family since I was a child. My mother had a fancy for garage-sale finds, and she picked up this wooden beast at one of those bazaars decades back, finding it amid a front-lawn litter of Barbie dolls and Pendleton shirts, lunch boxes with Charlie's Angels decals and shoes spongy with age. It always looked magical to me, especially as Mom would tell me bedtime stories about how the lion trapped in the table came alive at night, and ran around the kitchen looking for scraps. Dad displays no other mementos of her in this house—an expensive white tract-box with giant windows, and a cream rug that he's constantly spilling coffee on and then frantically cleaning with Spray Wash. He's lived here for five years, but it still looks as if he's just moved in: Besides the lion table and accompanying chairs, a leather sofa, a blond-wood bed, stainless-steel floor lamps, his guitar leaning against a wall, and about thirty silver-framed photos of yours truly are the only embellishments to be found. My father hasn't had any trouble finding success with the ladies, though he doesn't show any signs of getting married again even if he *loves* getting taken care of by women, and especially in the cooking department, which is why I never come over without a little something I've made. Now I take a knife and cut through the crust of the pie I baked this morning. Garlic, a pound of almonds, ginger, and orange water waft up. Black cardamom and saffron lace a dark meat. There are cups of wine on the table but no utensils—certainly no forks.

"You have to eat it with your right hand," I say.

"What is it?"

"Moroccan pigeon pie. Something I read about."

He raises his eyebrows. "Pigeon *pie?* Those stinky birds? *Yakka*, no way. Give me a regular burrito. Give me some normal steak with the little curly fries."

I scoop out some of the pie and put it on his plate. He leans over and sniffs it. Then he grins at me.

"Poor ugly pigeon. Smells *good*."

"That's what I thought."

My father rolls up his shirtsleeves, revealing his scar, and then we carefully dip our right-hand fingers into the dish. He starts humming while he devours the food. Sometimes he pounds on the table, though he eats as fast as a German shepherd and I can't see how he tastes anything. Half the pie disappears down his hatch, without a glint of sauce on the mustache, until he takes a breather by leaning back and looking at me.

"How's business?" I ask.

"Business is business. I got a job down in San Diego that's breaking my back. I got a thing there in Glendora that's giving me a migraine. Business is great. But the question is not how business is. The question is how you are. So?"

"I'm doing fine."

He squints. "You got a guy to tell me about? You having any fun? Or is feeding your dad weird food your idea of a good time?"

"I've been working a lot."

"Working's for the birds. You should go out. You should date, a pretty girl like you. My sweetie! Look at that face!"

"Dad."

"You know what I did last weekend? I took that girl, Veronica? The one I introduced you to? I took her dancing at a nightclub, we were up all night. I had a great time, I felt seventeen. What's wrong with that?"

"Nothing."

"That's right. That's what *you* should be doing, not an old moose like me." My father pauses and eats a few more bites, using the wrong hand.

"You're not an old moose."

"I am, and I'm gonna be a fat old moose you keep cooking for me like this." He tilts his head at me, frowns. "You're still not one hundred percent. You've still got the bug eyes."

I shrug.

"Is it because you read that announcement thing in the paper? That why you're in the dumps?"

"What announcement thing?"

He grimaces, looks back down at his plate.

"*What* announcement thing?"

"Honey, I'm sorry. The engagement announcement thing. For Karl and this girl." He presses on his forehead with his hand and begins rubbing it all around. "Well, maybe you should know anyway. They're getting married, in San Diego, on what—July fourteenth."

I nod.

He blows up his cheeks, lets out a big breath. Then he claps his hands. "Don't let it get you down, my baby! San Diego? Foof! For losers! When you get married, what do you say I fly us all out to Mexico? Cuernavaca, *muchacha*! You want to get married on top of a volcano? I'll hire a big band of mariachis and we'll party for a week."

"That sounds nice," I answer.

"Because you *are* going to meet somebody top quality," he goes on. "Somebody who'll treat you right. Somebody who'll make you feel beautiful, okay?"

"Okay."

We eat in silence for a few minutes here, while he worries at me with his eyes. He wipes his hand on a napkin and leans forward. "Look. Hey. If you have a pain, I want to know it."

"I'm all right."

"What you are is *not* all right, see? When I see you like this, I want to, I don't know. I want to . . . *yell*! I want to hug you so tight that I squeeze all the crazy out of you."

"Well, what do you want me to say?"

"*Mi vida*, tell me your heart."

I look outside of his giant windows, at the view of the palm trees and the Mediterranean tile roofs of neighbors' houses, and the sky darkening. "I just feel bad about it all the time."

My father reaches across the table and holds my hand.

"Once . . ." I stop. I'm having trouble talking. "Once, did I ever tell you this? Karl and I stayed up all night long. This is eight years ago. We'd gone to a party and afterwards we weren't tired, so Karl said, why didn't we stay up until dawn? That's what we did. We drove up to Pacific Palisades and parked on the cliffs. It was dark and kind of cold, but we stayed there, talking. I don't know about what. We stayed until the sun came up, though. That's the first time I'd ever done that. The stars disappeared, and the sky—the sun came out and you could see . . . everything. The water, and

Catalina. There were seagulls. And the light! It opened up over us, really soft. And then Karl turned to me and he said, 'That's how you make me feel.' "

My father squeezes my arm. "Sara."

" 'That's how you make me feel.' No one's ever going to say something like that to me again."

"*Course* they will."

I stare down at the patterns of oak in the table. "Is that how you thought about Mom?"

He drops his eyes. "Oh, your *mother*."

"Did you?" When he doesn't answer, I ask him something else. "Do you think about her a lot?"

"What do you mean?"

"Do you think about her now?"

He leans back. His hand is still on mine. "You think I don't?"

"You don't talk about her too much, not like you miss her."

"No, you're right." He nods. "I don't do that."

I run my hand over the table, tracing the patterns in the wood. "Dad, I shouldn't have brought it up."

My father continues looking at me for a while, grimacing a little. Now he stands up and tugs on my hand.

"Come on," he says.

"What?"

"Oh, I got an idea. I'm going to show you something."

Five minutes later we're in his car, a Mustang convertible, and sailing through the cool blue streets of Long Beach.

MY FATHER DRIVES me out of the suburbs. We move onto the freeway for ten minutes until he pulls into a renovated section of downtown. So much of Long Beach shines with steel-and-glass architecture; it is a smaller sister to Los Angeles, and due to an influx of funds from metro exiles it has become a modern Casbah made of gleaming new materials. The remnants of the scrappy town it used to be, full of tight-kneed Christians and well-to-do crooks, is barely visible in the spanking facades, multicultural billboards, and precision landscaping. But when Dad parks on one of these city streets, lined with transparent structures and lit by amber lamps with frosted-glass bulbs sculpted like candle flames, he points to one of the office buildings—a law office, with snowy stucco and the signature Pacific-green windows—and begins telling me about the jewelry store that stood there in 1964.

"That was Maharaja's," he says, leaning against his car door and looking out the window. "The fanciest jewelry place in town. It was owned by this guy Gus McMahon, who was *Mister* Money Bags. *Mister* Fancy Pants, let me tell you. Good-looking too, every hair perfect. Always very well dressed, and with a pinkie ring that must have weighed two pounds, with diamonds and rubies and sapphires in a pattern like the American flag. You imagine? What a numbnut this guy is? But back then, to me, he was . . . *wow*. Mr. America! And I have to say, he was a very smart businessman. He had that place decorated like a—like that Taj Mahal, you know? Because I guess Indians got a lot of jewelry or something, and people loved it. *Always* busy in there. Inside it was all silk this and velvet that, with the fringes and pillows and the girls dressed like belly dancers. Which I don't know if that's Indian or what, but that's why he hired your mom, because the dummy thinks Mexican, Indian, same thing. And she did look pretty, though. He had her all doozied up in this red silk whatchamacallit. With her hair fluffed up like Elizabeth Taylor and brass bells on her ankles and rings all over. She was a salesgirl, and when I'd walk by I'd see them bracelets and necklaces, and money clips, pure gold. And the men's rings with the big diamonds in them, though nothing as big as McMahon's. They'd be shining there in the window, foof! This was the world of the people on top.

"Then I'd look up and see your mom. She was eighteen. And like a flower. Like a tulip. Like a rose—with thorns. Her nose seems like it was in the air. She'd sniff at the customers, and she wouldn't even look at *me*, oh no, with the big eyes staring at her through the window, until Mr. Money shoos me off, saying, *We better not see you around here again, you no-good, you bum*. This and that. As for the girl, she belonged to *him*. He'd be patting her on the *cola* and following her with his eyes like she was the most expensive thing in the place. And then once, when the store was empty and he didn't think anybody was looking, he touched her on . . . a place he shouldn't, and she didn't like it. I banged on the window then, to make him stop, and he started, oh, yelling. It was *her* though, that made me nervous. She puts her nose in the sky. She wouldn't have any of *my* help. So what could I do? She was *too* good for anything, it seems. I thought she was like a thousand miles above me.

"Except there was this other day I walked by, and she was playing around with the window display, putting some more of those high-roller rings out. I was in heaven! I had never seen her so up close. And she brings up her head, and our eyes meet, and this time she doesn't raise one of those eyebrows at me, or sniff, or anything like that. She just . . . *looks* at me. No smiling, no flirting. But I knew she saw *me*. And then I look down, at what she has in her hand, and it's one of those rings, with a giant diamond in it. All gold, with white gold too. A big diamond in the center with a circle of little diamonds. Not as good as McMahon's flag one, but almost! I see the price tag, *wham*, but for some reason I know I have to buy that ring. If I buy that ring, maybe she will smile at me. Maybe I can bring her away from McMahon. Maybe I can be a big guy and get close to this life I see in Maharaja's, which I wanted more bad than anything.

"But of course, I have no money. I'm a little guy. She couldn't love me, a bum! I got no future. I owe the rent on my crappy place. But oh no, I was going to have that ring. For the next six months, I work *two* jobs, and stay out of too much trouble. I gamble, too, and have good luck. In the end, I have *just enough*, with my last penny. And so I go into Maharaja's, with my black eye (from a fight in a bar), and my tattoo, and my ugly clothes, and I do it. McMahon—he remembers how I rapped on the window, see? And he gets his boys to kick me out three times until I pull out all the cash and flap it around. Sure, he does not want anything to do with me in his store! He makes me fill out my name and my address on the receipt, and he says they don't sell to people like me. *I'm sure we wouldn't have anything you'd be interested in, sir. Our prices are quite high. There are many other fine establishments that would cater to your tastes, I'm sure.* Bah-ha! His face like he ate a gopher! Still, even he couldn't turn down the cold green. Not that it makes her smile at me, but she does look at me again, with her beautiful eyes. She *sees* me again, and I tell you, honey, I was one happy guy. I walked out of that store with the big diamond on my finger, with all the plans in my head. I could be like a millionaire. I could marry a girl like that. I could have a Mercedes—blah, blah, blah. Oh, I am big. Oh, they better watch out.

"And then I get back to my stinky apartment with the landlord screaming, *You don't give me back rent you're* out *on your ass, buddy*."

He stops for a moment, and looks out at the law office again and fiddles with his rearview mirror. From far off we can hear cars honking, the blare of a radio.

"What did you do?"

"Well of course, I have to give back the ring! Two days later, I go Maharaja's again and when McMahon sees me through the window, he knows. I know he knows. He's got a little smile on which is killing me. Your mother is there too, dressed like a goddess, untouchable, and biting her nails. And I don't think I can do it. So what I do is, I sit down on the curb outside the store. I sit there all day, I'm froze on the curb. A policeman keeps walking by me, saying I better move it. Finally, what can I do? Before the store closes I go in. There's McMahon, with his nice hair, the beautiful clothes, his big Mr. America flag ring in my face. The little smile. *Yaak.* I swallow my balls and give him the ring I bought. *I'm sorry this didn't work out for you, sir,* he says. *Would you like to see anything else?* And I can't even look at her. I leave.

"But that night, when I'm lying on my bed, here comes a knock on the door. When I open it up, there's a little girl with braids. Your mother! The real woman, without the paint and Taj Mahal clothes! And the poor thing looks so scared, she'd copied down my address from the receipt then took two buses through the bad part of town and walked up here past the hookers and drunks. She was shaking and crying a little bit. Finally, she wipes her eyes and hands me something in a tissue. A present for me."

"Your ring," I say.

He shakes his head. "Not the ring I bought. McMahon's ring, because she'd seen me looking at it. I said, 'What the hell you doing giving me your boyfriend's ring?' And she says, 'It's mine. He gave it to me, but he's not my boyfriend anymore.' And I say, 'Why not?' 'Because of you,' she tells me. 'I'm going to fall in love with you, I think.' She was a-shaking, she was so scared of what she was doing. McMahon helped her out with money, which she needed bad on account of your grandma was sick already. But I told her not to worry. I put my hand over hers, very gentle, very careful. Oh, and it was magic. Such a gift. Though two days later the police came, looking for that flag ring. I almost went to jail."

"She stole it, of course."

My dad begins a low chuckle, but then it cuts off in the middle and he stares out the car's windshield. "See, baby, I still have everything in me. But you understand, how can I keep these things on the top of my heart? My beautiful girl who died? What could I do? That love is very, very dangerous. I learned you go up, or you go down. And how could I go down with a daughter like you, mmm? Impossible. And so I went past all the bad. I make myself move on."

A warm breeze blows into the car's open cab, flicking our collars and my hair. Overhead, clouds drift in the sky, slowly, like white leaves in black water. Dad reaches over and weaves his fingers into mine. He looks at me.

"And that's what you've got to do too, honey," he says. "It's the way of the world."

He winks and smiles a little, waiting for me to agree. And maybe I should.

But I just kiss him on the cheek.

"I love you, Dad."

LATER THAT EVENING, after my father leaves, a white moon of lamplight brightens the leaf I am reading. Sofía Suárez's handwriting is bold, with flourishes, and the curled strokes look like dark scarves. The letters' bodies have straight backs, swelling curves, resembling generals and women. A gentle thumb on a lover's face would trace a line like this. A mother's stories should be transcribed in writing as lovely as this.

Maybe it is very dangerous. And maybe I don't know who I'm hunting for anymore in these pages—the juggler, or the priest, or even, somehow, Beatrice. But it doesn't matter. I'm going to finish what I started.

13.

During my days at the Getty I patch this book's cracked back, faded pages, and at night I explore the histories of Miguel de Pasamonte or plunge deeper into the thick sheaf of Sofía Suárez's letters. From these doors I enter a room filled with talk of Michelangelo. Talk of Copernicus. Talk of the impossibility of God and the possibility of love. Smuggled maps are spread out on the stone floor, exclaimed over by candlelight. Here are the conquered lands of New Spain, which spread wide despite de Coronado's hilarious failure not twenty years before. Women, lounging with each other in the giant bed, discuss the aftermath of Martin Luther's death, Charles's abdication, then slow demise in the countryside, Ferdinand's ambitions. These are the heady years in the mid-to-late 1550s, when Titian, in Venice, unveils his famous mythological paintings, which someone has seen and sketched. Sofía Suárez, tracing the image of Danaë with her fingers, looks up from the drawing, then walks across the room to the occupied bed. She bends over the languorous body of one of her lovers and takes a book from his or her hand.

SEPTEMBER 14, 1560

My dear de Pasamonte, what a sensation you will raise with this book of yours! I have just now finished the last page, and am dizzy with what our friends will say. Did I catch my influence in your work, perhaps? I thought I might have seen myself in your more lubricious witches. If so, I think I deserve an afternoon of agile employment of your tongue and a naughty bit of velvet glass. It is only fair re-payment for my services as a Muse!

OCTOBER 16

My tender girl. What a heavenly night I spent yesterday, pressed close to your balsam-sweet thigh. And I think I might have made you blush when I spanked you on my knee! Nevertheless, dear, I promise to behave in the future (unless you do not want me to). And oh, you looked lovely in that yellow gown, with the ribbon in your hair. At dinner, my breath escaped me for a moment, just from gazing upon your beauty. I am the luckiest woman in the world to have a wife as kind and generous as you are. But then why did you talk so much to that idiot, Mascheroni, with his ridiculous mustache and laughable clothes? Is he trying to seduce you, as I fear? If so I really must poison his wine the next time he visits (just joking, angel!). Still, do try to shoo him off, won't you? I become so jealous!

A few biographers of Suárez and de Pasamonte have posited various theories of how this complicated triangle maintained its peace, but the histories which focus on these years of the letters tend to concentrate more on the presentiments of another kind of trouble, that involving the Inquisition. For it was not too long after de Pasamonte circulated *Las Tres Furias* to the salon that the Inquisitor received word of this supposed heresy—and it was this flirtatious Italian Suárez mentions who turns out to be the spy that leaked the book.

Buosa Mascheroni, a mountebank, an ungifted poet, and a gambler, came to the attention of Inquisition officials in 1553 after cheating a Leonese nobleman out of two thousand reales in a rigged game of dice that lasted for three days. Mascheroni—who was also wanted for hawking a poisonous nostrum with supposed curative properties in Valencia the year before (eight suffered hideous deaths)—only escaped execution by becoming an informer, and specialized in infiltrating subversive and intellectual cliques. With his flashy attire (he was fond of velvet breeches and wore a mustache that stretched twenty inches) and penchant for quoting his own, lurid verses, he was accepted readily by Suárez's circle as a comic yet harmless addition. And he does seem something of a crass bumbler—a reading of Suárez's letters shows that he spent less time spying than attempting to infiltrate the knickers of the salon's more attractive members.

Still, on May 3, 1561, only a few seasons after de Pasamonte astonished his friends with the private circulation of *Las Tres Furias*, the governor of Spain's records show that he received Mascheroni at his mansion and took into his possession a copy of the famous novel.

Within the month, hundreds of copies were feeding the riots and cult hysteria that would shock a country already horrified by eighty-three years of Inquisition violence (Mascheroni is suspected of being the distributor). And in the last week of May, one hundred armed guards descended upon de Pasamonte's monastery tucked into the countryside, which was a twenty-day trip away from Madrid.

MAY 18, 1561

De Pasamonte, I have received some rather disturbing news from our friends. It appears that the velvet dolt we all laughed at might be the reason so many uninvited eyes have recently gazed upon your work. He has disappeared, hasn't he? Only yesterday I thought how I had not heard him recite his stupid poems in some weeks. Moreover, I have heard the most horrid rumors concerning the purges. The Inquisitor is interested in having a chat with us, it seems.

We must be as quiet as a mouse now, dear. And watchful as a hawk.

MAY 20

My darling girl, you are keeping me so brave! As you have told me, it is time to gather one's things together. Have you any weapons? I have swords, food, money, peasants' costumes, the horses. And poison.

I have word they will arrive here in eight days and thus we still have time to arrange for transport. Where will we go? France, did you say? Or Algiers?

It is late spring when she writes these words, and it is late spring as I read them in the museum library, touching the lines with my fingers. The coincidence gives me a chill. It's taken me a while to push through the letters because I have been so busy, of late, restoring the book. I've made much progress in the last few weeks, and the folio's burnished beauty is starting to emerge. Nevertheless, I've kept up my research at night, now I am nearly down to the last letter in this sheaf.

It seems that Suárez was mistaken in how long it would take the soldiers to reach them, since the army's interview of de Pasamonte's swarthy hunchbacked maid indicates that the priest escaped his cell by minutes. As I've mentioned, all of his books and papers were there, including these letters—and it's a wonder they weren't burned along with so many other relics. As I sit here in the archives, imagining the horses Suárez gathered, the money, and worst of all the poison, the Getty's lights start going off, as it's quite late. But I'm almost at the end. I have only two more letters to go.

I turn the page, to the letter dated May 24, which is the day before the soldiers marched into the countryside.

De Pasamonte:

All is ready, save for the 1,000 reales our friends will bring to me this afternoon. I must admit a great sadness that we must leave this place where we have found much happiness, and after so many years of sorrow to be turned into the wilderness again makes me afraid. But you, my bold girl, my Pasamonte, you will give me strength, won't you? As you always have.

Remember when we first met? Rome seems a lifetime ago, and we were so young. But you have not changed, you amaze me as you always have. Oh, how you shocked the Pope with your magic balls! (Now, do not think lewd thoughts at that! I am becoming misty-eyed with innocent reminiscences.) And how we shocked each other by falling in love. It does not surprise me that we should face this danger together all these years later. For I have always felt as if you held my soul in your small hands.

And then there is another note, written the same day:

Algiers, then, as you wish. And if you are correct, Isabella will be
a great help to us.

Are you certain she will send a ship? I suppose as a sea baron
she has access to such things.

We will leave in two days, then, darling.

The Getty has gone black. Everyone is gone except for the
guards, and I am left alone with these stunning letters that seem
to leap at me from across a chasm of more than four hundred years.

I am bent over them, my face feverish, and I am not breathing.

But I will not tell anyone tonight. I won't whisper a word of
what I think I have found.

I drive home and go to bed, grinning into my pillow.

I do not sleep.

THE NEXT MORNING, June 13, I get up very early and drive
immediately to work. My desk is a small fortress made of books. I
examine each history, each criticism, for the scholars' interpretations of these last two letters.

I spend another full day at my desk, without eating, and only
drinking coffee. There has been a good amount of academic conjecture written about these last dispatches. One professor of
Spanish literature at the University of Chicago posits that Suárez
must have been terrorized out of her mind in the days before her
scheduled arrest, and that her confusion is evident by her calling
de Pasamonte "my bold girl."

Another scholar, a linguist from Miami, mentions that Suárez's
reference to Rome may indicate that she was once a nun—though
he professes confusion about the mention of "magic balls."

No one, that I can find, knows who Isabella is, or the identity of the priest's swarthy hunchbacked maid. Not one of them knows who Sofía Suárez and de Pasamonte are. None of them knows that he did not spend his childhood in Barcelona, or what he looked like under his robes.

But I do.

ON MAY 25, 1561, the Inquisition soldiers, visible on their horses from the monastery windows, came charging over the hill bearing arms they would use to kill the heretic if he offered any resistance to his arrest. They clamored through the groves, toward the cloister, dressed in red and with plumes in their tall hats. They numbered so many one might have expected they came to fight a war and not to arrest a mere priest and a few armchair philosophers.

Bursting into de Pasamonte's cell, they only discovered a dusky hunchback tearing her hair and sobbing for mercy in an imbecile's unintelligible tongue. Scattered about the cell were the incriminating books, letters, and other documents, and the inspection of the stable revealed the missing horse. Back inside, one of the soldiers began gathering papers together to form a giant bonfire outside the building, although he was canny enough to save the papers in the event they were of interest to the governor.

The maid continued crying as the literature was confiscated and burned, until the guards finally left.

As soon as they disappeared over the hill, she rose from the floor and extracted the hump made of straw from her blouse. She may have donned the peasant's costume given to her by her lover, or perhaps she had some other disguise to wear. I don't think she put on the priest's frock—that she must already have buried. And then she left the monastery to retrieve the horse she hid in the forest or some other concealing place.

Helen climbed onto the horse and then raced ahead to the home of Sofía Suárez, the famous bluestocking and letter writer who lived on the outskirts of Cáceres; the woman who in earlier times had been called Caterina.

THE SUNSET POURS through the window and stains the office copper-red, so that the illumined vellum seems to blaze against my naked hands. Scholars and biographers wander into the wing to hunt for ancient texts on antiseptic shelves. Nearby, I hear someone whispering a Latin poem.

My mother used to whisper secrets to me. She taught me not to trust what I saw around me, to share a suspicion that gave her so much unhappiness, but which also let her detect what others did not. *Everything you see here is stolen*, she said, and then she showed me the beauty of an old book. *Don't believe it*, she would murmur. *Look underneath*. She had more faith in the lost and forgotten than in the plain and visible, and sometimes that creed made her strange. But I see now that she was right, if only in part.

Could Helen have known, as she sailed back to Rome to find her lover, that she would become part of a Church that had undone so many? That had undone her? When she landed on Italian soil, she began a new chapter of a life that would have a much different ending from the one she'd imagined back in Tenochtitlán. This is a chapter that no one knows. That only I can tell.

And it's at this moment, when I think of telling this story, that something else occurs to me. I imagine whispering it into his ear. Of weaving it like a web around him.

My thoughts now turn to Karl.

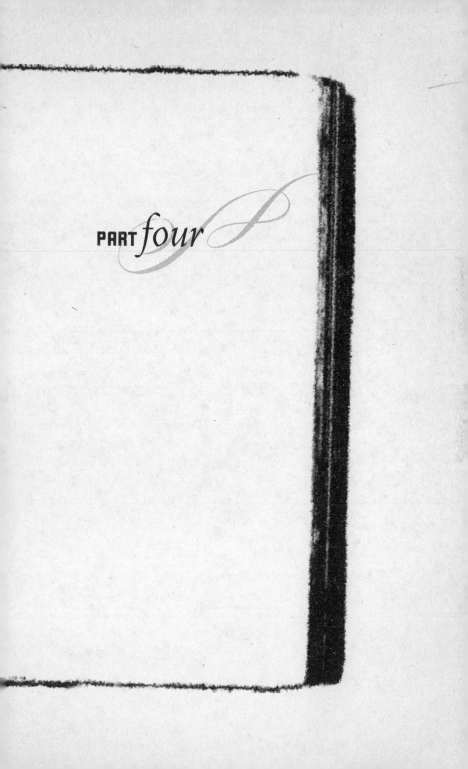

PART *four*

14.

When I returned to the Vatican in December of 1556, wearing a large sword and a nobleman's disguise, the first person I saw was a witch. Many had been born since I last lived in that place, at least so held Pope Paul IV in his infinite stupidity, as he had installed the Roman Inquisition for the purpose of vanquishing the succubi and incubi who infected the City of God. Everywhere he looked, this Paul saw Satan in the curves of women's bodies or shining out of the eyes of Jews. Books were burned like kindling, suspects pursued with dogs and crossbows. In that first year of the Holy Office, in that winter which was colder than any I have remembered before or since, I invaded that palace of Hell with only Caterina's safety on my mind. But as is usual with me, I soon found myself entangled in another adventure.

The white weather obscured the palaces from view as I drove my steed over the border from Rome. Making my way toward the fortress that held my bride, I saw forms appear through the mist. As I neared them I made out a stake and a bed of straw, a tall fat dame surrounded by a band of soldiers bearing torches, and a large crowd of weeping women, gaunt-faced men. The victim wore a black robe, which obscured her face and it was embroidered with yellow flames—the symbol of the unrepentant. When I halted my steed she removed the robe to reveal a quite stylish farthingale made of red silk, and although she did not shake with fear, I knew this Jeanne d'Arc could not have felt otherwise, for red, besides being the color of heretics, is also the color worn by martyrs.

She turned to the guard who held her by the arm and this is when I could see her face, which was familiar to me. She had great jowls, an honest brow, and an attractively voluptuous mouth.

This victim was none other than the Countess Mathilde, Caterina's old lover, and the same woman who had been so kind to me twenty years before!

"Oh my poor dear, how ugly you are," she said to the guard. "Your mother must have had quite a fright when she whelped you! Did she faint, boy, when she saw your atrocious nose? Does she weep when she inhales your reek? Well, no matter, I am sure she loves you anyhow, as a mother must. And it must be quite a comfort to her that you are so admirably employed."

"You die today, witch," the ugly guard answered, and the women in the crowd began to scream. Others, including the Countess's old butler and cook, had gone white with fear.

"Now, there you idiots go again, calling me this 'witch,'" she said, over the noise. "I must admit I find it somewhat tiresome. My name, you dolt, is Mathilde, and if you are accusing me of sleeping with the Devil, you are severely mistaken, as the Devil, as far as I have heard, is male in gender, and I only have eyes for women." The Countess looked at a young lady in the crowd. "Isn't that right, my sweet?"

The lady to whom she spoke shrieked out her name, and the butler and cook began pushing through the crowd toward their mistress, whom the guards tied to the stake.

"Stop them!" the horde yelled.

"Can't we do something?"

Still others cried out for fire and blood.

The ugly guard took a torch and put it to the straw. Flames began eating at the fuel and smoke wafted up to her face.

I hesitated no more, and charged my steed toward them. I discovered that if I poked my sword between the shoulder blades of the ugly guard, they went in rather easily and he was not at all stubborn about dying. The others, however, were. As I reached down to untie the Countess one of the soldiers whacked at me with his saber, and would have undone my arm if the Countess's butler had not now split his skull with a cleaver. Pandemonium soon set in. The women in the crowd, mad with fear, leapt on the guards like lions. I sliced at the cobs of many, several men joined in with rapiers, and our red casts, gleaming by the light of the witch fire, seemed the stuff of nightmares. In short order, women and guards lay dying on the ground, though the Countess survived. I approached her as she sat in the dust dazed and bleeding from the head while her lover nursed her. She turned to look at me.

"Do I know you, sir?" she said. And then she peered closer. "Or Madam?"

"Yes."

She stared at me even harder. "You aren't that frisky little Indian Caterina was so mad about?"

I nodded.

"I would recognize that color anywhere."

"Where is she?"

"Oh, she was wild about you, did you know that? She never recovered after you left."

"Where is she?"

The Countess Mathilde put her hands to her face and began to weep. "Lord, that was an age ago. Wasn't she beautiful then? With her gold hair? We Sapphists have not fared well under this new regime." She looked at me again, with her large wet eyes. "She's in the Castel Sant'Angelo, of course, in a cage like a dog with the rest of them. And you must go and get her now, before more soldiers arrive and kill us all."

I put my hand to the Countess's face for one moment, but did not delay any longer than that, though I was leaving her to certain death. I mounted my steed and fled from my old friend and that burning place, toward the horrifying chambers of Sant'Angelo.

THE GRUESOME CRYPT of the Roman Inquisition, the deadly prison of the Holy See, is actually a rather gorgeous tomb built by the Emperor Hadrian as his final resting place. I think it is telling that in this land of lies the house of so much suffering should be beautiful, with its ancient Roman friezes and its fabled bridge, the Pons Aelius. There were years when it was used as a fortress—the Pope himself hid here in 1527 during the

Sack of Rome, and Caterina once showed me the secret alley that extends between it and the Vatican. Otherwise, people say, the castle is as impenetrable as the moon, or (others might claim) as closed as Cortés's heart.

But it was in the stone heart of this dungeon where Caterina waited for death. And so I had no other choice but to find a way to her.

As I was stained from the battle with the guards, I disappeared with my steed into the trees around the castle. I waited until night fell, then slipped out from the black forest, toward the old tomb lit here and there with torches. It was a perilous crossing, though as I have learned through all these years to disappear when it suits me, I crept down the Aelius as silent as smoke.

There were three guards stationed at the great door, each of them with the purple face of a newborn babe on account of the cold. And they were not much older than that. These boys stood stamping and swearing and puffing out white clouds of breath, and I remained in the shadows, beyond the circle made by the torchlight. The cold must have weathered all the pity out of my heart, for I did not care one whit for their young lives. I sprang at them from the shadow, tucked my blade into one of their bellies as the others fumbled for their swords, mewing with fear. One of them cut me on the shoulder and I cannot allege any great prowess on my part, only the stark and precise insanity of a woman in love. All I can say is I killed the other two, I barely know how. My jumping sword and dagger found their way into their tender throats before theirs found mine, and once the children were on the ground, I finished the job. But when I saw their broken forms, my logic escaped me: I threw my dripping sword into the moat and beat my breast like a mad thing.

After some moments of delirium, however, I collected myself. I took their keys, avoiding their stares, and went inside.

Running my hands over the rough walls to find my way through that gulf, I was astounded not by the gloom barely brightened by the torches, nor the deathly winter of that place, nor the lunatic beauty of those Roman relics outlasting more fragile clay, but by the silence. I might have been surrounded by ghosts, it was so quiet, though I continued to tread as mute as the air and did not give myself away. Guards were stationed at intervals but they were so consumed by their own misery—many wrapped their coats over their faces to ward off the cold—that I slipped unseen through the shadows, up to the second floor that contained the terrible dungeons known, with good reason, as the Mouth of Hell.

I saw no sentries yet, but eyes glared at me behind bars, and the scabbed, shorn skulls of the penitent, their moving skeletons cracked my mind for I knew that my girl numbered among these shades. Up ahead, I heard a slapping sound and moans. When I turned the corner I came upon a guard's broad shoulders, just visible in the flickering light. He moved violently, and as I neared this fiend I saw the twisted face of a prisoner, a man the color of parchment, cringing before him while being beaten with a truncheon. The prisoner's eyes opened to see me and I nodded to him, and in that moment we both leapt upon the guard, strangling him and stabbing him with nary a sound, though our victim heaved in our arms with such wild strength he nearly crushed me. He took a very long time to die.

"Take his keys," I hissed to my accomplice, as I relieved the corpse of its sword.

"Who are you?"

"Helen." I looked at him. "I am—I am an Indian."

"I am Cagnazzo," he said, then grinned. "I am a pornographer."

"You are a pornographer no more, my friend," I said. "Now you are a Spartacus. Open the prisons."

We flung the doors wide but the captives were so stunned they stayed where they were in their cages, staring. Down the hall, I could hear the muttering of guards as they approached to relieve the duty of their dead friend.

"Get up! Get up!"

The frail bodies began streaming from the cages. I ran from cell to cell, whispering Caterina's name. Guards' boots chimed on the stone. I unlocked these caves of the dead, which are nearly without light, without air or moon, only despair crammed in filth and illness. The sick movement of rats. I left blood on the bars as I pushed them open. The scarred faces of the hostages were pale as bone, and I breathed in the stench of indignity and fear. How many cells? Where is she? As the guards arrived and began screaming an alarm, the prisoners coiled around me, then ran madly in all directions, over the guard's corpse, trammeling his friends. Cagnazzo stabbed one of the sentries then disappeared into the suck of the horde. Wails sliced the dusk. Bodies slumped onto the ground. More guards swarmed inside the pale, shaved crowd, hacking at the fugitives. I continued to break open cage after cage until I saw her.

I swear I might have missed her.

She was small as a fawn, shorn, and with a blank face, but when she turned and saw me some light glimmered there.

"Is it you?" she asked.

"Caterina?"

She began weeping. "Darling, I'm not dreaming? Or dead?"

I bent over her and inspected her face. This was my girl, still beautiful despite the years, though marked by hunger. I kissed her mouth. "I am real, and it is time to go."

I took her hand and we flew from that chamber, into the hot stream of bodies escaping. Prisoners battled guards hand-to-hand, and we slid past the weapons only because they were employed in murdering dozens of others. From memory, we tracked the path to the Pope's secret alley and ran inside the blackness until the light appeared again, and then we were in our old home, racing lightning-quick through the glittering halls, past the shocked guards, the heartbreaking art, the priests still as the marble angels guarding this empire of gold and God, out the carved doors and into the cape of the night, where we were free.

Once we reached my horse I stopped, then turned to look at her in the moonlight.

"I remember," she said, touching my cheek, "what a funny imp you were when we first met. Though I cannot believe you are the same girl."

"I am not the same," I said.

"No," she agreed. "But I am. I have never, never forgotten you."

"You once told me to forget everything."

"Then I was a brazen ninny, of course, and you should not have listened to me. When I thought I might lose my mind, I would talk to you in my memory. What a comfort that was, my Helen, you will never know. What a comfort you have been to me all these years."

"I have comforted no one," I said. "I have become something terrible."

She grasped my hands. "Who has not, my dear? Who has not in this madness?" She kissed me. "Let us go home."

"'Home'?" I shook my head at her folly.

She smiled. "Let us go to Spain, then. I will feed you oranges and wine there, and I will ravish you every night until you beg for mercy, and we will be happy."

"And you believe this is possible?"

"No." She laughed. "But we will do it nonetheless."

And so we climbed on top of my steed and I put quicksilver in its ears, and we sped through the black trees and the gold-drowned churches away from the Vatican, away from Rome. We purchased many costumes and seemed to be constantly changing our clothes, our titles, our manner of behavior in order to make our escape, but every time she touched my hand I could still feel my secret and true name glowing inside of me like an ember. Finally, six months later, while on a ship we had hired at an exorbitant rate, I saw the green hills of Spain for the first time.

She laughed with joy then, but I did not.

This, my new residence, was the country I had first spied in the standard carried by a man who called himself the beginning, but revealed himself to be the end. This was the home of my home's death, of my father's murder. It was the place that had birthed Cortés and nurtured his hellish industry. It was also the place where my love was born, and for a while, it had nurtured the gifts that she now gave me.

In all my years of living here, it has been my most difficult task to hold both of these truths in my heart at the same time.

WE WANDERED THROUGH *the countryside of Spain for more than a year, living off the fortune of our pirate sister Isabella. We rented manors, small castles, always moving whenever we caught a whiff of the governor or his guards. Caterina kept her promise, feeding me the region's splendid citrus and wine, and we could spend days under the trees, looking at the light glistening through the leaves, and tell each other amusing tales. But for all this, I still felt myself to be a fraud—and not for the clothes, not for the changed names, or the pretensions of manhood. No: I descried myself as false because of my many crimes. I continued to have visions of the boys I had killed, and I had dreams where my father instructed me in the art of murdering emperors. Whenever I peered into the different palaces of my heart—Aztec, daughter, juggler, lover, and that more ambitious system we call "human"—I found failure. And it was not until 1558, when we reached the cloister* of Yuste in Cáceres, that I thought I found the possibility of redemption.

Driving our carriage up a winding road, we saw in the distance a tree-lined abbey that bore a flag of the Holy Roman Empire. As we continued uphill, a farmer with a face like a walnut appeared on our right, picking grapes for wine.

"What is that?" I asked him, pointing to the building.

"The monastery of San Jerónimo, my Lord," he answered.

"Who stays there?"

"The Emperor, my Lord."

I stared at him, hard. "And which Emperor might you mean?"

He furrowed his brow at me. "Why, Charles, sire. He has come here for his retirement, though I hear he has not felt so well as of late."

Caterina and I continued up the hill.

"And what do you think you're going to do?" she asked. "You think you will kill him? You might as well slay the both of us here and now!"

I did not look at her, nor did I speak. The looming monastery grew closer, and as the blood began to beat in my head the world around me seemed to take on a sharper cast. I noticed every leaf, I saw each blade of grass. The sky seemed bluer than before. Caterina, fearing the high color of my cheeks, continued to admonish me, but for once I did not listen to her. Vengeance! I would sacrifice him to the forgotten god Tlaloc! I would snuff his breath with my bare hands, and the last word he would hear was the name of my father! No—better yet—I would start where Maxixa had left off, and stop this Emperor's heart with my old arts. I gripped the reins and drove us through the misty arbor to the monastery door, guarded by a stiff line of sentries.

One of them, noting my carriage's coat-of-arms with approval (it had been won off a count who had not seen the cards up my sleeve) approached us and bowed.

"And to whom may I be of service?"

I waved a fly from my face and gave him one of the names I used at the time.

"The Emperor welcomes your honor to this abbey, but he is too ill to receive guests at this time, having contracted brain fever from the sun."

"I am only here to have my confession heard," I said. "I will not trouble His Highness at all."

"As you wish, sire."

Caterina put her hand on my shoulder. When I turned I saw she was as pale then as the day I found her in Sant'Angelo, and her eyes were huge with fear.

"Do not go," she whispered. "Stay here with me."

But I only kissed her and reached for my bag of spheres, which I slung around my shoulder.

Streams of thin gold light floated from the windows to the stone floor inside the cloister. The cool air carried a small melody of whispers and two priests stood arguing by the confessional like a pair of ill-tempered birds. I witnessed a laundry-hauling maid exit a doorway down a corridor then disappear into a separate hall. Nodding to the priests I walked with my head held down like a penitent heavy with sins, and when the elder busied himself by boxing the younger's ear I entered the door of the maid. Here I found a washroom, filled with linen as well as several cassocks, one of which I quickly slipped on. It fit beautifully, and I must say I made a perfect priest.

I wandered through the abbey's maze, stealing a beaker of holy oil from another closet. I inspected every corner of two floors until I discovered a door at which four colossal sentries were posted.

"What do you want?" the largest of them asked me, a hill of flesh with eyebrows like wings.

"I am here for His Holiness."

"The Emperor is too ill for visitors."

"That is why I have come, to tend to him in his illness." I showed the brute my bottle of holy oil.

"I have orders that he is to see no one."

"And I have orders to administer extreme unction."

He furrowed his brows. "Did he not receive extreme unction yesterday?"

"No he did not, you muddlehead," I spat. "Now get out of my way. Do you want the Emperor to die before he receives last rites? If he burns in Purgatory it will be no one else's fault but yours."

The goliath relented, ordering his brothers to step aside. I brushed past them with a haughty air, into a room scented with violet water to eclipse the reek of illness. A body in a thin bed enjoyed a view of an open window, and next to the bed stood a table bearing a bowl of water and a basket of linen. A crude wood chair also stood nearby, upon which sat a fat maid, cooling the King's brow with a wet cloth.

The man on the bed, hearing my footfall, turned slowly toward me as I entered.

Charles.

The once plush and ugly head was now wasted by disease, without hair, without color except for two bright spots of fever on each cheek, and the massive jaw collapsed, as it was deprived of teeth. The savage who once grasped all of Europe in his fist could not now clutch even the thin edge of his sheet. His hand, mere bones, lay on his chest like a withered offering of flowers.

"Who is it?" he whispered.

I commanded the maid to leave us, and crept toward him on quiet paws. "I will not hurt you, Your Highness," I lied. "You will be safe in my arms."

But he was beyond all fear. Cataracts covered his eyes and he strained to see me. He reached for me with that awful hand, and a smile played on his face. "Lovely girl, is that you?"

I put my hand on his throat. "As ugly and as sick as you are, do you still long to breathe? Can life be precious to an animal like you?"

The smile faded. "You are not my wife."

"I am the daughter of Tlakaelel, old man."

He turned his head toward the window. "You could not be my wife. My wife died."

"And you will join her, soon."

The Emperor stared out the window. "There are flowers out there, I think, though I cannot see them. I imagine fields of violets, I can smell their perfume. Roses, perhaps, on climbing vines? The sweetbriar and Columbines? The spectral Helleborus orientalis? As I grew older gardening became a balm for my heart. When I brought my wife roses I knew they could not match the sweetness of her, the beauty. I will throw them away, I said. You are the only bloom in my life. Though now I find those roses are inside of my mind, filling up my head with their thorns—or is that the fever? My wife's cheeks were the color of roses."

I bent down as if to give him a kiss. "Come to your senses," I hissed in his ear. "I am the servant of Montezuma. I am the daughter of Tlakaelel. It is in his name that I murder you."

"Murder?" the Emperor whispered back, his face warping in confusion. "I am murdered?"

"You are dead," I answered, and stripped the bedclothes off his body, revealing what appeared to be a bundle of cracked twigs and the thin chest laboring. I reached under the cassock to retrieve my purse and then poured the spheres onto the bed. Pulling the chair close to the Emperor, I took my seat and prepared to levitate all one hundred.

Snatching them in handfuls, I sent ten, now twenty, then forty in the air, and began weaving Maxixa's spell. They spun in the sun-shot air as the Emperor continued to stare blindly out the window, crooning small songs about roses.

I trembled as I added ten, next twenty spheres more. And then, as the eighty balls flew too fast for my eye to follow, I could hear the blessed sound: The underwater sound of a heart beating.

Hup-hup. Hup-hup.

The Emperor's heart.

Charles V shuddered in his bed and I could see his eyelids flickering as he descended into his death. His mouth gaped like a fish's mouth, and his clouded eyes widened as if that might help him see. I added ten more spheres, thrown up like hail, and a physical pleasure began to flood my body with warmth. Hup-hup. At one hundred he would be dead.

And it was here the Emperor turned and touched me, very gently, on my leg. The savage called me his wife's name.

"Darling, let me comfort you," he rasped to a dead woman, and the blood now shone from his forehead. Blood appeared on his lips. "This illness is nothing. You are in no danger while I am here. Do not be afraid, my sweet girl, my sweet wife."

My body continued to tremble with pleasure. The spheres twinkled like stars over our heads. And my father's face appeared to me as bright as when I was a child, and he told me to finish my work.

End him. Kill him. Dip your hands in his blood. Spear his head on a spike.

Was it in me?

If I could be one thing of my own choosing, I thought once, it would be love. And I did not believe I could choose that.

But now I closed my hands into fists. I let the spheres fall to the ground.

The Emperor breathed, and my dear father's face vanished from my eyes.

In that moment I failed him once again. Yes, I became a traitor. I would not number among the great ones who used memory as a shield against villainy and death, because I could not pay the cost of that gift. I would not add this man's ghost to my haunting.

In the next ten hours I did not move from his side, and as the priests wandering in and out of the room appeared to accept me as one of their own, I was able to nurse the Barbarian until his death. I can barely discern why I gave a gentle hand to my enemy. Words like forgiveness and kindness do not transfix my heart. For I did not forgive, nor shall I ever. But while I wiped that broken figure with cool cloths, and spoke to the madman of his wife, I felt as if I nursed someone else. Each time I bent down to his ear and whispered, "Suffer not, old man," and "Sleep peacefully, King, without pain," I imagined that I did not care for the Emperor who killed us, but instead comforted my beloved father's starved body, giving him a succor I could not when he died.

Charles V expired before the sun rose and only then did I exit the monastery, leaving my spheres behind, though I did still wear the cassock. I climbed aboard the carriage to find Caterina awake and rigid with fear.

"I did not know if you would return," she whispered in the dark. "I have been so afraid, I have not moved once since you left."

"I am sorry I left you for so long."

"Did you kill him?"

"No."

"Is everything all right?"

I did not answer that question, though I did touch her hand to my face.

"Let us leave this place, sweetheart," she said, taking up the reins again.

"Yes. We will depart now."

Caterina and I drove through the night until the light polished the glade again, but I discovered that I regretted our retreat from the province. We remained in Spain as it is the last place I saw my father, and have lived

here now for several years. My hope was unfounded—
I have not seen him again, and can barely recall his face
anymore, a lapse that brings me much grief. There are,
however, other aspects of the region that we find agree-
able: It is a place where we can vanish, untraceable and
undiscovered.

We are invisible here until we look at each other.

EVENING DESCENDS AS I sit at my writing desk,
and a blue-plum dusk filters through the window, covering my love's body while she looks at me from her bed. I
am still in costume, while she undresses for me, slowly,
shedding her false colors until she emerges like a pearl
lifted from the sea.

"Take off your disguise, darling," she whispers,
"and I will call you your name."

Only she can bring me back home, though I do not
always want to return. There have been times when this
mask I wear has seemed to lock onto my skin, and
locked away too the shades, cracked temples, seraglios,
and summoned moons that still glitter inside of me. A
gorgeous, diamond-clear nothing floods through my
mind then, and it is a happy madness that I swallow
like medicine. I feel myself growing thinner, lighter, and
floating into blue space, but then Caterina touches me
and I grow warm and solid as the world charges back
with all its beauties and old demons.

A few years back, I met a young priest with a cunning S-shape to his nose and a copper cast to his skin,
which I recognized as the inimitable legacy of Ixtlilxochitl, who was my old juggling partner at the Vatican.
The mixture was quite curious—like a drop of ink in

milk. When I asked him who he was sired by, he said he had been born in an orphanage and knew his ancestors not. On account of my randy brothers, our splendid blood will linger here for decades after we die, marking their children's faces with a secret code that no one can read.

And then we will disappear.

But not yet. Not yet.

For here on these pages is a record of all we lost.

And here in this bed is the dusk-lit beauty of my wife.

I stand, and slip off these skins so that I may approach her as an innocent. She reaches for me. Under her hands I feel my name rising to the surface of my body, and she whispers it into my mouth.

No, we will not disappear yet. And perhaps we may never vanish. For I believe this love will endure. I must believe it. Despite the fire of time that consumes the clay and the air and all our thoughts, I think we will leave a print in this dust, or a disturbing murmur in the wind. We are writing it here, now, this lasting thing. This constitution, this rumor. This code someone, somewhere might decipher through the dark veils of the world.

15.

The museum is bright this morning. A cataract of gold light pours from the windows and burns the bronzes in this gallery. Naked, sun-gemmed girls and satyrs turn hard in the glare, and look like they will last longer than any of the rest of us here. I move from the room and out of the wing, stepping onto the esplanade with its view of the ocean and the horizon beyond that pure blue. I once thought I could see Mr. Getty flitting through the tabernacle his money built, but he's not strong enough for this sun. This is no weather for ghosts—there are no mists for them to emerge from, suddenly, in order to scare the docents to death; nor are there winds that would carry their disgruntled murmurs. It is even too warm for sweaters and I remove mine, drape it over my elbow, as I enter the library.

It is early on Saturday, June 14, only one month before Karl's wedding day, but I need to run one errand at work before I make any other moves. I take the elevator to the third floor. There's almost no one on this level today, and no one should be at work, though when I first enter the lab I hear a shuffling and knocking sound coming from my office, and I grow worried. No one but staff is allowed back here, but last year a guest did wander in and try to filch a six-hundred-thousand-dollar book of hours by slipping it into her purse. I move through the first room of the lab, where we store manuscripts and other rare items, and when I enter our work space I see Teresa, with springing gold curls and a rosy face, sifting among cardboard boxes and an effulgence of gorgeous mess.

Here is the radiant detritus of twenty years in book arts, pulled from shelves, unearthed from drawers, littered about like party favors and streamers. I note the collection of antique bone folders, made of glowing ivory. The cobalt Murano glass horses picked up at the conference where she gave a talk on eighteenth-century French endpapers. The small plough knife that once belonged to the illustrious Roger Payne. The flame-red vase she's stocked with flowers every week since I met her (it's now empty). The assortment of rosewood lettering pens on the desk, along with the glossy bottles of India ink and the worn oilstone that sharpens edging knives. The antique oak book press lies already in a cardboard box. Marbled papers flutter in the breeze coming from the window, lengths of linen and rich leathers lie curled on the floor.

Teresa looks up, then picks up one of the rosewood pens, approaches me, and places it in my hand.

"I know you always wanted these."

"What are you doing?"

"My tests came back *clean*, isn't it fabulous?" she says, and then laughs. "And so I'm quitting."

She begins talking about the future she's decided on—travel-agenting, which should give her *scads* of opportunities to see the world, she says. And she speaks without any sign of the dread of what has passed before—though it is still on her face, the lines she pressed around her mouth yesterday when she waited on the phone. But she doesn't want any part of that. Instead, she first listens very politely to my findings, and then jumps into an ebullient description of her plans, which are so soaringly forward-looking that I wind up listening to them for hours, despite my anxiety to dispatch my errand and get back to Karl before I run out of time. "I will first go to Kenya with the object of having a rather naughty Dinesenian love affair," she says, "and then perhaps scoot off to Peru in order to help build public housing as well as sample what I understand is the most *delicious* chocolate."

While she talks, I can't help but marvel at this difference between us that's cemented my unlikely friendship with Teresa. It's a disagreement about how to survive, and what really matters. But though her reckless forward gaze made me so nervous before (those crumbling books she ignored; those scofflaw parties), I now get that there's something wonderful and necessary in her amnesia. Even if I'm a restorer by instinct, I know I can't turn my back on that gift of forgetting any longer, as I'm starting to see it's as potent, dangerous, and sublime as memory.

Though when I bring this up to her, she surprises me again with her answer.

"Well, of course you have to forget *some* things, dear," she says, "though for today you should probably concentrate all your efforts on retrieving that big, sexy *sailor* of yours, who I believe is about to marry some frightful redhead in a matter of weeks."

TOWARD THE AFTERNOON, after Teresa packs up and goes home, I finally return to my errand. I glance up at the volumes awaiting repair—a twelfth-century herbal with gilded roses, a reproduction of Mercator's *Atlas*—but ignore them, reaching instead for the finished folio on my desk. The leather boards glow like a saddle; the spine invites the fingers to grasp it. The vellum pages look like the face of a still-beautiful dowager. Turning the leaves, I read the letters that I carefully repainted with Teresa's rosewood pens, and the ones I allowed to remain faded; a few are blurred or chipped. These are imperfect marks of *her* hand.

Now I rise from my chair, carrying the book, and walk to the computer that contains the files of our collections. I click into the entry for the folio which I recorded a few months before:

AUTHOR   de Pasamonte, Padre Miguel Santiago

TITLE   *Untitled Manuscript*

IMPRINT   Cáceres, Spain; Sixteenth Century

NOTE   A fanciful novel set in the era of Holy Roman Emperor Charles V.

I change this entry to:

AUTHOR   de Pasamonte, Padre Miguel Santiago/Helen/Anonymous

TITLE   *The Conquest*

IMPRINT   Cáceres, Spain; Sixteenth Century

NOTE   The autobiography of an Aztec woman brought to Europe in 1528 by Hernán Cortés; author wrote several well-known books under the name "Padre Miguel Santiago de Pasamonte."

My fingers rest lightly on the keys. My entry vibrates on the screen like a living thing. Patrons filter into the gardens outside my window while I stay in my seat, staring at those words, and the sun slants through the glass panes lower, then lower still.

I think of my mother's dark hands, when they smoothed the stolen *amoxtli* fragment on her bed. Then I just think of her, before that day. I almost call out her name. I want to yell it. "I miss you!" I do say, out loud. And then I realize that I am very tired.

The Conquest is open on my lap. I finger the soft, almost furry pages. I close the book.

I stand up, get my keys, and exit the library.

THE TRAM DESCENDS the Getty's hill toward the city glittering with the stalled afternoon traffic, stop signs, other assorted barricades of the modern world, a world that I know I'll have to start paying more attention to from now on, and that I should embrace in a fully functional way, but that nevertheless makes tiny fireworks of dread detonate in my chest.

It takes me nearly an hour to get out of the city and onto the freeway that leads to Oceanside.

AFTER EXTRICATING MYSELF from Los Angeles, I speed south, whizzing once again alongside the brand-new baby mansions and scattered habitats of trailer parks until all the cerulean beauty of San Diego comes charging at my windshield like a gorgeous tsunami about to crush me. On the street where Karl lives, weekender leatherneck dads knock back Diet Cokes and watch the children lurching over the sidewalks on their motorized skateboards, or playing sweet games with buxom dolls, or hunkering on gutters with their faces pressed so close to GameBoys they appear to be giving the screens a tender kiss—but he is not out here, nor does he answer his door. I prowl around until I attract the attention of a Latina, close-cropped, very pregnant marine who, while weeding her garden daisies, gives me a look of such bemused goodwill that it sends me fleeing back to my car. I drive off, and head toward Camp Pendleton to circle its perimeter, but do not see my whisker-headed boy entering or exiting the base, nor is he at the beach or the park, with the softball-playing daughters and tattooed pops. In the local mall, I wander through stores packed with American flags and somewhat scary Devil Dog T-shirts and other U.S.M.C.–suburban fun that I swear I would wear and wave with only slightly ironic enthusiasm if I could call him mine, but he's not there or in the supermarket, the bridal boutique, the shake-and-bake suntan salons, and I maneuver past the arcades, toward other residential quarters, though losing confidence.

Until, that is, I veer away from the shops and commons toward an elegant quarter of Oceanside. Here I hit a particular street called El Cielito. I came to look at this very place nearly a year ago, touched then, as now, by morbid curiosity and just plain staggered grief after Karl told me about meeting Claire here. The sky now begins to relax into twilight, but I recognize the leaf-laced, stately row of groomed manors fronted by perfect salt air–defying lawns. These are the citadels of lucky 1960s real estate investors, as well as the old-school east-coast expats—and retired, arts-and-crafts aficionado generals.

The hacienda of General O'Connell, grandfather of the winning Claire, has its hoary oak doors and windows thrown open so that I can see within the twinklings of fairy lights and candles, the shine of swinging girl-hair, the sounds of high heels and man-laughs and party music. I park my car in a streetlamp-lit space that has just been vacated by a departing reveler, and feel as if I float out into the street, up the glowing porch steps, and into the flame-bright mansion, which receives me as if I were any other invited guest.

The foyer and ballroom are thronged with coiffed, silky women as well as marines in full dress, but it isn't until I spot Karl's father from the back (I have not seen him for years and that large disciplinarian is withered suddenly, nearly unrecognizable to me), as well as one of his grandmothers with her intricate tower of hair, that I understand how epiphenomenally unwelcome I must be as this is the formal and apparently extremely expensive *engagement* party. Slipping under the elbows of giant soldiers and the polite smiles of their dates, I note also a stately redhead in a flowered shift comforting a general who blinks at the scene in pink-eyed amazement. This pair, I figure, is Claire's.

I list past a scarred major, wall-mounted Japanese swords, a butler wielding minuscule food, and move into a parlor. Three guests clustered by a display of model destroyers look up at me expectantly, and then with bafflement, when they note my jeans and bunged-up ponytail. I nod and bare my teeth in a sort of smile before making my escape through a side door which leads to a labyrinth of boudoirs and powder rooms where other merry-makers' gum-revealing hilarity signals the first stages of serious inebriation. An excessively attractive sorority gathers by a bath-room, weaving slightly while yodeling about the impressive size of their (as yet unseen) friend's diamond ring. I'm half in tears by this time and U-turn toward an opposite hall, expecting to see the fiancée rushing at me in a blaze of Laura Ashley and blasting ammunition, or that mother-in-law who I'm sure wouldn't think twice about hauling a home-wrecker like me out by the hair. But nobody like that shows and I keep going, brushing by a moist-looking lady wearing a silk suit the color of Paris green and a marine sneaking a smoke by an open window, until I spot another marine, with nearly invisible blond hair—a friend of Karl's I've met a few times, his name is Peter, I think—coming out of a room at the very end of the next corridor.

Inside of this small bedroom, I find Karl.

He's sitting on a jacquard-draped bed, and is dressed in his gold-buttoned blues. He's staring at his gleaming shoes. When he realizes someone else is in the room he glances up and half-hops to attention, but then sits down and keeps his large eyes on my face.

"I'm here, Karl," I blurt, "because you can't marry this woman."

He doesn't say anything. Not, How did you get in here? Not, What are you doing?

"You can marry me instead." I pause. "Even though my timing's bad."

"Bad?" he asks. "*Bad*?" He glares back down at his perfect shoes. "Sara."

"Things won't be different, even if you do this."

"Okay, hold on. Listen to me."

I start to cry. "We'll say this was the closest call ever. We'll tell people, 'Oh god what a drama that was.' And I'll say, 'I was scared to death.' And you'll say, 'She dragged me out of my own engagement party, can you believe that?' "

He reaches up and touches my hand. "Here, no," he says. "Shhhh. You're all right."

"Let's get out of here."

"I can't."

I begin to see Karl in a kind of darkening tunnel vision, I am focusing so hard on him.

"Hon, you've got to see why it happened," he tells me. "You know that all these years, there wasn't anybody else for me. Only Sara, you're all I could think of. Only you. How could I leave you? You *know* I couldn't leave."

I try to interrupt, but he doesn't let me.

"You know it's not me who left," he says, while still holding my hand. "*You* did. In your way. And I'm not talking about who took what job where or not even the not getting married. You'd just take off on me."

There's a silence here, and I can hear the music and jabbering outside the door.

"I know I left. In a way, all those times, I left you."

"And I didn't want to feel like that anymore. It was too rough on me."

I look down at my shoes too, now, which are a pair of navy Keds. I look at his hand with its huge, white, walnutty knuckles. "Then what are you doing in here alone?"

He doesn't answer that, but only scuffs his shoes against the carpet, which is a flat honey Berber, overlaid with a daintily woven Oriental. "There's something else, I might as well tell you. I was accepted to Houston this week." He grins in an unhappy way. "Can you beat that? I swear, I'm almost thinking about not taking it."

He lets go and presses his hands together between his knees, and in my neural shakeup I somehow notice that the room's immaculate, and looks unused. This is a hideaway room designed for an unwanted overnight guest, or a maid, I guess, but seems less suited for sleeping or sex, and instead is just perfect for a purpose like this—to make a space for a last-ditch, fretful air-clearing where you get a good, gory look at your future. I sit next to him on the hard little bed.

"Of course they'd take you."

"You always said that."

I scrape my hand against the bed's jacquard. "Well. You *are* going."

Now Peter the marine pokes his head into the room.

"Okay, buddy," he says. "What the hell? You still hungover from all the booze last night?" His jaw drops when he sees me. He goggles at us for a couple of seconds, then pulls the door shut.

I gesture at the door. "Did you guys go out?"

"Yeah, but I wouldn't say a good time was had by all."

"Karl, don't say I'm too late."

"I've been sitting here thinking that maybe the best decisions can be the saddest ones, too, you know?" he goes on, as if he didn't hear. "I'm getting the idea that they can be the hardest ones."

I can't think of anything to say to that, since it is so obviously true.

"And that maybe you can need someone, and feel like they're a part of you," he says, "and still not be with them. It's tough, like watching your dad getting older. Facing up to things, all that. Trying to do what's best by good people, and Claire is a good person. A real pistol, too, not that you need to know that." He nods his head, and now does look at me. A second passes. "You're a part of me, and this is the hardest thing, but you did come too late," he says.

I hear the music again, the chattering, the tinkling sounds of the party down the long, snaky hall, and have the slow, stunned realization that my relationship with Karl is over.

I take his hand again and I am gripping on tight, without any idea of what to do. A warm sadness heats my face. Someone is complaining about the drunks outside the door.

I lean toward him, wondering what step to take next. I put his hand to my mouth and kiss the palm, with the ramifying lifeline and the hard, square tiny calluses.

Finally I whisper: "A wonderful thing happened yesterday, and I want to tell you about it. Remember the story about the juggler and the nun?"

My voice is as soft as fur. I can feel the old skill thrilling through me.

He nods; he doesn't stop me.

And I begin the next part of the saga, the part where I last left off.

I lead him away from this house with my voice, and in my own words I carve out the black Mediterranean where a ship is sailing into a storm, then the dunes of Süleyman the Magnificent where a girl lies in the sand and glares up at the booming sky. Karl's large hand rests in my hand as he travels with me to the desert. His eyes are on mine and a small smile plays on his mouth. And we've never been as intimate as this. When I tell Karl a story I'm delivering pieces of the world that he assembles with his gifts for listening and patience and perception, and the tales were never just of my own making, but something we built together. I describe to him now the gloomy Castel Sant'Angelo with its Roman relics, its half-dead victims, the escape through the Pope's corridor, while the party laughter floats over to us from some far-off place and I know I have to hurry to tell him all of it before it's too late. Once, years back, we squeezed in lovemaking during a fifteen-minute break, and this feels like that did—I want to pour everything into this small space so that nothing is wasted, nothing lost. A knock comes on the door, but we ignore it and the interloper's feet shuffle off again. I talk of the countryside of Spain, and the Emperor's madness as he lay dying. I reveal the secret of the insane priest, the bluestocking Suárez, and their attempted capture. I talk until I'm exhausted. I use everything up.

"That's the end," I say. I give him a kiss.

Then I let Karl go.

I could almost imagine I'm moving to another country when I walk away from him, because the look on his face makes me feel like I'm sailing off on a barge while he grows smaller and smaller on the shore. Still, I push through the door, and down the hall, walking so fast I am nearly running (though I do *not* run) through these shimmering rooms, this jewel-strung gang poised on the edge of Claire's party. The women crowded around Peter now step away from me like a flock of nervous bluebirds (one begins pointing), and as they part, they reveal a strawberry-haired girl dressed in a long rose gown, with gold bracelets at the wrist, as shimmering as a Klimt. She is pearl-dewed, and when her face isn't bent like that I know she is beautiful. The bride! The wife! The gorgeous Claire, red-cheeked with confusion. I'd like to tell her, "Take care of him because he's the best there is," but I can see she's praying for a bolt of lightning to come down and turn me into a quivering cinder, and I decide not to take my chances. I keep moving, through the corridors, past the busy kitchen and ballroom, the toy destroyers, the fish-eyed General O'Connell, the battalions of marines and the mounted Japanese swords hailing from some questionable provenance, as well as Claire's mother who's got a face on that tells me she'd like to give me a good pistol whipping with one of their guns, Karl's handsome, shrunken father, and his tower-haired granny who gives me a friendly little waggle of her fingers until I am finally outside, in the cool gloaming, where it is quiet.

I sit in my car, with my hands on the wheel, staring out the windshield at the gold lamplight frosting the street. No one rushes out of the mansion to give me a talking-to or otherwise run me off. An elm tree stands just to the side of the car, and I hear how its leaves pick up a bit of wind; it appears to awaken.

I am cold.

I am freezing, and feel hard to the touch.

And—here it comes again—this feeling brings me back to the first story I ever told Karl, when I was fifteen years old.

That night at the beach I told him about a princess who fell in love with a soldier. *She removed her dress for his pleasure*, I'd said, while floating around him in the water. *She loosened the ribbon of her gown so it fell to her feet.* I had described how a war came to her country. How the soldier, arming himself with his spear and shield, left to repress the rebels, and after kissing him good-bye the woman hiked to the top of a mountain so that she might see his standard as he marched into the jungle. The woman, I told Karl, waited there on the mountain for years but he never returned. She waited, but there was no word from him, no message. Though she did not forget him. And at the end of her life on the top of the mountain, she felt her breast shudder and a blazing temper flood from it. Her arms hardened as all her hot blood flew to her heart. Her hands darkened and cooled and developed fissures, which matched the grain of the volcano. Her eyes formed into purple crystals like the crystals born in rock. Her tongue was made of rock, and her thighs widened into a cliff. Her belly was formed of black rock and the diamonds made by violent earth. She was cold, the way granite feels to the touch, and she discovered finally that she wasn't a girl anymore but a mountain, a rough thing.

I sit in my car and stare out the windshield, thinking of that.

After some time, partygoers begin to seep out of the general's manor, moving toward their parked sedans. I watch beautiful brunettes step into Jeeps with the help of burly men. A group of laughing daters wander down the darkened street, the spaghetti-strapped women shivering against the cold. I sit in the car and do not move, but listen to the sounds of traffic drift over from some unseen freeway. The dopplered lilt of a convertible's radio wavers in the air as a speedster races off, and waiters and maids can be seen still serving shrimp to the vivid-faced guests laughing behind the general's grand windows. An orange cat slinks across the porch steps, its fur sparked by the lamps and candle glow. A marine walks straight and stiff down the same steps, with a cheerful blonde on his arm.

At this, I've had enough. I start up the car. The manor stands black against the city-lit sky, with its gold windows giving it a Halloween face. I maneuver out of my tight spot on the curb, and follow my spotlights through the darkened street, toward the freeway. There's nothing else to do or see. I go home.

AT HOME IN PASADENA, on my porch, I have a blue-and-white garden in terra-cotta pots—pansies, mostly, with silky light petals and inky eyes. The flowers are sturdy, and thick with moisture, though they will bruise a staining indigo if handled too roughly. The softness and lightness of feathers, kissing lips, infant hair—all that is in the pansy. The petals and leaves are lovely when pressed into books, as they resemble the thin, revenant ghosts of old women. The living petals are bright tongues. When they are held up on a day like this, the light reveals wavering veins that look like warnings penned in ancient Arabic.

It is two days later.

The sun is out, printing the white porch and, beyond the burned-grass path leading to the sidewalk, carving shadows out from the spaces beneath the curbside trees, which are glossy from this spring weather. A line of light inscribes my forearms as I work in the pots, reconfiguring loam, nursing hieratic roots with my green watering can. The flowers were not dry or dying when I came out this afternoon to tend to them, I simply wanted their company. I stripped them of soil, I bathed them and fed them. I had been looking at *The Conquest* in bed, and could not read the words, so I began gardening.

My sadness is a kind of blurred language, chattering and baying at me. I have no idea how to listen to it. I do not want to translate it.

The sun slants across my wrist and lights the suddenly copper, articulate hairs. The cracks scribble over the porch concrete, and there are the scrawls of flaws in the terra-cotta. My hands, working in the purchased dirt, look strange to me, and separated. I try to think of beautiful things—the gilded Islamic writing in the Getty's Andalusian Qur'an with its Mixtec annotations, the tooled foliated leather of the 1719 *Robinson Crusoe*, these lucid white petals and their naked, barky roots. I try to see Helen, dressed in her deerskin. I try to see my mother.

I can't. None of it helps.

The flower heads flutter in my palm as I tuck them into the soil, which has a texture to it like flesh. There are limits to beautiful things. Not many, but there are, and important ones. I can see a looseness in the skin between my thumb and index finger I hadn't noticed before, a displeasing, cellophane pull to it. I will bury the roots here. I have a suspicion that when I am done I will go back inside. I will handle the book again, perhaps give it another polish. I may restitch a section of the binding. I'll do anything to make myself feel better. Because I don't want to feel like this. I may cut some of the transparent kozo and spread it like good skin over the vellum, pasting and repasting. There might be a small comfort in the act if I try it again. I know that I might spend the rest of the day repairing that old folio—gluing, stitching, washing, gilding—even if it doesn't need it.

IT IS THE MIDDLE of July. I try to notice things, to let the weather teach me. Los Angeles rocks like a river around the canoes of freeways. Old books must be fought for here—the light is an eater of such things, nibbling at the fore-edges with its chemical air and peeling the morocco with its bright breath. A woman sitting in a Pasadena park reading an expensive old folio as if it were a paperback commits a great crime, even if she is not caught. But now, in the hot mouth of this city, I see that I was wrong, as not even the famous L.A. contains the perfect climate for forgetting. It is true that the images of my mother have started to fade in my mind—but the shiny surfaces of the buildings reflect back faces resembling those that were once carved into caves. And the metropolis's cups and wells are filled with old things. Innovative archaeologists have begun to orchestrate digs in the musty spaces beneath the freeways, and find 1890s engagement rings there, 1920s valentines, bits of hair twined into love knots.

The city, I think, was built on the dreams of people like me, and in order to escape their heartaches they touted its amnesiac effects in such clamoring terms that many who listened eventually believed these mountebanks, perhaps for similar reasons.

While I'm sitting in the park, with my old book, a child approaches me, under the keen-eyed gaze of her mother.

I let her sit next to me, even turn the pages. I describe Spain in the sixteenth century, and begin to translate the gorgeous Rotunda script. Except for two people, no one yet knows about my discovery, but I tell her the old love story inside the book.

There was a juggler once, I say. There was once a nun who loved to read.

The girl turns another page and touches the gorgeous script, the delicate rubrication.

And then, even before I realize what I'm doing, I am telling her another love story, a more recent one.

IN THE FALL, after July, I return to my porch and replant the small garden. Sisters of the last pansies still last here, and I try to recall if my mother planted these, back in Long Beach—and can't. I am even having trouble remembering what she looked like the day that she walked out of the museum holding the remnant. Though her spicy perfume is still preserved and frozen inside of me.

Other things, however, remain hot and perilous in my mind. His large hands on my body, as an example. The last, barge-leaving look.

The sun is strong yet and showers my lawns, bends toward me on the porch, while the quiet, friendly scenes of south Pasadena pass me by. Dogs and women, husbands and daughters. Across the street, a family—though we've been neighbors for four years I just recently learned their names—the Chos, all dressed in khakis and fat white sneakers, climb into a gigantic car and drive off to shop somewhere, their dalmatian barking wildly in the backseat.

As I crouch on the porch, holding the flowers, the sun slides over my forearms, my knees, yellow as pollen, and, now, with pollen's gift of information. For the light curving across my body flickers suddenly, then disappears.

I stop what I'm doing.

I hear the rustle of grass. The sound of breathing. An idea comes to me. I stare at this small bit of shadow. I do not look up.

The light reappears on my knee, wavers. I touch the flickering gold on my skin very tenderly, as if it will break. My eyes fix onto it.

When I look up, I see that Karl has walked up my burned grass path so that his long shadow stretches toward the place where I sit. He stands in the center of my lawn, and I can make out his large eyes, his bare, pale face under his shorn hair, and his hands caught in mid-gesture.

Karl stands, awkward, on the edge of my house. He doesn't take another step.

He stares at me across the distance between us, with his arms stiff at his sides. His arms rise, higher, then higher. They open.

There's love in his face.

LATER, WE RETURN to the shore and float together again in the gold water.

The pure sky of early-summer Long Beach drifts down onto

our faces; our shoulders bump and touch, then glide apart. Karl extends his hand and touches my fingers and when I look over I see his profile, white against the green waves. His pale chest hovers above the ocean and his arms stretch out through the water. His eyes are closed. His mouth opens slightly. Farther up beyond him, I can make out shifting, busy color on the strand. There are more people here than I remember; Long Beach has grown since we were kids.

He smiles now, and opens his eyes. He reaches up to smooth back my hair.

"Well, I'm surprised," he says. "Usually by this time you're telling me a story."

I roll over and tuck myself under the water, then open my eyes for a moment in the startling, smarting green space. I surface again and swim toward him. My feet find a solid patch of sand. I press my lips to his shoulder, shake my head.

For once, I keep this mouth of mine shut. I'll always have a hankering for tales but right now I find that I have no need to make myself up into a strange river girl, or Karl into a dragon or a *kalif*; I don't need anything to make this afternoon sweeter or to soften the rough spots, either.

At this thought about the rough spots, I try to remember my mother as well as I can. I work to see her face in the water and make out a glimmer of her laughing mouth before my own reflection sifts over the waves.

Now Karl turns in the ocean, and embraces me.

"No stories today," I tell him. "I'll treat you to one later, in Houston."

IT'S PAST MIDNIGHT NOW, and my bags are only half-packed, but I'm still up rereading this book, which I've managed to keep my hands on for these past months even though the restoration job has long been finished. I've had some trouble giving her up, I admit, and I'm enjoying these last few hours when *The Conquest* is still all mine, before I return it to the Getty's shelves and call up those de Pasamonte scholars with my news.

Helen's been a private comfort to me this year, but I know it's time to hand her over to the professors, and the truth is I can't wait until she's loosed from this book like a genie from a bottle, then barrels through the imaginations of all those Boswells, knocking down their rock-solid stories and leaving nothing but awe and beauty in her wake. I think there's just enough between these pages to dynamite a small section of reality, and when the Ph.D.s catch a glimpse of the layers beneath the surface, which are pure gold and go too far down for the eye to follow, they'll probably hold their heads in astonishment for a while. If *he* could be *her*, then what else have we got wrong? they'll wonder. I'm liable to believe nearly any possibility now. Maybe there *are* Sirens beneath the ocean. Maybe that cold wind spooking you *is* the breath of the dead and buried clamoring for justice. Maybe there are spirits in the rocks, and you are a thief, and maybe your heart is as big as this giant world that belongs to you as well as to me.

Yes, I want to say to all that, though the best affirmation of those possibilities that I can think of are expressed with the old tools of the trade—tattered books, glue, kozo, and bone folders. For I did not quit my job. I have old morocco in my blood and can't get lost libraries out of my brain, and besides, the Getty couldn't let me go. Though I am, in a sense of the word, a traditional girl, I am becoming smart enough to take advantage of the modern world, which means I'm trying to have my book and read it too. It makes me nervous, but now I think that if Karl can call off a wedding and make it up to the stars, then I might be able to balance leatherneck babies on my hips and hop flights to keep the universe safe from deliquescing Etruscan and *cuir-ciselé* binderies (and the Hellenic secrets they contain). Or maybe my part-time plans will all go to hell and we'll have to work something else out—something messy and difficult probably, as it'll have to make room for those seeming irreconcilables like books and Jupiter and the Long Beach–born passion I have for Karl.

But I am set on stepping out from the beautiful unreliabilities of the museum and into the heat and contingency of the life I used to spy outside my office window. I suppose I can do this now that I've disturbed the peace of Mr. Getty's dazzling galleries and so dispatched the duty I inherited a long time ago. It also helps that I've proven to myself that the one act, that one afternoon when my mother lifted a page from a very old book and stole it from under the docents' noses, wasn't just born out of the craziness that everybody else saw, but also a kind of common sense. My finding that out was one of her more important bequests to me (she of the disbelief in genuine inheritances), but there was another one too, a tool, the tricky tongue she used to mourn that which was stolen and nearly forgotten as well as to make something new.

Come here, I'll whisper to you. There's nectar and myrrh under this tongue of mine. I know incantations that will take you to magic places. Once, a long time ago, there was a witch who fell in love with a wicked queen . . . a fortune-teller read the name of God in her cards . . . a court jester slew the king and ascended the throne. . . In *The Thousand and One Nights* the fables dry up because their author gets the king in the end, but that hasn't happened to me yet.

Take the other evening—I phoned my father for a few minutes before he was about to set out on another date, and I started telling him one of my adventures.

"There she goes again," he said, "Miss Crazy Brain, just like your mom! If you just had a *little* bit of a level head, I'd die happy. Maybe if there was a *tiny* bit of practical thinking in that piñata you call a brain, I wouldn't be having a heart attack all the time!"

But he listened anyhow, and he must have liked the story, because he'd lost track of half an hour before he realized he was late.

After I hung up, I considered all the life lessons he's tried to teach me through the years, that business about birthrights and spring-in-your-step, the tough-it-out, the move-on, and then I thought about my mom, and the mnemonics *she'd* tried to teach me, and for a few moments both angles locked in together with a big *snap*. I could see how both their ideas about birthrights and heists were right, and how both the surface and shadow worlds were real—and the way, too, that cold fact of her dying could coexist with the incredible mystery of the juggler girl who turned herself into an assassin-priest.

And I swear, I had it all figured out then. I could feel the real and hidden worlds flow right through me, and it didn't hurt, and it was a wild mix of nonsense and logic that was sweet as honey and easy on the nerves. I was a damned *philosopher* then, juggling not just the moon, but Jupiter and Venus, too, and I felt like I could have set even the great Maxixa on the run.

It ended, though, just a little while later. After some minutes I lost the thread of what I'd been thinking, and things got complicated again.

I have settled on something, though, which is that I agree with Helen, because love's the only thing that ever kept me from swimming off into the distance like that cow she wrote about. My darling husband, of the straight teeth and square head, you stole my heart a hundred years ago, and every time I look at your sweet pale chest I see that little blue polestar on it, which appears to be leading me in the direction of . . . Houston, for now. I don't know after that.

And just the idea of these next steps makes this quilted ticker of mine go *whumpa-whumpa*, as hard as Charles's and the Pope's. I'm getting the idea that those steps don't lead to any straight line, but are more of a dance inside the soft or strangling arms of then and when. Oh, I can make it clearer than that: *I love you, Mom, with all my heart, but good-bye.* Teresa and my father were right, it seems, for I did have to forget someone, in a way. Just as I've fixed my mother's expressions in my memory, a downy, gentling mist has started to wander over her face, obscuring the more harrowing as well as beautiful features that I never had to draw in my mind because they were already burned there—and even as I think this, I think too *don't go!* Don't leave! How much I can control or keep I don't know. Nor am I sure how much I should take with me or leave behind, though based on past experience I'll bet I'll try to travel with the heaviest bags I can.

But I do know this. I am in love with all that is left for me to restore and remember and lose: The secret cartography of Karl's blue-compassed chest, the brass-tacks sweetness of my father, even the split-hearted ache I feel when I imagine my mystery-loving, fading mother—and these are more than private things, even larger than consolation. They've thrown me a rope I wouldn't have had otherwise, and I'm stringing it out tight and stepping lightly over it like a girl in the circus, though still looking down at the view; if I'm lucky it just might lead me over this territory of promises and stolen gold, birthrights, amnesia, the riddle of history, the heart's puzzle, this unrecoverable past that is our inheritance and our legacy.

acknowledgments

My loving thanks go to: Andrew Brown, Renée Vogel, René Alegría, Fred and Maggie MacMurray, Maria and Walter Adastik, the faculty of Loyola Law School, Michael North, Victoria Steele, Eila Skinner, Ken Murray, Eileen Paris, Mona Sedky Spivack, Elizabeth Baldwin, Ryan Botev, the fellows of the Los Angeles Institute for the Humanities at USC, the MacDowell Colony, Thelma Quinn, and Daniel Mulligan.

In addition, the Getty Museum, where I am a stack reader, had a tremendous influence on the writing of this novel. (And I would like to emphasize that all the exploits depicted here are absolutely fictional; the character of Teresa Shaughnessey is not based on an actual person.)

Several books, also, were crucial to the writing of this novel. Details concerning the siege of Tenochtitlán were taken from William H. Prescott's *History of the Conquest of Mexico*, Miguel León-Portilla's *Fifteen Poets of the Aztec World*, and Bernal Díaz del Castillo's *The Conquest of New Spain*, Margaret F. Rosenthal's and Catharine R. Stimpson's *The Honest Courtesan: Veronica Franco, Citizen and Writer in Sixteenth-Century Venice* also proved instructive.

I also want to thank the following publishers for permission to quote the following:

The quote from the story of Tiresias on page 147 is from Ted Hughes's *Tales from Ovid* (Farrar, Straus, and Giroux, 1997). The quote from Dante on page 94 is taken from Robert Pinsky's *The Inferno of Dante* (Farrar, Straus, and Giroux, 1994). Emerson's cryptic phrase quoted on page 186 will be found in his essay on Montaigne in *The Works of Emerson*, and St. Augustine's prayer to God quoted on page 147 will be found in his *Confessions* (Vintage Spiritual Classics, 1997; Maria Boulding, trans.). Lines from Petrarch's poem quoted on page 83 are from *Petrarch's Lyric Poems: The Rime Sparse and Other Lyrics* (Harvard University Press, 1976; Robert M. Durling, trans.). Finally, the last lines of *Don Quixote* found on page 183 are from the 1964 Signet Classic edition (Walter Starkie, trans.).

a reading group guide to

THE CONQUEST by
YXTA MAYA MURRAY

INTRODUCTION

"I glanced up, then, at these shelves of sleeping books and thought how each hid the ember of a hot heart that beat after passions now long forgotten. This fact holds unbearable ramifications. Doesn't it? Or is it a blessing?"

Sara Gonzáles lives in a solitary world filled with dusty, broken books. A restorer of rare books and manuscripts, she spends her days—and many of her nights—within the confines of Los Angeles's Getty Museum. Sara finds it easier to navigate the intricacies of the museum and its rare and ancient artifacts than she does her own life.

When Sara is assigned to restore a scandal-filled book that was banned in the sixteenth century, she does not yet know that the story of *The Conquest* will consume her both intellectually and emotionally. Reputed to have been written by a notorious Spanish monk, *The Conquest* recounts the adventures of an Aztec princess enslaved by Cortés after his conquest of what is now modern-day Mexico. Skilled at juggling, she is taken to Europe to perform before the aristocracy. Given the name Helen, she soon becomes all the rage at court, an artist's muse and an assassin determined to exact revenge for the destruction of her family and her homeland.

Convinced this is no fictional tale written by a monk, but rather the story of Helen's life written in her own hand, Sara sets out to prove the book's origin. As Sara immerses herself in Helen's story, it captures more than just her professional curiosity. *The Conquest* gradually becomes a cultural allegory of her own frustrated existence, for Sara has not yet resolved the conflicts of her broken family. While her father refuses to remember the past, she cannot forget—or overcome—her mother's turbulent life and untimely death. Sara's painful history also threatens her romance with the man she's always loved, and it is *The Conquest* that ultimately leads her to an understanding of what she values most.

Filled with swashbuckling adventure and scholarly mystery, *The Conquest* is a perfect combination of history, passion, and imagination.

DISCUSSION QUESTIONS

1. The manuscript Sara is restoring is untitled, and she gives it the name *The Conquest*. Hernán Cortés's conquest of Mexico is just one of the many incidents that take place in the story. Why else do you think Sara chose this as the title? Why is it so important to her to give the manuscript an identity by naming it?

2. Sara has been a restorer at the Getty Museum for many years, breathing new life into countless rare books and manuscripts. What is it about this particular book, *The Conquest*, that draws her in and captures her imagination?

3. Sara is the sole dissenter of her colleagues' hypothesis that Padre Miguel Santiago de Pasamonte authored *The Conquest*. She says, "If I prove my hypothesis I will be as clever as any necromancer, for all the dark women of history have lost their tongues. If I show my colleagues that an Aztec woman wrote this book, it will be as if I'd tapped on the shoulder of the great volcano Ixtacihuatl and bade her speak. And that's exactly what I'll do" (pg. 5). Why does she feel so passionately about proving that an Aztec woman wrote this manuscript—and that it's autobiography and not fiction? Does she start out with one reason and develop others as she spends more and more time with Helen's story?

4. Why did Sara choose to become a book restorer? In one instance Teresa says to Sara, "What we do is ridiculous. What we're doing here is totally ludicrous and irrelevant" (pg. 186). Why do you think Teresa says this? What is Sara's reaction to this statement about their profession?

5. About her mother, Sara says, "She trained me from an early age to distrust this kind of zoo. . . . A Mexican, she taught me, and a woman, can only have an uneasy rapport with these menageries. My mother died two decades ago, but I know that if she were still here she would tell me to quit this job that I love. She would want me to be an *enemy* of museums" (pgs. 37-38). How does Sara reconcile her choice of profession with knowing that her mother would never understand her decision? Why does she specifically reference her gender and her race?

6. Discuss the scene where Sara's mother, Beatrice, steals the valuable manuscript page from a museum. Twenty years after her mother's death, this is still a very vivid memory for Sara. How did this experience affect her? What does it reveal about Beatrice's character?

7. Sara's father tells her, "Your mom, you know. She'd look at things and want it all to be different.... I think maybe you've got too much of her in you, and not just the good things" (pg. 171). What does he mean by this statement? How does Sara react to it?

8. How would you characterize Sara's relationship with Karl? Why is she unable to commit to him after all these years? If she had really wanted to, could she have found a way to balance both her professional pursuits and her relationship?

9. In one instance Sara says, "It was in that moment that I discovered my only talent, which is to tell Karl Sullivan stories, and I felt strong enough to mesmerize him all night" (pg. 14). Sara adopts the practice of storytelling with Karl, spinning tales from the first night she meets him. How does she use storytelling in their relationship? How does she specifically use *The Conquest* as a means to interest him?

10. In one instance Helen writes, "Little did I know that my worst enemy was myself" (pg. 138). Could the same be said of Sara? Despite their having lived centuries apart, are there any similarities between Helen and Sara?

A CONVERSATION WITH YXTA MAYA MURRAY

1. *In* The Conquest, *we learn that Sara came by her storytelling ability from her mother. Where did you get your inclination and ability to tell stories?*

I always wanted to be a writer; like all children, I wanted to have supernatural powers, and I learned that telling stories was the closest I'd ever get to witchcraft. As a novelist, you're like a little demiurge, conjuring planets, people, and philosophies.

Moreover—this is an old response of artists, but it's still true—writers can sometimes be attracted to the order that writing fiction promises. In the chaos of everyday life, it can be comforting to look down upon a world that makes some sense to you.

2. *What inspired your writing of* The Conquest?

The specific inspiration for *The Conquest* came from my reading of William H. Prescott's *The History of the Conquest of Mexico*. Late in the book, he writes of how Cortés ordered his men to load up his ships with booty from the Americas to send back to the European rulers and Clement VII, the pope. These treasures took the form of gold, silver, emeralds, feather work, and people—Aztec jugglers and dancers and buffoons who had survived the siege. When I read about these dancers being sent off as playthings and slaves of the pope, I tried to imagine their lives at the Vatican.

Soon enough, I began dreaming of Helen, the Aztec master juggler, muse, sybarite, and assassin.

3. *The magical realism that you inject into your writing is reminiscent of authors like Gabriel García Márquez and Isabel Allende. What writers do you admire?*

Certainly Márquez and Allende are influences, though I'll admit the phrase *magical realism* doesn't have too much resonance with me. I grew up in a religious and somewhat superstitious household, where the likes of God and Jesus were well known, as well as the specters of ghosts and psychics and bugaboos and demons. If you're hanging out talking to God, and sort of hear him answer, and in the other room Grandma is chatting up her spirit-walker, and Satan is lurking in the house's corners—well, from a perspective like that, having Helen toss up one hundred juggling balls in an effort to assassinate Clement VII is not such a stretch after all (though one might worry about heresy).

Magical realism is really just a philosophy.

As for the writers I like: Borges, Tolstoy, Morrison, Calvino, Homer, Woolf, Ellison. Among others.

4. *Tell us about the research you conducted for this novel, particularly the historical aspects.*

I did massive quantities of book research for this novel. I studied the reign of Charles V, and the careers of Suleyman the Magnificent and Barbarossa, and the biography of Titian and his circle. I also researched the physical environs of Italy during the sixteenth century, which apparently were undergoing a kind of constant accretive transformation as all this amazing art was continually piled onto the place. For example, I studied the architecture of the Vatican's Castel Sant'Angelo—which plays a prominent part in the book—and found that it has a bridge that is called the Bridge of the Passion Angels, as it's lined with stone sculptures of angels, who all represent the passions of Christ. Helen runs down this same bridge as she's storming Sant'Angelo in her effort to save Caterina from the dungeons. The only problem was that the Passion Angels were simply not there in the sixteenth century, as any good art historian will tell you, but I was laboring for quite a while under the misapprehension that they were there when Helen was. Imagine my sense of shock and horror when I discovered that I was wrong. Really, I was shocked and horrified and very scared of making such idiotic mistakes.

It's just such details that drive historical novelists nuts.

5. *Are any of the characters based on actual historical figures?*

Charles V, Barbarossa, Suleyman, and Titian and his scandalous poet friend Aretino are real historical personages, and I had a great, great deal of fun both researching their lives and then resurrecting them in the world of my novel.

Sara, as it so happens, as she is just a teeny wee bit based on myself, is a name that I used to give at parties, as I find that whenever I tell someone my name, Yxta, from the Aztec, it inevitably brings up questions concerning pronunciation (upon which there is some debate), spelling, the legend behind the name (sad story involving princess and warrior), whether the Aztecs are still alive, and especially inquiries concerning my racial identity—questions that I am happy enough on many occasions to answer—but then again, sometimes you just want a beer. My little moniker disguise, however, would occasionally backfire, such as when resourceful suitors would get ahold of my phone number, and then call me up at home. Then, I'd have to of course tell them what my real name was—"Eeek-stah, my good man—no, no, try it again, Eeek-staaah." And then they'd think I was completely crazy.

But back to the historical personages. What do you think about de Pasamonte? He's the one I get asked about the most. I am both sad and happy to report that he is a product of my imagination.

6. *Why did you decide to have Sara be a book restorer? Were you familiar with the process of book restoring prior to writing this novel?*

I made Sara a book restorer because it is one of my projects to—via the imagination—restore the history and art of the Americas that has been irretrievably lost through the conquest. Also, I stationed her at the Getty, which is such a temple to the artistic supremacy of Europe. Whenever I wander through that museum, in Los Angeles, I feel both a kind of awful melancholy, because I see that not only are these beautiful works, but that they are also forms of propaganda once used to help encourage and justify the expansion of the crown into the Americas. Titian's work—he painted a portrait of Charles V himself—is just one such example. But at the same time, I'm also a complete fan of European art. And so I wanted Sara to tangle with these contradictions in the same way I do.

As to the other part of the question, no, I am not a book restorer. Nevertheless, I am completely respectful of books. I almost never dog-ear my pages.

7. *In the story, Sara's mother makes reference to the fact that Latinos' history has been stolen, which she cites as the reason she takes the manuscript page from the museum. What are your thoughts on this?*

Beatrice is a complicated character—furious, mournful for the lost history I've already been writing of in these pages, and very, very intelligent. Her act is an ambiguous one: From one angle, if not justified, then perhaps understandable; from another angle, absolutely not. It is this ambiguity that lodges the theft in the mind of Sara, and steers her on a particular course in life. Her later career, where she works to retrieve signs of the lost Americas between the tattered bindings of books, is a non-felonious version of the act her mother committed when she was a child.

Both Sara and her mother are trying to give the past back to America.

8. *The story of the burned library that Beatrice tells Sara has a particular resonance in the novel. Did this event actually take place?*

I will cite two sources for the destruction of these libraries.

Bernal Diaz del Castillo was a soldier of the conquistador Hernán Cortés, and he went with Cortés into the besieged city of

Tenochtitlán, and later reported what he saw there. In his book, *The Conquest of New Spain*, he writes thus:

> I remember at that time his steward was a great Cacique whom we nicknamed Tapia, and he kept an account of all the revenue that was brought to Montezuma in his books, which were made of paper—their name for which is *amal*—and he had a great house full of these books. But they have nothing to do with our story.

As so little of the original city of Tenochtitlán has survived, these books were apparently destroyed.

It is by reading the words of another European, however, that makes one begin to suspect that the library described by Diaz may have been burned. This European was the Franciscan Bishop of the Yucatán, Diego de Landa, and he was a great burner of American libraries. He once wrote:

> We found a large number of books in these characters and, as they contained nothing in which there were not to be seen superstition and the lies of the devil, we burned them all, which they regretted to an amazing degree, and which caused them much affliction.

I quote this from Coe and Kerr, *The Art of the Maya Scribe*.

9. *You tell Helen's story intertwined with that of a modern-day woman. Why did you choose not to tell Helen's story alone, as an historical fiction novel?*

I wanted to show how we actively engage with the past all the time. Sara, through her historical and literary detection, is doing a very intense kind of reading of the past, the magnified version of the kind we do whenever we read histories or biographies or old novels. She's asking the question that we all do: What can I learn from what's gone on before; what does it have to do with me? And she certainly gets the answer to that.

Moreover, she was too spicy and fun not to write about; I think she's a great sister to Helen.

10. *How would you sum up Sara's journey in* The Conquest?
She's the luckiest girl in the world, isn't she?
She finds what she's looking for.